THE
MISSING
HALF

THE MISSING HALF

A Novel .

ASHLEY FLOWERS

WITH ALEX KIESTER

BANTAM
NEW YORK

Published in the United States by Bantam Books, an imprint of Random House, a division of Penguin Random House LLC, 1745 Broadway, New York, NY, 10019.

BANTAM & B colophon is a registered trademark of Penguin Random House LLC.

Hardback ISBN 978-0-593-72698-3
Ebook ISBN 978-0-593-72699-0
International edition ISBN 978-0-593-98325-6

Printed in Canada on acid-free paper.

randomhousebooks.com
penguinrandomhouse.com

9 8 7 6 5 4 3 2 1

First Edition

Book design by Caroline Cunningham
Title page image: AdobeStock/Dave

The authorized representative in the EU for product safety and compliance is Penguin Random House Ireland, Morrison Chambers, 32 Nassau Street, Dublin D02 YH68, Ireland, https://eu-contact.penguin.ie.

To the two women, who long ago as girls, taught us

what sisterhood meant. Allisa Flowers & Rachel Kiester,

this one is for you!

THE
MISSING
HALF

PROLOGUE

A sharp twist of underbrush clawed at her knee as she ran past, like fingernails brittle and slicing. She yelped out in pain, then clapped a hand over her mouth. Quiet. She needed to be quiet. But the swampland was deceiving at night, and although she'd passed this place many times, she'd never before been inside. The canopy of trees was dense, consuming the light of the stars, and the air was thick around her, filling her nostrils with a murky, earthy scent.

Solid ground turned to mud beneath her, swallowing her feet. She took a few more blind steps, then she was in the water, its algae-slick surface lapping against her thighs. Just as she yanked her foot free of the sucking mud, the toe of her shoe caught on something—a rock? A branch?—and she lurched forward with a splash, announcing her presence as loudly as a siren.

She looked over her shoulder, but all she saw was black.

She waited, not moving, not breathing.

As she stood motionless in the water, some dark part of her brain not engaged in self-preservation unexpectedly spat out a flash of memory of her and her sister at the lake. Her sister's face was cracked wide with laughter, their tankinis billowing beneath the water's surface, both their noses red and peeling. She thought about the way it felt to make her sister smile and realized that even if she was caught tonight, at least she'd lived a life with some small, happy moments.

Then a twig snapped behind her, and there was only one thing she could think.

Run.

CHAPTER ONE

2019

I'm mopping up vomit by the claw machine when I notice her watching me.

She's sitting in a booth where the tables end and the arcade begins, near the old pinball machines no one uses anymore. In her early to mid-thirties, with the slightly haggard look of a parent, she fits our customer mold here at Funland, the go-to birthday destination for every preteen in Mishawaka, Indiana. But there's none of the usual evidence of kids around her table, no gnawed-on cheese sticks or packet of wet wipes or discarded action figures. Just a half-drunk soda. When she notices me looking, she nods, then turns away.

There's something off about the gesture that makes me think she's nervous, like a bad PI going for casual. I keep watching to see if she's checking up on a kid in the throng of the arcade, but she just stares at the side of her drink, rubbing her thumb against the glass. Our dinner options are greasy pizza or rubbery burgers, the undersides of the tables are speckled with wads of gum, and the background noise is the shouting voices of children. If she doesn't have kids, what the hell is she doing here?

The woman flicks her gaze in my direction and then away again. The hair on the back of my neck rises.

I do a last few rushed swipes at the puddle of yellow sick, rinse out the mop and bucket so I can stow them back in the cleaning supplies closet, then scan the place for my manager, Brad. I spot the back of his head as he makes his way over to the computer where we ring up customer bills and half walk, half jog to catch up with him. "Hey, Brad?"

He turns, an affable smile spreading across his face. "Nic, hey. What's up?"

Brad Andrews gave me my job at Funland eight years ago, back when I was working summers in high school, out of sheer nepotism. He was the best man in my parents' wedding, and growing up, our families vacationed together every summer. He and his wife, Sandy, are more of an uncle and aunt to me than those related by blood. Neither of us could have foreseen how long I'd be here though, and sometimes our relationship shows the wear.

"That woman." I nod in her direction. "I think she's here alone. We may want to keep an eye on her."

"What woman?" Brad peers over my head. "That one in the blue?"

"She doesn't have any kids here." I don't need to elaborate. We get a certain kind at Funland every once in a while—childless middle-aged men whose eyes linger too long. We usually ask those people to leave.

"She looks pretty harmless to me. A little lonely, maybe, but harmless. Don't you think?"

I roll my eyes. Brad's brand of sexism manifests as an unwavering faith in the fairness of the fairer sex. He probably thinks his wife, Sandy, doesn't masturbate when he's away, or ever fantasize about a one-night stand with the young cashier at the grocery store. The idea of a female with actual bad intentions would gobsmack him.

"She was watching me." I regret the words before I finish saying them.

He glances over in the woman's direction again, but she's looking at her drink. "Are you sure?"

"You know what, never mind. I'm probably just . . ." The end of my sentence hangs in the air between us. Brad doesn't need me to tell him my paranoia and suspicion are habit. He was there seven years ago when my life flipped upside down, and he's seen me almost every day since.

"You sure? I can go and check it out if you—"

"No," I say. "It's fine." I know he's just offering for the brownie points anyway.

Brad studies my face. "You doing okay, Nic?"

"I'm fine."

"It's just—I know you have a lot on your plate right now, what with the . . . program and all that."

At first, I tried to keep the details of my "program" quiet, but my hometown is small, and a DWI is a juicy piece of gossip. Plus, I never had a shot of keeping it from Brad. He and my dad have a beer together every week. "I'm fine," I say again.

"Good. Good." Brad bobs his head. "Well, listen. You'll let me know if you need anything, yeah? If you ever want to talk . . ."

I soften a little at this, but we both know I won't take him up on it. Between working this job to pay off the state fine, going to my weekly AA meeting, preparing for my appearance in court, and fulfilling my mandatory community service at the local animal shelter, I don't exactly have the emotional bandwidth for a heart-to-heart. But more than that, I learned years ago that numbness is better than pain. I've been not talking for so long, I'm not sure I'd even know how to start.

My gaze flicks to the woman in blue, but she's gone, her table empty, her drink still half-full. Did she see me talking to the manager and leave before we could kick her out? *Stop,* I tell my churning mind. *You're being paranoid.*

"I should probably get back to it," I say to Brad.

He claps my shoulder. "You should come over for dinner soon. Sandy would love to see you."

As he turns to walk away, I scan the place one last time for the woman, but she's nowhere to be found.

We close an hour later, and I walk out the double doors of Funland into the Indiana summer night. The near-empty parking lot sprawls before me, telephone wires crisscrossing the black sky above. The heat is a muggy slap. I unlock my bike from the rack, then slip the lock into my backpack.

"Nicole! Nicole Monroe."

I turn and see the woman in blue emerge from the shadow of a tree on the edge of the parking lot. My fingers tighten around my bike handles. Most people's reaction when they're confronted is fight or flight. I freeze. And I hate myself for it.

"I just wanna talk." She lifts her hands as if she's approaching a wild animal. "About Kasey."

My sister's name is a fist in my gut, and I want to smack it out of this stranger's mouth. Although no one has showed up at my work like this in years, there have been countless like her in my life. Reporters, podcasters, bloggers. People who expect my eager participation as they turn my tragedy into their dollars. "Unbelievable," I mutter, turning to leave.

"Wait!" There's a flicker of desperation in her voice. She probably has a tight deadline, and I feel a stab of cruelness. *Good,* I think. *Let her squirm.* "I just want a minute of your time. Please."

"I have to catch a bus." My lawyer petitioned the court for an occupational license to drive to work, but until it goes through, I'm stuck like this. Hauling my bike onto the bus, riding five miles to the stop nearest my apartment, then biking the remaining two miles to my door. This bus is the last one of the night. If I miss it, I'll have to bike the entire trip in the dark.

I've already started to walk away when she says, "I know it hurts to talk about—"

I whirl around. "You *know*?" I don't have time for self-righteousness right now, but this is my button. People thinking they can empathize with my pain because they listened to a fifty-five-minute episode about it once.

"I . . ."

"Go on," I say. "Really. I'd love to know how you, a perfect fucking stranger, could know how it feels to talk about *my* sister." Over time, my grief has morphed to anger. Now it lives just beneath my skin. Prick it and I bleed. "Are you some sort of psychic? Or wait, no, let me guess. You're an empath. Right? You just feel everything *so* deeply?"

"No, I—"

"You don't know what it feels like. You couldn't. So please just leave me the fuck alone."

This time I've already hopped onto my bike and am pedaling off when she calls after me. I didn't think there was a single thing this woman could say that would make me stop, but I was wrong.

CHAPTER TWO

It feels as if I've been plunged into water. The air is viscous around me, the sounds muffled. Everything is blotted out by the woman's words echoing in my mind.

"My sister disappeared too. Just like Kasey."

I so rarely say my sister's name aloud anymore—my life is a little less painful that way—the syllables thrum through me like rushing blood. *Ka-sey, Ka-sey, Ka-sey.* It tugs me backwards into the past, and though I try to resist, it's like trying to hold on to a wet, writhing fish. Then suddenly, for the first time in years, I'm back in 2012. It's the summer after my junior year of high school and Kasey is still alive.

I woke around nine-thirty with a dull sort of hangover. My mouth tasted like beer, and when I looked in the mirror, my eyes were black. Like I had so many times before, I'd forgotten to wash my face when I got home. My day stretched before me like all the rest that summer—a mind-numbing shift at Funland during the day, then whatever diversion Kasey and I could come up with at night.

I padded barefoot down the hall to her room, knocked softly on the door. "Kase? You up?"

I wanted to sprawl at the foot of her bed like I'd done so often these past few months, chat about the night before. It was an irregular tradition of ours, something we did whenever we had time. We'd lie together, Kasey under the blankets, me on top, our voices still thick with sleep, and we'd talk until we were both laughing so hard we couldn't stop. It was our most beloved competition: who could make the other laugh harder. My favorite Kasey stories were the ones where she did impressions of the clumsy, fumbling guys who'd hit on her that summer. "They're such boys," she always said in her placid voice. "I need a man, Nic. A real fucking man."

But it was quiet in her room today. "Kase?" I said again. When she didn't respond, I cracked her door. Her room was empty.

At the end of the hall, our parents' bedroom door was open a few inches, which meant they weren't in it. The door to the bathroom I shared with Kasey was flung wide, the light off. I walked into the kitchen. Empty.

Mom and Dad had always had a hands-off parenting style. As kids, Kasey and I were downright feral, spending summers perpetually barefoot and skinned-kneed, sleeping in the same bathing suit for days on end so we didn't have to change to go to the pool. That summer, our parents' already long leash had been effectively cut. I guessed, because Kasey was in college now and living most of the year hundreds of miles away, they figured what was the point and then just lumped me in too. Even with both of us working nearly full-time, Kasey and I lived a little like nomads, sleeping at friends' houses and staying out all night.

And unlike a lot of kids in town, our mom and dad both worked, Dad at the fish hatchery, Mom selling vitamin supplements from a phone bank in South Bend. They both left in the morning before we got up.

Which was all to say that waking up to a house with no one in it was not unusual.

I got ready for my shift at Funland, washing my face and pulling my hair into a ponytail. I changed into my uniform, which smelled like pizza grease, and chugged a glass of orange juice. I kept expecting Kasey to walk through the door. We both worked on Grape Road, a commercial strip home to over a hundred different businesses rife with summer jobs, places like Olive Garden, Best Buy, Payless. Kasey worked at an old record shop called Rosie's Records about a quarter mile south of Funland. And because we shared a car, we usually drove to work together. But by the time we needed to leave, she still hadn't come home. I checked my phone. No messages.

"Thanks, Kase," I muttered. I was guessing she spent the night at her friend Lauren's and was planning to get a ride from her. Lauren worked at the record shop too, and they did this often, but a heads-up would've been nice.

I walked into the kitchen to grab the car keys from the counter, where we were supposed to leave them, but they weren't there, and I couldn't remember who'd had the car last. A group of us had taken a case of beer to one of the cornfields outside town last night, but I'd gotten a ride from a friend, and Kasey had stayed in.

I searched the house. My room, her room, the living room, the bathroom. Finally, I went outside, thinking maybe one of us left the keys in the car, but when I got out there, the car was gone.

"Are you fucking kidding me." I tugged my cell from my pocket and called Kasey. It rang through to voicemail, so I called again. Voicemail, voicemail. I shot off a text: You planning on picking me up or what?? And another: I have a job too you know. Then: Kase, wtf? I'm gonna have to run to the bus. Are you gonna pick me up tonight or are you planning on ditching me again?

I ran to the bus stop, making it to work twenty minutes late and sweating. I told Brad what happened and he gave me a grudging smile. "I understand," he said. "Just try not to let it happen again." Then, my attention was swallowed by balancing trays of food, exchanging arcade tickets for animal-shaped erasers, and singing Funland's noncopyrighted birthday song. I didn't think about Kasey again until I got off nine hours later. But when I called her, it still just rang through to voicemail. I disconnected before she could tell me to leave a message at the beep.

I felt a tick of worry, like a gear cranking one notch tighter in my chest. There was an explanation for it all, I was sure. Something had come up and she had her phone on silent. And yet, Kasey was the responsible one. Forgetfulness, spontaneity—those were my territory, not hers. I slung on my backpack and started the quarter-mile walk to the record store.

The shop air smelled like old books, and when I walked in, it was pulsing with the sound of some obscure band I'd heard Kasey play before but couldn't remember the name of. The rows of records were overflowing, and when I walked by, I ran my hand over their edges, reminded why Kasey loved being here so much—it was like disappearing into music.

But when I looked to the front of the store, she wasn't there. Lauren seemed to be working alone.

"Hey, Lauren. Where's Kasey?"

She shrugged. "I don't know. She's not here."

"She already left?" I said. "She's supposed to give me a ride."

"No." Lauren shook her head. "She didn't leave. I haven't seen Kasey all day."

CHAPTER THREE

"**N**icole?"

My head snaps up to see the woman in blue. She's standing beside me now. I'm in the Funland parking lot, straddling my bike.

For the first time in years, I let my mind slip into the past, and it's just as painful as I always imagined it would be. Knowing everything I know now—that right around the time I was writing those angry texts to my sister was more or less the time she was in unspeakable danger—makes the little flame of self-loathing that lives inside my chest grow.

"Are you okay?" the woman says.

"Who are you?" I ask. By now I already know, but I need to hear her say it to make it real.

"My name's Jenna Connor. My sister was Jules."

I begin to see it in her face: the pieces of Jules Connor reorganized—the upturned nose, small blue eyes. This woman, Jenna, has the same hair too, dark ruddy blond. Maybe this sounds shitty, but there was nothing particularly memorable about Jules Connor. I can't think of a single superlative you would stick in front of her name. She wasn't the smartest or dumbest, prettiest or ugliest, funniest, boldest, meanest. She was average, in her early twenties, from Mishawaka, working as a bartender in the next town over. Yet I will know her name and face forever. Because she was one of two branded the "Missing Mishawaka Girls": her and Kasey Monroe.

"Sorry to show up at your work like this, Nicole," Jenna says. "But I had to talk to you."

"It's Nic."

"Right—Nic. Sorry. I just need an hour, tops. I'll buy you a drink."

"No," I say quickly. "And I don't understand. What do you even want to talk about?"

"Well." She hesitates. "Our sisters' cases are connected."

You wouldn't have to read even a single article about the disappearances to know that. It's common knowledge—at least around these parts—and it strikes me suddenly how odd it is that we've never met. The Connors have held a lot of real estate in my mind over the years, but no one in either family—hers or ours—has ever gotten in touch with anyone in the other.

And because our sisters went missing from different towns, their cases were handled by separate jurisdictions. I've spoken with the detective on her sister's case, and I'm sure she's spoken with the one on mine, but we've never overlapped. Until now.

"And?" I say.

"No one knows why. After all this time. Why the two of them?"

What does she expect me to say? Does she not think the police explored that question? Or that every journalist and podcast host hasn't gone down that road a dozen times? I don't know the answer because no one does. And if she thinks the two of us are going to figure out in an hour what no one has in almost a decade, she's delusional.

"I know it sounds . . . farfetched," she says. "But talking to you is the only thing I haven't done. If there's any similarity between their lives—"

"The police looked into all of that."

"I know. I know. But no one knows them like us. The police missed something, and I think we have a shot at figuring it out."

"They're not coming back," I say slowly. "Kasey and Jules are dead."

I'm nervous for a second that Jenna is still holding on to the hope that I gave up long ago—the hope that because the bodies of our sisters were never found, they could still be out there, alive. But she just says, "I know."

"Then why are you doing this? What's the point?"

"It's . . . complicated."

There's something in her eyes, something she's not telling me, but according to my phone, I now have two minutes to get to the bus stop. "Right. Well, I'm sorry. But I have to go."

"Nic, please. Just give me an hour. I promise I'll leave you alone after that."

"Look," I say. "I've spent seven years trying not to think about everything I lost when Kasey disappeared. Seven years getting over the fact that my sister is never coming back." Although the truth is I haven't been getting over anything. I've been methodically numbing myself to it. And even so, any semblance of peace I have feels as if it's balancing on the edge of a knife. One breath and it would all tip over. "I'm not about to undo that for the sake of some stranger."

I turn again to leave, but Jenna grabs my forearm. "Wait! Wait. I get it. I do. But there's something I haven't told you. The reason I'm doing this—the real reason. I found something the police didn't have during their original investigation."

Her words hit me in the knees. And for the briefest moment, a millisecond in time that makes me hate myself, I don't want to ask what she found because I'm too scared to know.

"Jules's old diary," Jenna blurts out before I can say anything at all. "She, um, wrote something about that summer that the police didn't know. And if our sisters' cases are connected like we think they are, information about hers is information about Kasey's too."

I stare at her in silence, but inside I'm screaming. Screaming for her to go away, for my body to run, for something—anything—to get rid of this new ache in my chest. When I open my mouth though, all I can say is, "What did she write?"

"First, talk to me about Kasey's disappearance."

"Are you serious?" I say. "You're not gonna tell me?"

"I'll tell you, I promise. But only after you tell me about your sister's case."

"That's insane. I have a right to know."

"Look," Jenna says, "you just made it very clear that you don't want to talk about your sister or her disappearance. So if I tell you what I found out, how do I know you're not just gonna walk away? Think of it as collateral. I'll talk when you do."

I glance at my phone. My bus will be arriving any moment now. "Do you have a car?" I say.

"A—what?"

"A car, Jenna. Do you have a car?"

"I have a truck," she says.

"Good. I'm gonna need a ride."

"So, you'll talk?"

I give her a look. "You just told me you know something new about my sister's case. Of course I'm gonna fucking talk."

We make awkward small talk on the drive and walk into my apartment fifteen minutes later. I try to refuse to be embarrassed by it, but it doesn't work. My rent is necessarily cheap and my place depressing, one of those prefabricated apartments with a soulless interior—low ceilings, beige paint, wooden cabinets made in the nineties that swing unevenly on loose hinges. And right now, it's a disaster.

Dishes fill the kitchen sink, smears of food hardened on their surfaces. In one of the corners of the living room, the leaves of an old houseplant have withered on the stalk. Next to it is a litter box that hasn't been used for over six months now. Last year during a fit of optimism, I adopted an underfed tuxedo cat, bought a handful of toys from Goodwill, and told myself I was "turning my life around." I named him Slink, and soon I'd fallen deeply in love. But a month in, I realized he deserved someone better. Someone who'd feed him properly, not just leftovers, someone who could afford to take him to the vet, someone who didn't use wine to fall asleep. I took him back to the shelter and tried to forget he was ever mine. The litter box catches my eye and I seethe with embarrassment. The proof of my inability to see things through.

"So," I say to Jenna. "What d'you want to know?"

She glances around. We're standing across from each other in the middle of the small living room. "I was sort of thinking we could have a conversation. You know, sit down, maybe have a glass of water?"

I'm not an inherently inhospitable person, but I want to know what her sister wrote in that diary. Still. We made a deal. "Fine," I say. "You sit. I'll get the waters."

I fill two glasses from the tap in the kitchen and bring one to Jenna, who's now sitting on the couch. I take the other with me to the small table where I eat my meals and make a show of taking a sip. "What do you want to know?"

"I thought you could just start by telling me what Kasey was like. I mean, I know what was on the news, but it's not the same."

My stomach lurches, a knee-jerk horse's hoof in the gut. Her question sounds like a softball, I know, but it isn't. When someone dies, most people's reaction is to slap some reductive, feel-good label on their legacy. *Her smile could light up a room. He was the life of the party.* The claims are so blanketed, they leave no room for nuance, for reality. Even I, who've spent years learning better, still do it. Hadn't I, just a few minutes earlier, searched for some superlative to stick in front of Jules's name? As if *prettiest, smartest,* or *funniest* was the only thing that could give her life meaning. *Hypocrite,* I think acidly.

"Kasey and I were kind of opposites," I say. "She was . . . steady, I guess? Responsible. That summer was her first summer back from college, and even though she was going out and seeing friends and working, she was also taking summer classes online."

"What college was she at again?" Jenna has gotten out a little notebook and a pen.

"Arizona State. She was basically the only one in her high school graduating class to leave Indiana."

"What was she studying?"

"Nursing. She wanted to be a nurse." A hook tugs in my chest. She would've been a good one.

"So she liked medicine."

"Not really. I mean, yeah, she liked it fine, but I think it was more about helping people." And there I go, making Kasey sound like some kind of angel. Which she was and wasn't. "Our parents weren't around often, so Kasey sort of took care of me. You know, fixing me dinner and making sure I did my homework."

"Where were your parents?" Jenna says.

"Dad worked a lot. Mom drank a lot."

"So, Kasey was older than you?"

I nod. "Two years."

A memory fills my mind from over a decade earlier. I was probably eleven or twelve, Kasey thirteen or fourteen. It was the peak of summer and our AC had broken, our house turned sweltering. Dad said he'd called the repair company, but they were in high demand and the earliest they'd be able to come out was in three days. That first night, Kasey and I made a pallet in the enclosed front porch to sleep. We flung the windows wide and turned the fan on full tilt. But even so, the temperature was oppressive, and my long hair stuck to my sweaty back. I flipped around on top of the blankets until finally I couldn't take it anymore. The house was quiet as I tiptoed into the bathroom Kasey and I shared, grabbed a pair of scissors with one hand, a hank of my hair with the other, and cut.

It wasn't until the next morning when I looked in the mirror that I realized the damage I'd done. My hair hung in uneven chunks around my ears, a few uncut strands whispering against my collarbone. Kasey woke to the sound of me crying, and when she saw me her eyes widened, but only for a second. "It's okay," she said. "We'll fix it." She dragged one of our kitchen chairs out onto the back lawn and wrapped a towel around my shoulders, pretending like we were in some high-end salon. I remember she took such care wetting my hair and combing through it, her fingertips confident and gentle on my scalp. Eventually my hiccupping sobs faded.

"It must've been hard for her," Jenna says. "Being a kid and being responsible for a sibling."

I don't respond. I've guilt-tripped myself enough for this over the years. I don't need a reminder.

"I didn't mean it like—" Jenna cuts herself off. "She was your big sister. That's what they do."

I can tell by the way she says it that Jules was younger than her. So, she lost her little sister, I lost my big one. Suddenly, I want a glass of red wine so badly it hums inside my limbs. This is why I didn't want to talk about the past. My emotions get too heavy to hold. I stand up and walk to the kitchen. Cutting back on alcohol feels like something someone in my position is supposed to do, so I've been trying. But I think there may be a bottle of wine somewhere. I bang through my kitchen cabinets, look in the fridge, rearrange the items beneath my sink, and still I can't find it. I was doing better before tonight. I grab a bag of peanut M&M's instead. Some woman named Ilana from AA recommended candy as a booze replacement, and even though I'm not trying to quit drinking altogether, I tried it once and then again, and realized somewhere along the way that I was hooked.

I offer some to Jenna, but she shakes her head. She's flipped to a new page in her notebook, her pen poised above it, like it's a scalpel and she a surgeon.

"Can you tell me about that day?" she says. "The day Kasey went missing."

That's when I see it, the old familiar scene, the one that has haunted both my sleeping and waking mind for years. It's something I've never actually seen, but rather constructed to fit the police report on Kasey's disappearance: It's a country road at night, dark and quiet. Trees loom black against the night sky. The only car in sight is the one I share with my sister, and it's pulled over where the pavement meets grass. The car's interior light flickers with an almost inaudible tick, tick, ticking. Her door is wide open. She is gone.

CHAPTER FOUR

I tell Jenna everything I remember about the day Kasey disappeared, from the moment I woke up to the moment I talked to Lauren in the record shop.

When I finish, Jenna says, "I assume it was unusual for Kasey to miss work?"

"Oh yeah. She never did that. Kasey may've gone out and drank and stuff, but like I said, she was responsible. Super responsible. There's no way she would've skipped work without at least calling in some excuse."

Jenna jots this down. "Then what happened?"

"I asked Lauren for a ride. It was the end of her shift too. She drove me home and when we pulled up, there was a police car parked out front."

This next part is a blur—getting out of Lauren's car and running inside, seeing the officer sitting on the couch. I don't remember who broke the news to me, who said what first. All I remember is shouting into the room, "What happened? Where's Kasey? Where is she?"

"We had to have the fucking police tell us Kasey was missing," I say. "She'd been gone for hours by that point and none of us had even noticed. Or I guess I had—I just hadn't cared enough."

Jenna gives me a look. "Nic, you can't—"

"I know," I say. "I know." But if I'd put the pieces together earlier, if I'd understood something was wrong that morning, Kasey might still be here today.

"Her car was reported as abandoned on the side of the road," Jenna says. "Right? That's what the police were there to tell you?"

"Yeah. Up in Michigan. Some little feeder road off I-131 just north of Grand Rapids."

"Do you know where she was going?"

I shake my head. This is the part that always sticks in my throat, the piece I can never swallow. Kasey and I were the kind of sisters without walls. We shared eyeshadow and bras and lip gloss. Hair from both our heads intertwined in the same brush. When one of us got too much sunscreen on our hand, we'd slap it on the other's thigh. Both of us knew every boy the other had ever had a crush on. The night before she went missing, she told me she was staying in. Had she changed her mind? Had something—someone—changed it for her?

"A family called it in," I say. "They were taking a road trip, I guess, and had pulled over because the car door was open and they thought someone might need help. They said it looked suspicious."

"The driver's side door," Jenna says. "That's the one that was open."

"Yeah. And all her stuff was there. On the passenger seat. Her purse, phone, everything. There was cash in her wallet, and bank cards. Nothing had been taken. But she was gone."

"Just like Jules."

I've always known Kasey's and Jules Connor's disappearances were nearly identical, but when Jenna says this, the magnitude of it settles on me like an anchor. When we first learned of Kasey's disappearance from the police, all the information was so overwhelming, it took me days to realize that they, and we, knew next to nothing. In fact, they would've had exactly nothing to go on had it not been for Jules going missing the same way two weeks earlier.

"The only difference," Jenna says, "is that Jules's car was broken down. And I was the one who found it."

"I didn't know that. But how? You were out driving and just . . . happened to see her car?"

"No. I was looking for her. We were living together in Osceola at the time, but she was working over in South Bend, at Harry's Place." Osceola, Mishawaka—they're all just offshoots of South Bend, the area we call Michiana.

"My friends and I used to go to Harry's sometimes," I say. "It was the only place around that took our fake IDs."

Jenna's mouth tugs slightly at the corner. "Yeah. That tracks."

A memory emerges. "Actually, that's how I first learned about Jules going missing. I went there one night and these cops were hanging around inside, asking everyone questions."

"Did they talk to you?" she says.

"Me and my friends, yeah. For like a second. At first, we were terrified because we thought we were gonna get in trouble for underage drinking, but they said if we cooperated with their investigation, they wouldn't do anything about it."

When I hear this out loud, I realize how self-absorbed it must sound. Here Jenna's sister was missing and the teenage kids who could've known something were too distracted by the thought of getting punished to help. Though the truth is I told the police everything I knew.

"They showed us a photo of Jules," I say, "told us she was a bartender who'd gone missing. Mainly, I remember they wanted to know if there were any sketchy guys who hung out there."

"What'd you say?"

"That half the people in there were sketchy guys. They had us describe some faces, but we couldn't give them any names. Then they gave us their cards and told us to call if we thought of anything."

"She was working the night she went missing," Jenna says. "That's why they were so focused on talking to people at the bar. Jules usually got home late, around one or two. But that night, I woke up around three and she wasn't there. I called her cell and it went straight to voicemail. I wasn't worried exactly—not then, anyway. But she had a shitty car and sometimes forgot to charge her phone. And I didn't like the idea of her being stuck at the bar after it closed. Like you said, lot of sketchy guys.

"So, I decided to drive over to make sure she was okay, but she wasn't there. On my way home, I took a different route and found her car pulled over on the side of the road. It was the middle of nowhere, a cornfield on one side, trees on the other, and it all looked so . . . wrong. The only light was her car's interior one. Her door was wide open."

I suppress a shudder. It's eerily similar to the scene I've imagined all these years.

"I learned later from the police that her car had broken down," Jenna says. "That's why she'd pulled over. I just . . ." She shakes her head. "She was fifteen minutes from home, you know. If her car had lasted fifteen more minutes, she wouldn't have pulled over and he wouldn't have found her."

He. He is the part we haven't gotten to yet.

CHAPTER FIVE

One woman who disappears from the side of the road, according to the police, is an anomaly. She could've run away to start a new life, could've been high on something and wandered into the wilderness, could've been tracked by an angry boyfriend / ex-lover / fill in the blank, then lured out of her car and murdered. It was a setup, an accident, a personal attack. It was a one-off. On the flip side, if there had been a string of disappearances, it would have been foul play, perpetrated most likely by a stranger. A Ted Bundy. A Zodiac Killer. Some people still argue this theory, say a serial killer was just getting started but then got locked up for another crime. Or died. Or moved because the investigators were getting too close. But that's just people on the internet sensationalizing the story.

Two women from the same area who disappeared under almost the exact same circumstances points to someone on the periphery of their lives. Someone who knew Kasey and Jules, at least in some small way. Someone with a screw loose who believed that if he wanted something, he should have it.

That has been the extent of the prevailing theory among local law enforcement since 2012, which is such shit—not because it's not accurate but because it's nothing. It's like saying the victim who was stabbed thirty-seven times in the back died from murder.

I remember one of the many visits from Detective Wyler, the detective assigned to Kasey's investigation. It was squeezed in between Christmas and the New Year, and he'd called ahead of time, which was unusual. My mom made coffee, poured a little something into her own, then she, my dad, and I sat in the living room to hear what the detective had come to say. I could tell by the way he was staring at the carpet that it was going to be bad news.

"You all know how we've profiled the perpetrator in Kasey's disappearance," he began. "The man we're looking for is probably hiding in plain sight. He has a job, not necessarily a good one, but he pays his taxes. He functions in society and most likely owns or is familiar with some sort of property where he took Kasey after the abduction. But in a case like this . . ." Wyler rubbed his hands together. "In the case of an abduction, it is unlikely that this man would keep a hostage alive indefinitely. I want to let you know we're still doing everything we can to find out who took her, but I also feel I need to set expectations. After almost six months, the odds of finding Kasey alive—well, they're not good."

He walked out shortly after this, coffee untouched. Before the front door even shut behind him, Dad dropped his head into his hands, and I heard the choked sounds of him trying to stifle his sobs. Mom stalked wordlessly into the kitchen and poured herself a glass of her favorite grieving drink, vodka Diet Coke. Without even deciding to, as if I were one of those puppets with the strings, I followed the detective out the front door and onto the driveway. I'd been drinking soda out of a coffee mug, and as Wyler pulled out, I smashed it onto the concrete and screamed.

"I don't know how it worked with your sister's investigation," Jenna says, and my head snaps up to look at her. For a moment, I'd almost forgotten she was in the room with me. "But when the police talked to me, they were so focused on Jules's present day-to-day life. Like, they asked about her co-workers and people who went to the bar. They asked about our family and whether or not she was seeing anyone. But then they never really dug into her past, you know. I didn't think much of it at the time. I was so . . ." She waves the fingers of one hand vaguely. "But now I wonder—what if they were focused on the wrong thing? What if Jules knew this guy years before she went missing and then crossed paths with him again right before it happened?"

"I mean . . ." I suddenly feel exhausted, scraped out. I know I agreed to this, but I just want to hear whatever her sister wrote in her diary that summer. Did she mention a person the police never interviewed? A place they never checked out? And how could it possibly connect to Kasey? After years of disappointment, I know I shouldn't get my hopes up, but maybe this would all feel less futile, less painful, if I understood whatever new puzzle piece Jenna discovered. "Yeah. That seems possible."

"Right?" Jenna says. "So, I was thinking we could go through Kasey's and Jules's past together. You know, sports teams, schools, after-school programs, all the places they worked, friends, friends of friends."

I pop an M&M into my mouth. I want to track down Ilana from AA and tell her to go fuck herself. Candy will never replace a glass of wine. "Don't you think this would be easier if you told me what Jules wrote in her diary? Right now, we have nothing to go on. It's a needle in a haystack. But if you told me what you found, we could work backwards from there."

"Right, I get that, but . . ." Jenna's gaze flicks over the carpet.

"Oh my god," I say, "it's not like I'm gonna hear your thing and just stop talking."

"No, it's not that. I just—I don't want to plant some idea in your head and then have us only look in one direction. I want you to stay objective, you know? Open."

"Okay. Fine."

"Look," Jenna says. "Your sister got the Grand Rapids police on her case. Jules got fucking Podunk Mishawaka PD. I honestly don't know if they botched her investigation because they were shitty or because they just didn't care, but if I'm doing this, I'm gonna do it right."

I lift my palms. "I said okay, didn't I?"

"Thank you." Jenna glances at the little notebook open in front of her. "So. What part of town are you from?"

"The south side, kind of. Near the train tracks. You?"

"North. Up Grape Road, past the memorial park, just east of the apartment complexes."

I know the neighborhood she's talking about. Kasey and I didn't grow up with much, but I realize now Jenna and Jules might've had less. From everything I've gleaned about Jenna so far, I would've guessed the opposite. She seems to have salvaged so much more of her life than I have. "Why'd you guys move to Osceola?" I say.

"That was all Jules. It happened about three years before she went missing. We were living together in an apartment in Misha-waka, working there too. Then one day out of nowhere she woke up and announced she wanted to leave. She'd already found a place in Osceola and a new job in South Bend. I didn't really care where I lived, I just liked living with her, so I said okay."

"That seems pretty sudden. Did she say why?"

Jenna shrugs. "She said she wanted a change. We'd lived and worked in the same square mile our whole lives, and she'd sort of gotten into a funk. She'd stopped going out, stopped seeing friends. I think she wanted a fresh start. To shake herself out of it."

"By moving from Mishawaka to Osceola?" I say. They're all of ten minutes apart.

"I didn't really understand it either at first," Jenna says. "But she really leaned into it. She'd saved like crazy since she got her first job at, like, fifteen, and she used the money to buy a house, put down roots. It wasn't big or nice or anything, but she was happier there. Do you know anyone in Osceola?"

"I don't think so. No one I can think of."

She jots down a note. "What schools did you and Kasey go to?"

I list them—elementary through high school—and am not surprised when she nods blankly in response.

"We went to schools closer to us. Over on Bittersweet Road. And you said Kasey was in college, right? When she went missing?"

"Yeah. Arizona State."

"Oh, that's right. So, far."

I nod.

"What about jobs?" she says. "Where all did Kasey work over the years?"

"Well, she worked at Funland during high school. Just during the summers. The manager, Brad, is a family friend, so he got both of us jobs there. But that summer she was working at that record store, the one on Grape Road. Rosie's Records."

"And that's it?"

"That's it," I say. "What about Jules? I know she was working at Harry's Place that summer, but what about before?"

"By the time she went missing, she'd been there for three years—since we moved. Before that, she worked at a barbecue place waiting tables. It's on Grape Road too, called Famous Jake's. Have you heard of it?"

I scrunch up my face. There was a barbecue place by the record store, but that was called Mesquite or something. "I don't think so."

"Okay," she says. "Let's keep going. What about extracurricular activities?"

We go back and forth on life details, striking out with each. Kasey played soccer as a kid. Jules took dance classes until their mom decided they were too expensive. They went to different parks, different skating rinks. We play the name game, and it seems impossible that, even in our small area, we come up completely dry. It feels like we're stuck in a loop: running into a brick wall, dusting ourselves off, then running into it again. After a while, I look at my phone and see over an hour has passed.

"The problem is," I say, my voice sharp with frustration, "the guy is the connection. The man who took them. He could've shopped at the record store a few times and had Jules as a bartender at Harry's. He could've worked near Jules's high school and brought his kids to Funland." Picturing my sister's killer out in the world with a job and a family does bad things to my body. My skin starts to hum with hatred. "Hell, he could've coached Kasey's first soccer team and then, ten years later, eaten at the restaurant where Jules was a waitress. There'd be no way to ever fucking know."

"That's why I'm taking notes," Jenna says. "I've written down all these places so we can go back and look into them more. Here. I'll take a picture and send it to you now." She asks for my number, and a moment later my phone pings with a new text.

"I don't get it," I say. "How can you be so . . ." I wave a jittery hand in her direction.

"What?"

"So . . . I don't know, calm? There's nothing we've brought up that the police haven't looked into, so how can you think this isn't futile? Aren't you frustrated? Aren't you angry?"

Jenna stares at me. "Nic, I've followed my sister's case from day one. I've consumed everything ever made about it. And now my mom has cancer, and she's probably gonna die without knowing what happened to her youngest daughter unless I can somehow, de-spite being a dentist's receptionist and completely unqualified to do this, uncover something new. I'm calm because I have to be. Being calm is the only way we're gonna find anything out."

I know she didn't intend for her words to dagger into my chest, but that's what they do. She has spent almost her entire adult life looking for her sister, while all I've done is numb myself to the fact that I lost mine. "I didn't know about your mom," I say. "I'm sorr—" But then something hits me. "Wait. You said you're *trying* to un-cover something new?"

"Well . . . yeah? That's sort of what all this is about?"

"But you've *already* uncovered something new. Right?"

"I don't—"

"The thing you found in Jules's diary?" I say. "The thing you think connects to Kasey? That's what you were gonna tell me in exchange for talking."

"Oh, right. Yeah. No, I just meant, something else new. That's all." But her eyes dart down as she says it.

"Okay," I say. "So, what is it then?"

"What is what?"

"What did you find, Jenna? What did you read in Jules's diary? And don't say I still owe you. I relived the worst day of my life for you. And the months after. And the years that led up to it. Now it's your turn."

"Nic, I . . ." Jenna lifts her head to look into my eyes and that's when I see it—the truth. She has uncovered nothing.

"You lied."

She doesn't respond.

"I don't get it—what's in the diary? Just a bunch of nothing?"

"There is no diary," she says softly. "I made it up."

I stand so quickly my chair falls over behind me, landing on the carpeted floor with a dull thud.

"Look." Her voice is urgent, pleading. "You don't understand. I had to get you to talk. My mom—"

"Oh, your mom with the probably fake fucking cancer?"

"She does have cancer. That part was true."

"That doesn't give you a pass for lying to my face."

"I know it was shitty," Jenna says. "I do. But my mom, she's . . . Even before the cancer, she was—unwell. Sometimes, she won't get out of bed for days. Other times, she rages at everyone she sees. I'm sure there's a diagnosis somewhere, but whatever it is, Jules's disappearance made it worse. The cancer was the cherry on top."

"All right, Jenna, I get it." My voice is cold. "You can leave now."

"I just need you to understand—"

"I do. And now I'm telling you to leave."

"I will, I will." She stands from the couch, hastily stuffing her notebook into her bag. "But please, just listen. These days, all my mom can talk about is missing her baby girl. When she goes into a rage, it's at me, because I'm not Jules. I feel like if I can just give her this one thing, if I can just give her an answer before she dies, then maybe . . ." She doesn't finish the thought, but she doesn't have to. It's already corkscrewing through me, leaving an unexpected pang of sympathy in its wake. But I'm too angry to let it take hold.

"Good luck with that," I say, opening the front door. "Now please. Get the fuck out of my house."

I wait a few minutes to make sure she's gone, then I bike to the grocery store—the only place that'll be open this late—buy as many bottles of wine as I can afford, and drink until the pain turns to sleep.

CHAPTER SIX

The website of the local animal shelter is splashed with colorful photos of glossy-haired dogs licking faces and fluffy kittens sleeping curled in palms, but the actual shelter is a pretty depressing place. It has the kind of kibble-y, wet-fur smell that stings my nostrils and clings to my skin long after I leave, and walking past dog after dog with sad, lonely eyes makes my chest cave in. On top of that, it serves as a weekly reminder of my own inability to take care of Slink, but when presented with the list of community service options from the court, the animal shelter was the only one that didn't sound terrible.

I'm here now, sitting on the floor of the air-conditioned cat room, my mouth cottony and my head throbbing. It's been twelve hours since I kicked Jenna out of my apartment. Twelve hours since she took a pickax to my finely tuned numbness. In the short amount of time since then, I've been a live wire, jumpy and suspicious. Every woman I've seen is either Jenna, following me again, or Kasey, come back from the dead.

I've also had this strange nagging feeling since Jenna walked out my door last night, the kind you get after you leave for a trip and know you forgot to pack something but can't remember what. Maybe it's just Jenna getting to me, but I can't stop replaying what she said: *No one knows our sisters like we do. If there's any similarity between their lives, maybe we can find it.* I resent Jenna for dredging up a past I've worked so hard to forget, and I'm still furious at her for lying, but I can't help wonder if she could be right. What if this feeling is something important? What if it's something everybody else missed?

Trying to remember is a sensation I'm not familiar with. In the past, whenever memories of Kasey invaded my brain, I'd bury them. Now, for the first time in years, I want to reach out and grab them, but they're murky and ethereal, impossible to catch.

I hear the door open, and I look over to find Pam, one of the animal shelter employees. "Here you are," she says.

As far as volunteers go, I'm the lowest in the pecking order, below the new empty nesters filling their time and the high schoolers who are only here for a line on their college applications. I have to get Pam's signature on my community service sheet every week, and even though she doesn't know what I did to wind up here, it's clear she thinks I'm a criminal. Which, I suppose, I am.

"You were supposed to hose out kennel three," she says. "I just walked over there and it clearly hasn't been—" Her eyes lock on my lap. "Is that Banksy?"

Banksy is a skinny calico with a crook in his tail and a missing eye, and he's currently asleep in my lap. I met him on my first day here and knew the moment I saw his face, with one surly-looking eye and a sewn-shut hole where the other should be, his chances of getting adopted were slim, but the first thing I do when I walk through the door every Saturday is check to make sure he's still here. Every time I see him curled in the far corner of his cage, glaring through the bars, I feel both relieved and sad.

"Yeah," I say. "I just had to get him out of his cage, because he threw up in it and I wanted to clean it out." I can tell she doesn't believe me. And even if she did, I'm still breaking protocol. There's a separate room where we put the cats while we're cleaning their cages, and I am not in it. Nor am I allowed to interact with the animals until all my other duties are done.

"We're not here to provide emotional support animals for our volunteers to feel better," Pam says. "Our volunteers are here to help us."

"Right. I get it."

"Then start helping. I moved all the dogs from kennel three to the exercise field half an hour ago. I had to get Hillary to man my post to come find you." Pam always has a way of making volunteering at the animal shelter feel like working at NASA.

I scoop Banksy up, and he glares lazily at me with his one eye.

Pam opens the door, making a show of shaking her head. Just as it's closing behind her, she turns. "And, Nic? When you say you're gonna do something, please just do it. Don't make me come track you down."

When she leaves, I lock Banksy back in his cage, avoiding his gaze. "I know," I mutter. "Sorry, Banks."

I close the cat room door behind me and make my way to kennel three. As I do, my mind flashes to something Jenna said yesterday. *One day, Jules woke up and announced she wanted to leave. She said she wanted a change. She'd gotten into a funk. Stopped going out, stopped seeing friends.*

The exchange is sticking in my brain like a popcorn kernel between teeth. There's something there I'm not seeing, something I'm not remembering. What I told Jenna was true: Osceola, where Jules and Jenna moved, means nothing special to me. I don't know anybody there. I've driven through it plenty of times, but I've never thought of it as anything more than one of Michiana's many towns. Is it possible, then, that I know something about Jules Connor? I did go to the bar where she worked quite a few times that summer, but back then she was just one face among many.

I pass by a dog, a little yippy-looking thing with tangled white fur. He starts barking, and then the whole kennel is barking, and whatever memory was tapping at the edge of my mind is gone.

Two days later, I'm in the church basement where my weekly AA meeting is held, sitting in a circle of chairs. The room smells, like it always does, of pine cleaner, coffee, and cologne.

I resent having to be here, but AA is a requirement of my probation, so I've been going every Monday night for the past four months. I still haven't gotten used to the rubbed-raw way it makes me feel though. Like going into surgery without anesthesia, hands digging in open wounds. Each time I walk through the door, I hear the sound that's been haunting me ever since getting my DWI. A squeal of tires against pavement, the metal crunch as I clip that tree, all of it muffled through a fog of booze.

Today though, memories of my accident are buried beneath the nagging sensation I've had ever since talking to Jenna. Far from dissipating, the feeling's only gotten stronger over the past few days, like a vibration that's gone up in frequency. Something about Jenna and Jules moving to Osceola is important—I'm sure of that now—but I can't figure out what.

People make their way to the circle, Styrofoam cups of coffee in their hands. My AA group is made up of an unlikely assortment of people, old and young, rich and poor, high-functioning addicts and the opposite. Numbing oneself, I suppose, is universal.

Nancy, a woman of perpetual flowing layers and long chunky necklaces, is our meeting chairperson. "All right, people. Let's find our seats," she says, then gives a few introductory words about the program. After that, the man I call Sad Henry, a middle-aged man I've only ever seen in a suit and tie, does a reading about step eight while Candy Ilana streamlines Skittles beside him.

"Thank you, Henry," Nancy says when he finishes. She looks around the circle. "Who'd like to get us going tonight? Step eight is a doozy. It'll take guts."

There's scattered laughter. Step eight is making a list of all the people we've harmed. As she scans the room, Nancy catches my eye, and it throws me off guard. My mind had been circling: *One day Jules woke up and announced she wanted to leave.* I cut my gaze away.

From the opposite side of the circle, a voice says, "I'll go."

I look over to see Michaela. She's probably ten years older than I am, but her skin is like leather that hangs too loose over her bones. She's wearing a pink sweatsuit even though the high today was ninety-seven. The top is zipped all the way to the hollow of her neck.

"Um, yeah, hi," she begins. Her voice is like crunching gravel. "The people I've harmed are my girls. For anyone who doesn't know, three years ago I drove me and my girls home from a Fourth of July party. And, uh, I'd been drinking and I got into an accident. My oldest, Lexi, was okay. Few cuts and bruises, nothing too bad. But my youngest, Natalie—she broke her collarbone. I lost custody after that. They're staying with my mom now. She loves them, but she doesn't wanna be raising young kids anymore. She already did that. So, she's another person I've harmed."

I'm half in the room, half in my head. I hear Michaela's words, but I'm fixated on Jenna's: *Jules had gotten into a funk. Stopped going out, stopped seeing friends.*

"Anyway," Michaela continues, tugging the sleeves of her sweatshirt down over her hands. "I saw my girls this weekend, which is great, but also tough because it reminds me how much of their lives I'm missing. Every time I visit, Lexi's wearing clothes I've never seen before. And she learned how to do a cartwheel without me there to teach her. And Natalie, she had her hair in these little braids, and they looked so cute. But I started crying when I saw them because I used to be the one who braided their hair, you know? That used to be me."

Michaela keeps talking, but I'm no longer listening. Because it's hit me, the memory that's been clawing at the edge of my mind. And with it, a realization has suddenly come crashing through: Something I told the police that summer wasn't true.

CHAPTER SEVEN

It was a few weeks before Kasey went missing. I knocked on her bedroom door and opened it before I got a response.

"Jesus, Nic," Kasey said. She was sitting cross-legged on the bed. "Knock next time, will you?"

I flopped onto her covers. "I did."

"You know what I mean."

"You okay?" I asked. Her tone was unusually sharp.

She didn't look at me. She had a textbook open in front of her, a notebook beside it where she'd been taking notes. "I'm fine. Just studying."

"Okay . . ." I chewed at a nail, my gaze roaming around her room. She'd always had this obsession with old music, and posters of the Rolling Stones and the Beatles overlapped with academic stuff—her high school diploma, her acceptance letter from ASU. There was a piece of computer paper where she'd drawn and decorated the words of her favorite song lyric from "Strangers" by the Kinks: *We are not two, we are one,* and another where she'd doodled her full name over and over: Kasey Marie Monroe. Littered among it all were photos printed at Walgreens. In one, she and I were wearing heart-shaped glasses, our lips glossy and pink. In another, I recognized our aunt's backyard in Dayton, where we used to road trip every summer. Kasey and I were in bikinis, our hair styled with pool water, slicked back from our foreheads in what we called the George Washington. My favorite was from when I was a baby. Kasey, all of two years old, was sitting on the couch we still had today, her little legs straight out in front. She was holding me swaddled in the hospital blanket, looking down at my sleeping face with a kind of ferocious love, as if she was the one who'd just had me, the one whose job it was to protect me.

"You wanna hang out tonight?" I said. "Zach Walton's parents are out of town. He's having a party."

"A party?" Again with that knife-sharp tone. "I'm good."

"Okay . . ." I started to get up.

"Wait," she said. "How're you gonna get there?"

"Brianna's picking me up. Hey . . ." I didn't know what to do with her mood, but I took a gamble. "Would you mind braiding my hair? Kyle's gonna be there, and you know how cute I look in French braids." This would have usually made her laugh, I thought, but her face was stone.

"Is that why you came in here? So I could do you a favor?"

"Uh . . . no?"

"I can't do everything for you for the rest of your life," she said.

"What are you talking about? I came in here to invite you out tonight."

"Well, I'm studying. I just told you."

"Jesus. Fine." I stood up. "You don't have to be a bitch about it."

She let out a breath of bitter laughter. "God, Nic. Sometimes you can be really fucking self-absorbed."

"What is that supposed to mean?"

She flipped the page of her notebook violently. "Nothing. Never mind."

Kasey and I didn't fight often, but when we did, we battled. One time, when she discovered I got a C on a paper, she told me I didn't work hard enough in school. I told her she wasn't my mom and could shut the fuck up about it. The argument turned into a shouting match, but just a few hours later, we were splitting a bag of Oreos and watching a movie on the couch, everything forgiven. Our fights were like lancing a wound. We didn't hold off until we bled it dry. So Kasey's passive-aggressiveness now felt more ominous than if she'd slammed the door in my face.

"What's going on?" I said.

"Nothing." But she still wasn't looking at me. "I'm just stressed, okay?"

"Kase, you know you can tell me if something's wrong."

Finally, she looked up and her expression slowly softened. "I know. I'm just . . . I really am stressed. This summer course is harder than I expected, and with school about to pick up again . . ."

"Hey," I said. "You're, like, the smartest person I know. You're gonna be okay. You're gonna be a really good nurse."

She smiled, but it wasn't quite right. After a moment, she said, "Oh, fine. I'll braid your stupid hair."

As I was walking out the door a few minutes later, she called out to me. "Hey, Nic? Be careful tonight, okay? Don't drink too much. Don't, you know, go anywhere alone."

"Don't worry," I said. "I'll be fine."

"Nic . . . Nic. Nic!"

It takes me a moment to register that I'm in AA, and for some reason, I'm standing. A dozen sets of eyes are on me as Nancy asks me if I'm okay. I realize I've interrupted Michaela's story. "Oh," I say. "Sorry, Michaela, I . . . sorry. I'm fine."

"That's okay, Nic."

I sit, and everyone's attention shifts back to Michaela, but I feel Nancy's eyes on me, so I give her a reassuring nod.

When Jenna approached me outside Funland last week, I thought revisiting our sisters' disappearances was futile and masochistic. I believed her lie about finding a new development because I wanted it to be true, but I think a part of me knew better. Over the course of seven years, two different police jurisdictions have been able to come up with nothing more than a theory. How could we, a Funland waitress and a dentist's receptionist, uncover anything they did not?

And yet this memory *is* something. I can feel it in my gut.

Jenna said that three years before Jules's car was found on the side of the road, she'd wanted to move because she'd been in a quote-unquote *funk*. And now I remember that sometime in the weeks before Kasey went missing, she was acting strange too.

I'm not sure how to make sense of the timing, and I have to admit the connection is far from concrete. Maybe they aren't even related at all, but this memory feels pertinent—to Kasey's investigation at the very least. And now that it has risen to the surface, other snippets of memories are rising too. This wasn't the only time that summer that Kasey acted this way. For a while there, maybe a week, maybe two, something was off. I remember telling Detective Wyler that just before she'd disappeared, she'd been stressed with school, but could that really have been all it was? Because if I let myself sink into the memory rather than let it blur past me like I've always done, I can see something I've never before let myself examine: There was a look of fear in Kasey's eyes when she told me to be careful that night.

For some reason, late that summer, my sister was scared.

CHAPTER EIGHT

I walk through my front door, head to my room, and sit on the edge of my bed, where I pull my phone from my back pocket. For the first time in what feels like ages, hope spreads its small wings in my chest and starts to flutter. Could there really be avenues in my sister's case that no one's explored? I try to smother it. As I've learned, optimism only ends in pain. Still, I have to look into what this memory means. It seems like an enormous stretch, yet I can't help but wonder: Could Kasey and Jules have had the same reason for suddenly acting so off?

The only thing I can think to do is to look into any overlaps between Jules's life before she moved to Osceola and Kasey's before she went missing. Did they interact with any of the same people? Go to any of the same places? Thank God Jenna sent me pictures of the notes she was taking during our conversation before I kicked her out of my apartment, so at least I have those to reference.

But as I go to pull them up, I see a series of new texts from a number I don't have saved. I tap on them and realize with a jolt they're from Jenna.

Hey Nic, thought I'd give you some time before I reached out but I just wanted to apologize. It was really shitty of me to lie . . .

especially about that. I hope you know I was just desperate. Not that it excuses it or anything but maybe you can forgive me?

I also wanted to let you know that I'm not done looking into our sisters cases. I know you're probably still upset but I really believe if we team up we could find something.

Please just give me another chance. I promise I'll do everything I can to make it up to you.

Conflicting emotions war inside me. She's right about one thing: I am still upset. But a part of me understands why she did what she did. Hope is an intoxicating sensation. I got a mere taste of it and here I am digging into the one thing I promised myself I'd never revisit. Jenna's hope may make her delusional and a liar, but in the wake of uncovering this memory, it's harder to blame her for it.

I stare at her words for a long time. Finally, I tap the reply box. My cursor blinks at me. I click back out.

Jenna's notes are messy but thorough. On one of the pages she photographed and sent, she wrote a timeline of both Kasey's and Jules's lives side by side, their entire existences reduced to two little columns of facts. According to this, three years before Jules went missing, just before she and Jenna moved to Osceola, she was living in Mishawaka and working at a barbecue restaurant on Grape Road called Famous Jake's. I remember Jenna asking about it, but it hadn't rung any bells. It still doesn't. But at least it's a place to start.

I type "Famous Jake's" into my internet tab, and up pops the restaurant's profile complete with a location, photo gallery, website, and menu. Below are the words *Permanently Closed.* It's not surprising. Jules worked there ten years ago. I copy the old address on Grape Road, paste it into my maps app, and see that it's about a quarter of a mile south of Funland. I can take an early bus tomorrow morning and bike there before work.

Sitting on my bed, I feel my legs itch to start moving. All that separates now from then is the span of a few hours, but if the bus operated at night, I'd be on it. Patience, as people have told me throughout my entire life, is not my strong suit.

When I approach 2452 Grape Road on my bike the next morning, I'm confused. I must have entered the wrong address, because I've never been to Famous Jake's—have never even heard of it before the other night—but the commercial strip I'm pedaling up to now is a place I've been hundreds of times.

I brake and hop off my bike, my breathing heavy. I didn't think to wear anything other than my uniform, and I've already sweated through my thick collared shirt. Leaning my bike on the kickstand, I pull my phone from my back pocket and squint at the map on my screen. I pull up my internet tab and search for Famous Jake's again, comparing the listed address with the one I typed into my maps app. They match.

"Holy shit."

I look up at the storefront. There are two business signs in front of me, two doors. Maybe this is a coincidence, but it doesn't feel like it.

I click over to my messaging app, to Jenna's texts, but hesitate, my finger hovering over her number. Do I really want to call her, the person who used my own sister to trick me into talking? But I have to tell someone, and who else am I going to call? The person I used to tell everything to was Kasey. I had friends once upon a time, but I vanished from their lives the summer my own was turned on its head. My mom's been emotionally unavailable since she remarried and moved to Florida six years ago, and I think a lead about Kasey's disappearance might break my dad if it turns out to be nothing.

I stare down at Jenna's text: I really believe if we team up, we could find something. Maybe it's wishful thinking, but I'm starting to believe it too. Plus, if there's one person in the world I can empathize with, one person who deserves my solidarity, it's this woman. Because we are the same, she and I. The two sisters of the two Missing Mishawaka Girls.

I tap her number and she answers before the first ring is over.

"Nic! Hi."

"Hi."

"I'm so sorry about the other night. I should never have lied to you and I've honestly been feeling really terrible about—"

"Look," I say. "Forget about that for a second. I mean, I'm still angry, but . . . I think I might've found something."

"Really? What is it?"

"Remember the other night when you said that just before you and Jules moved, she was acting weird? She wasn't going out, or seeing friends, or anything like that?"

"Yeah?"

"Well, that reminded me." I start pacing. "Sometime before Kasey went missing, she started acting strange too. It was kinda the same stuff you said about Jules, staying in and isolating herself. She kept saying she was stressed with school stuff, and at the time I believed her, but now I'm not so sure."

"Okay . . ."

"When Jules started acting like that," I continue, "three years before she went missing, she was working at that barbecue place, right? Famous Jake's?"

"Yeah."

"Well, when Kasey started acting weird, she was working at the record shop, Rosie's Records."

"I don't—"

But I keep talking. "Listen, I googled Famous Jake's, and at first I thought it had closed, but it turns out"—I glance at my phone's screen—"it's still here on Grape Road. It just changed names." I've been walking aimlessly, but as I say this, I turn to face the commercial strip and the two businesses in front me. "Famous Jake's is called Mesquite Barbecue now. Mesquite and Rosie's Records—Jenna, they share a wall."

CHAPTER NINE

I follow Jenna up the path to her front door. Her home in Osceola is a white one-story, small and old, but well-kept. She unlocks the door, and we go inside.

After I told her about the proximity of Mesquite and Rosie's earlier, we decided to meet up at her house to talk through everything this evening. When I asked about the bus route, she offered to pick me up from work and drive me to my apartment after we were done. It was a bit out of the way, she admitted, but her place had food and, from glancing at my laptop the other day, a better computer. I suspect though that she just wanted to go somewhere that didn't look like a hurricane had hit.

I follow her through the front door, the wood floorboards creaking beneath our feet.

"Is this where you lived with Jules?" I ask. I'm still mad at her, but in the wake of what I found, it feels as though we've slipped into a temporary truce. The storm is on the horizon, but it's not here yet.

"Yeah," she says. "I thought about moving, but . . . I don't know. She loved this place so much."

We walk into the living room, and I stop short. On the side wall, covering almost its entire surface, is a collection of research—

newspaper clippings, printed articles from online publications, maps marked up in Sharpie—all about our sisters' cases. The other day, when Jenna said she'd consumed everything about the two investigations, I thought she was being hyperbolic. It's clear now she wasn't.

"Oh, right," Jenna says when she sees me looking. "I know it's a lot."

A *lot* doesn't come close. This is the kind of wall serial killers have, or detectives in TV shows when they're slipping into obsession. The sheer amount of information in front of me makes me dizzy. I don't think I've seen even half these articles before, and it's a reminder that I'm the shitty kind of survivor while Jenna's the good kind. Unlike me, she went looking for her sister the night Jules went missing, and she hasn't stopped searching since. I walk closer and touch my fingertips to the curling edge of a newspaper cutout with the headline "Another Missing Mishawaka Girl—Are the Cases Connected?" My sister's name in the article catches my eye: *19-year-old Kasey Marie Monroe . . .*

"Nic?" Jenna says and I jump a little. "Hey, are you hungry? I could make us sandwiches."

Ever since the DWI, my expenses have skyrocketed. At first it was the legal fees that were drying up my bank account, now it's the payment plan to cover the state's fine. For months now, all I've been able to afford in the way of food is Cup Noodles and leftover pizza from work. I may still be angry with Jenna, but I'm not turning down a free meal. "Sure."

We head into the kitchen and I sit at a little round table while she moves around, pulling out sliced meats and cheeses, whole grain bread. She piles salt-and-vinegar chips onto plates, slices a fat tomato, washes crisp lettuce. With my first bite, I realize how long it's been since I've had a fresh vegetable. I can almost feel an influx of my vitamins and minerals. We eat in silence for a while. Then, as we're picking at the last few chips on our plates, Jenna looks up at me.

"I'm glad you decided to work with me on this," she says. "I think we should—"

"Whoa, whoa, whoa." I wave a hand. "Hang on. There's no 'we' yet, Jenna. I mean, I want to do this—obviously, because I called you—but we need to hash some shit out first. For starters, you lied to me. You deliberately misled me about my own sister's case. That's a pretty fucked up thing to do."

"I know. I'm sorry."

"I mean, honestly, how furious would you be if someone did that to you?"

"I know," she says again. At least she sounds genuinely contrite. "It was a really shitty thing to do. But it wasn't like it was premeditated or anything. I wasn't trying to hurt you, it just came out. Honestly, I was probably as surprised to hear me say it as you were. Normally, I have everything all planned out. But I didn't think there was any chance you wouldn't talk. I just assumed you'd want to figure out what happened too. When you didn't, I got desperate and made something up. Not that it's an excuse for lying, but that's why I did."

"It's not that I don't want to know what happened," I say. "Jesus, I'd sell my soul if it would help me understand what happened to Kasey. But when I think about that summer, about my sister, I . . ." I shake my head. "Look, the good memories just make me miss her, and the bad memories—they make me feel like shit. Plus, I thought what you were trying to do was, you know, futile. I didn't think learning anything new about her case was even possible."

"I get it," Jenna says. "I do. But what about now? You learned something new."

I eat a chip, then another. I'm already in—I was in the moment I biked up to the commercial strip this morning—but I want to make her sweat like she made me. "If I agree to help, you have to swear on your life you won't lie to me again."

"Done."

"I'm serious, Jenna. If I do this and I ever find out you're lying or holding something back about our sisters' cases, I'll . . ." I look around her kitchen. "I'll make you wish you hadn't."

It sounds both petty and dramatic, but she just says, "I get it. I swear."

"And you know, I don't have a car right now . . ." I haven't told her about getting a DWI, but biking everywhere isn't common in Michiana, so I wouldn't be surprised if she suspected something. "Which means if we ever need to go anywhere, I'm gonna need a ride."

"Right. No big deal."

"And . . ." I rack my mind. I don't have anything else to ask for, but I still feel like I have the upper hand, and I want her to pay. Not suffer, not sacrifice, just pay. I glance around the kitchen. "I want that tomato."

Jenna follows my gaze. "You want *that* tomato?"

"I haven't been eating enough vegetables, and I don't have time to go to the store."

"Right." The corner of her mouth twitches. "It's yours."

She's chewing her lips now, fighting to keep a straight face. Despite myself, I feel her amusement catching in me. She presses her fingertips to her mouth, but a laugh escapes them. "I'm sorry," she says, her shoulders shaking. "But you asked for my *tomato.*"

"Shut up." But I'm laughing now too.

"You *demanded* it."

"I don't know, I felt like I needed something physical. A token of your regret." This makes us laugh harder.

After it fades, Jenna picks up our plates and puts them in the sink. When she turns back around, she's all business. "Should we get started? There's more space in the living room if we wanna work in there."

We walk in and I settle into an old, threadbare armchair. Jenna sits on the couch, her laptop on her thighs.

"Okay," she says. "If the reason for both Jules and Kasey acting weird was because of something that happened where they worked, then we need to find someone else who worked there too. At either place, I mean, during 2009 when Jules was at the restaurant, or in 2012 when Kasey was at the record store." She bows her head, rubbing her hairline irritably. "I can hardly remember my own co-workers from back then, let alone any of my sister's."

"I can," I say.

Jenna looks up.

"Yeah. Lauren Perkins? I told you about her. She gave me a ride home the day Kasey went missing. She worked at the record store that summer too."

"Do you still know her? Can you reach out?"

The idea of seeing someone from my old life, of showing her what a dead end my new life has become, makes my skin prickle with dread. "I might have her number saved," I say.

But when I check my contacts, she's not there.

"Are you on any social media?" Jenna asks.

"I have Facebook, but I haven't been on in a long time. Like, years."

She puts her laptop on the coffee table, slides it toward me. "Why don't you log in? See if you're friends."

I have to reset my password because I can't remember my old one, but pretty soon, I'm in. When my profile fills the screen, the breath kicks out of my chest. I'd forgotten my banner photo was an old picture of me and Kasey. I'm probably seven or eight in it, Kasey nine or ten. We're both dressed up as witches for Halloween. Our arms are around each other's necks, cheap silver rings stacked on our fingers. We're wearing gauzy dresses and pointed hats, our lips painted black. When I realize I'm staring, I look away.

In the search bar up top, I type "Lauren Perkins," then scan the list of results.

"None of these are her," I say. "At least, I don't think."

Jenna walks around the table and looks over my shoulder. "Click on them to make the picture bigger. Just to be sure." I do and this confirms it: none of these Laurens is the Lauren I knew. "Try googling her," Jenna says. I open another internet tab and type in her name, but again there's nothing. "Hmm. Maybe she got married and changed her name."

I laugh. "Lauren is Kasey's age. She's twenty-six—she's not married."

"Nic, we live in the Midwest. At thirty-three, I'm practically an old maid." When she says this, I realize how little I really know about this woman I'm now working with. I know about her sister's disappearance and her mom's cancer, and I know she's a receptionist at a dentist's office, but that's about it.

"It's just hard to imagine," I say. But what I'm really thinking is that if Lauren got married, it means she's moved on from the devastation of losing my sister, moved on from Kasey herself. It shouldn't feel like a betrayal, but it does. This is what I do, assume everyone else is frozen in time because I am.

I click back to Facebook and delete Perkins from my search. When I hit enter again, a list of Laurens materializes, two of whom are my friends. A Lauren Maxson and a Lauren Tate. Neither name triggers any recognition, but in the thumbnail picture next to the latter, I recognize Kasey's old friend. Her face is no bigger than a pea, but it's her. Lauren Perkins. Now, Lauren Tate. "This is her."

"You're still friends."

"Mm-hm." I click on her name and Lauren's profile fills the screen. "Yikes."

"Not what you were expecting?" Jenna says.

"Not exactly."

In high school, Lauren was the kind of girl who loved indie bands and Jane Austen. She wanted more than anything to get out of Indiana, explore the world. Her current Facebook profile seems to be for someone else entirely. It's one of those shiny-happy-family ones, with a small picture of her beaming down at a baby, her hair and makeup perfect. The banner photo behind it is a professional: Lauren sits on a grassy knoll alongside a clean-cut man who looks like he could be a political candidate with a little time and money. There's a baby in her lap and a little girl in front. All four are in matching white and denim. Beside the word *From* on her About page, it says: Mishawaka, Indiana. Beside *Lives in*, it says the same.

The mean part of me whispers that Kasey would have done it all better, lived a life more worthy of existence. For the first time, I briefly let myself visualize a future for my dead sister. She would have become a nurse, traveled the country, dated all types of different men before settling down with someone interesting and kind.

Jenna and I dig around Lauren's profile and discover that it revolves around the same four things: her husband, Matthew; their daughter, Beth Anne; their baby son, Thomas; and their church, Holy Mount Presbyterian. That's another surprise: Sometime since 2012, Kasey's former best friend found Jesus. We sift through post after post, going back in time. Matthew and Lauren with their kids at Beth Anne's birthday party. There's a candle in the shape of a four on a cake and a bounce castle and young moms in sundresses talking to young dads in polos. Matthew and Lauren with their kids at their church's Easter egg hunt. Beth Anne runs around in white patent leather shoes and bunny ears. Thomas is tiny in seersucker shorts and a white collared shirt, asleep in Lauren's arms. Matthew and Lauren in the hospital, holding newborn Thomas. Beth Anne sits nestled in the hospital bed, smiling down at baby brother. Somehow, Lauren looks fresher and more put together after giving birth than I ever do.

"I can't believe she has two kids," I say.

If Beth Anne is four, it means Lauren had already had her by the time she was my age. The idea of me raising a baby right now is absurd. I couldn't even take care of a cat.

"Should we message her?" Jenna says.

"Yeah, okay." I scroll back to the top of her page and click on the message button. My cursor blinks in anticipation. "What do I say?"

"Just say you've been thinking about Kasey and you'd like to talk, ask her a few questions. Does she have an hour sometime over the next week or two for you to buy her a coffee? Keep it vague and upbeat, something that's hard to say no to."

I type out the message, and when I hit send, a bubble of anticipation rises inside me. It's as if I'm expecting Jenna's front door to fly open and Lauren to be standing there, ready with all the answers to our questions. Beyond the walls of Jenna's house, I hear nothing but the chirping of crickets, the buzz of cicadas.

"Thank you, Nic. I know I dragged you into this, but I appreciate your help."

"I'm not doing it for you," I say. "I'm doing it for Kasey. And like you said, we found something new. I'm in it now."

I check my Facebook obsessively after that. It's the first thing I do in the morning and the last thing I do before I close my eyes at night. I start pulling out my phone so often at work that Brad asks me if everything's all right, and when I say it is, he gives me a rueful smile and gently reminds me that cellphones are only to be used on breaks. Four days after I sent our original message to Lauren, I send a follow-up telling her to please respond because what I'm after is important. Then I send another two days after that: We can talk over the phone if that's better for you.

"What's under the messages?" Jenna asks me on the phone Wednesday night. It's been a full week since we met up at her house and reached out to Lauren. Jenna's been asking for updates over text every day, but I've had none to give her. Her last text, which I saw after work this evening, said, Let's touch base. Call when you can.

"Under the messages?" I say. I've just gotten home and am sitting on the edge of my bed. "What do you mean?"

"You should be able to tell if she's seen the messages or not. If there's a timestamp, like *sent seven days ago*, she hasn't read them. But if you see her little profile photo, it means she has."

I pull the phone from my ear and put it on speaker so I can search my screen. "Shit," I say. "She's seen it. She's seen them all."

Jenna sighs. "Which means she doesn't want to talk."

"What the fuck?" I haven't seen Lauren in years, but once upon a time, she was a relatively big presence in my life. Sure, I only knew her through Kasey, only talked to her when they were together, but she was in and out of our house a lot during high school. I remember one time before Kasey went away to college when she, Lauren, and I went driving late one night. We rolled down the windows and put on some mix CD we still had from middle school and shouted the songs at the top of our lungs. I may not have wanted to write her, but I assumed if I did, she'd write back.

"Maybe it's time we track her down," Jenna says.

"We don't know where she lives. Her profile just says she's in Mishawaka."

"We don't know where she lives, but we do know where she goes."

I think back to Lauren's profile page, all those photos of her and her family on Sunday morning. "Damn it."

"Yeah," Jenna says. "I think we have to go to church."

CHAPTER TEN

A t 8:30 the next Sunday morning, Jenna picks me up from my apartment to take us to Holy Mount Presbyterian.

"You look nice," she says as I climb into her truck and stuff my backpack into the space by my feet. I have a shift after the service, so it's fuller than usual today with my uniform.

"Thanks." I'm wearing the nicest thing I could find in my closet—a purple cotton dress with tiny white flowers that, from afar, look like spots. I couldn't get myself to put on heels though, so I've paired it with my high-top Converse.

Jenna, on the other hand, looks like she's made a real effort. She's done her hair in loose ringlets and painted her lips pink. Her outfit though—a midnight blue satin halter dress and black slingback heels—makes me think she's never been to church before. And the way she's drumming her fingers nervously on the steering wheel seems to confirm it. I know with a sudden clench of dread that the good Christian socialites of this town will take one look at her and know she's playing a part.

"Hey, do you want borrow a cardigan or something?" I say.

"Why? Do you think I need one? Is this not appropriate?"

"No, no, no. It's not that. You look great. But these churches, they're fucking cold."

She lets out a relieved breath of laughter. "Okay. Sure. Thanks."

I run back up to my apartment and grab a white, loose-knit cardigan from my closet. At least now the whispers won't have the word *slut* in them. I wouldn't care if they said it about me, but for some reason it bothers me to think of Jenna on the receiving end of that kind of petty cruelty.

"So," I say after I've made it back to the truck and tossed the sweater into her lap. "You and Jules didn't grow up going to church, huh?"

"No. I can't imagine our mom ever stepping foot into a church. She never really believed in anything but herself."

This is the same woman who rages at Jenna for not being Jules, the same woman for whom Jenna is doing all of this. It shouldn't make any sense, but I understand. Family is complicated.

"What about you?" she says. "You and Kasey go to church when you were kids?"

"For a while. Kasey was better at it all than I was."

Back when our parents still loved each other or at least pretended to, back when drinking was more of a hobby for our mom instead of the priority it eventually became, she used to wrangle us to church. We were never going to be an every-week sort of family, but every third Saturday or so, Mom would announce we were going to service the next morning. I didn't know what the hell it meant to be Christian, but I did know that church meant putting on an uncomfortable dress and sitting still as some man droned on about God and Jesus and the Holy Spirit, who were all the same person but also weren't. Oh, and money. There was always a special part of the sermon to ask for money.

"Quit squirming," Mom would say every time we went. "Quit tearing that program to shreds." Even during the half hour after church when our parents would talk with the other adults and Kasey and I would play on the church's playscape, I managed to get in trouble—for cursing, for getting my tights dirty, for messing up my hair. One Sunday morning, when our mom shepherded us to the car,

I refused to get in. I was probably nine or ten at the time, and I stood in the driveway, arms crossed over my chest. "I'm not going."

"Nicole Monroe," Mom said. "You get in that car right now."

I shook my head.

My mom looked to my dad, who just let out a weary sigh.

"Nic, you are a Christian and that means you are going to church."

But I stamped my foot and used the word I'd learned only a few weeks earlier during, ironically enough, Sunday service. "I am atheist," I shouted. "And I'm not going."

This time, my mom looked to Kasey, the only one in the house I really listened to. "What do you want me to do?" Kasey said with a shrug. "Apparently, she's an atheist."

It wasn't long after that that our parents gave up on church.

Holy Mount Presbyterian is one of the older churches in town, gray stone with ostentatious columns out front. We pull up beside an enormous magnolia sprawling over the lawn, its waxy leaves casting stark shadows in the summer sun. People are still milling around outside, but the men are glancing at watches while the women call out to their kids. It's almost time for the service to start.

"I don't see Lauren," I say to Jenna as she walks around the truck to join me on the sidewalk. "Or Matthew or the kids."

"They're probably inside already."

We file through the church's double doors with the rest of the congregation, looking exactly like the wide-eyed tourists we are. People are shooting sideways glances at us and smiling too broadly when I catch their eye. We sit in the back, and I crane my neck to search the pews. There are dozens of women I think could be Lauren, but I watch each until they do something, turn their head or laugh, and I realize they're not.

A man with thick dark hair and unnaturally white teeth stands in front of the crowd and welcomes everyone, inviting us to join him in a song of worship to get started. It's then, as the congregation stands to sing, that I see her—a head of blond hair, an eyelet white dress, a baby in her arms. I elbow Jenna and nod in Lauren's direction.

After the sermon, something about unconditional love that I only listened to pieces of, Jenna and I hurry outside and wait at the bottom of the stairs on the front lawn, where every person in the church will walk by on their way out. We wait for what feels like forever for Lauren and her family to emerge through the double doors, and I start to get antsy. I don't have long before I need to leave for work. Finally, we see them.

"Lauren," I call, waving a hand.

With Thomas in her arms, Lauren scans the crowd, a bright, expectant smile on her face. But when her eyes land on me, it falls. She turns to touch a man's shoulder—her husband, Matthew—then slowly makes her way over.

"Nic!" She's plastered a friendly smile back on, but I can see through it. She's not happy to see me. "I'm so happy to see you! It's been ages. Are you a new member here?" She knows I'm not. She knows why I am here.

"Just visiting," I say. "This is my friend Jenna."

"Hi," Lauren says. Her voice has a put-upon sweetness that chafes my skin. It was obvious from her Facebook profile that she'd turned into somebody else over the years, but seeing it in person is disorienting. "I'd shake your hand, but as you can see"—she nods at her arm wrapped around Thomas—"mine are full."

Matthew walks up to us, holding their daughter Beth Anne's hand. "This is my husband, Matthew," Lauren says, then introduces us. She doesn't tell him how she knows me. "And this is Beth Anne."

As Jenna and I shake hands with Matthew, Beth Anne starts to pepper him with questions and the two of them retreat a few steps away to talk. An awkward silence falls over the three of us that neither Jenna nor I try to fill. I'm hoping Lauren will take the bait, and she does.

"Listen, Nic," she says, sounding somehow embarrassed, apologetic, and defensive all at once. "I'm sorry about not responding to your messages. I kept meaning to, but with two little ones running around, things can be chaotic."

"That's all right," I say. "But since we're both here, I'd love to talk to you now."

"Oh!" Her eyes widen, and I can see her Midwestern manners

battling her desire to get away from us. I just don't understand why that desire is so strong. If I can stand here and talk about my own sister going missing, why can't she? "You know, I'm so sorry, but we've got to get home to feed Thomas, and then there's nap time. I'm not sure if you have kids"—she says this in a way that makes it clear she knows I don't—"but if you get their schedule off by, like, a minute, the entire train can fall off the rails."

"It won't take long," I say. "Promise. I have to get to work in a bit, so it'll be few minutes, tops."

Still, she hesitates.

"Lauren, please." I think back to that first night outside Funland, to how Jenna lied to get me to talk. While it infuriated me then, now that I'm standing in front of a source of potentially new information, I understand. "She was my sister."

Lauren stares at me for a moment, then lets out a breath. "I'm sorry. Of course. Sometimes, I just get wrapped up in parenting and . . . Anyway, I really don't have too long, but I'll help if I can." She turns to Matthew, who's now got Beth Anne on his shoulders. "Honey? I'm gonna catch up with Nic for a minute, okay? I'm fine with Thomas, but maybe the two of you could go to the playground for a bit?"

"Sure," Matthew says as Beth Anne shrieks with delight. "It was nice meeting you."

He walks off and Lauren turns back to us with a resigned-looking smile. "So." She shifts Thomas to her other hip. "What do you wanna know?"

Jenna and I look at each other. I told her I wanted to take the lead, but I don't really know where to start. "Well," she jumps in. "You spoke to the police after Kasey went missing, right?"

"I'm sorry." Lauren flicks her eyes briefly to Jenna's satin dress. "What was your name again?" By her sweetly acerbic tone, it's clear the real question is: Who the fuck are you? It's weird. Kasey and I used to make fun of those people. Phony, we called them. Now her best friend is one of them.

"This is Jenna Connor," I say. "Her sister was Jules Connor, the other girl who went missing from the side of the road."

"Oh. Oh, I'm—" Lauren shakes her head. "I'm sorry. I didn't realize."

"That's okay," Jenna says.

"Um, but yes, to answer your question, I did speak to the police."

"Do you remember who you talked to?"

"Some detective. He came over to my house. What was his name?" She clicks her tongue.

"Wyler?" I say.

"Yes. That was it. Detective Wyler."

Jenna looks to me so I can take over, giving me an encouraging nod.

"Right," I say. "So, that summer, you and Kasey—you basically saw each other every day, right?"

"Well, when I was working at the record store, we did."

"What d'you mean by 'when'?"

"I worked with Kasey at Rosie's Records, the record store on Grape Road?"

"No, I remember that," I say. "But the way you said it—it made it seem like you didn't work there the whole summer."

Lauren gives me a look as she hitches Thomas higher on her hip. "I didn't. I worked there with her for about two months. Then I left to go waitress. Kasey never told you?"

Her words, spoken innocently enough, worm into my brain: *Kasey never told you.* But Kasey and I had told each other everything. For a moment I can't speak, and Jenna fills the silence.

"Where did you work as a waitress?" she says.

"Just the place next door. It's called Mesquite."

"You worked at Mesquite Barbecue?" Jenna shoots me a glance. She looks as thrown as I feel.

"Yes . . . ?" Lauren says.

"That's where my sister worked."

"Jules? Really? I don't remember her there. I don't think."

"No, you wouldn't," Jenna says. "By then, she was working in South Bend. She worked at Mesquite a few years earlier. Back when it was Famous Jake's."

"Oh." Lauren's voice is light. "Huh."

"I don't understand," I say, and Lauren shifts her attention back to me. "You and Kasey were attached at the hip. She loved working at the record store with you. Why'd you leave?" I feel frustration wafting off Jenna and realize too late what I've done—bowled over the revelation about Jules to ask about Kasey.

"Bah!" Thomas shouts. Lauren brushes his wispy hair with her fingers, then says, "The waitresses there made really good tips. I was in college. I needed the money. Plus, it wasn't like I was going far. It was literally next door."

"When did you switch jobs?"

"July, I think?"

"No." My voice is louder than I'd intended. A few of the church goers glance in our direction. "That can't be right. You were working at the record store the day Kasey went missing—August 17th. I walked over after work to look for her and you gave me a ride home."

"That's not how it happened."

"What do you mean?" I say.

"I was working that day, but I was at Mesquite. I saw you through the window. You were on the sidewalk out front, on the phone. You looked upset, so I came out to see if you were okay and you asked me for a ride. I remember because I had to ask my boss to leave early and he was a jerk about it."

I feel as if I'm in a snow globe that's being flipped upside down. That day was the most pivotal of my entire life. It's unfathomable that I could misremember it. And yet, Lauren's memory is already distorting my own. I think back to that summer evening: crossing Grape Road, sweat rolling down my back. The sound of that obscure band over the record store speakers. Lauren working alone. "No," I say. "I remember asking you where Kasey was, and you said you hadn't seen her all day."

"Right. Because I hadn't."

"But we were in the record store when we talked. Why would you have been in there if you weren't working there?"

"I wasn't in there," Lauren says. "I wouldn't have been. You probably went in looking for Kasey then came back out again. That's when I saw you outside."

Jenna's eyes are on me. "Nic. It was seven years ago. It's okay. You just misremembered something."

I nod but feel unmoored. First I learn that Kasey hid something from me that summer, and now I find out my own memories have betrayed me.

To Lauren, Jenna says, "Can you tell us about that summer? What was it like working so close to Kasey?"

"Well, the record store was a pretty cushy job. It was super slow, so Kasey and I just hung out most of the time. Oh, and there was this cute boy who worked at the yogurt shop across the street. We'd take turns going over there and seeing what free stuff we could get from him. Usually, he'd just give us tastes of the different flavors, but sometimes he'd pour sprinkles into a little cup. We'd take it back to the shop and eat them as we talked."

Lauren smiles softly, and I can see that to her, this memory is golden and light. If it were mine, it would carve a hole in me.

"And we worked well together too," she continues. "At first, we both did a bit of everything around the store, but Kasey was the one in love with the music. She'd spend hours deciding which records to play and in what order. She was a real perfectionist about it. You know how she could be. And she loved getting in new albums and making sure they were shelved properly. She even started joking about dropping out of nursing school to work there full-time."

"I remember that," I say. It sounds defensive.

"And I didn't really care about the music. So, I worked the cash register and answered the phone."

"What did you guys talk about?" Jenna says.

As Lauren had spoken earlier, I was starting to catch glimpses of the girl I used to know. But now, she clears her throat, straightens Thomas's shirt, and continues in her sweet, airy tone. "Oh, Lord, who knows? School, friends, Channing Tatum or whatever actor was hot that year. We were teenage girls."

"Did she ever say anything about leaving?" I ask. "Or even just taking a trip? Like, do you have any idea where she could've been going the night she went missing?"

"Well, by then, I was working at Mesquite, and we weren't really seeing each other as much."

"Yeah, but you were still friends. You talked. She didn't say anything about where she was headed?"

"I'm sorry," Lauren says. "No."

"What about . . . Did you ever notice that she was scared that summer?" I'm not being methodical about any of this, but I don't care.

"Scared? I . . . no. No."

"What about guys?" Jenna says. "Did she ever talk about who she liked?"

"Kasey was pretty focused on school."

It's true. And while my sister might not have mentioned her friend changing jobs, she would have told me if she had a crush. Of that, I'm certain.

"Plus"—Lauren shoots me a look—"she probably would've told you before she told me." It feels like a finger prodding a fresh bruise. *Kasey never told you.* I can't tell if it was intentional or not.

"What about the guy who worked at the yogurt shop?" Jenna says before I have the chance to respond.

"Oh. That was nothing. He was just fun to look at."

"Can you remember his name?"

Lauren's eyebrows jump. "You think he might've had something to do with Kasey's disappearance?"

"Right now, we're looking for anything."

"Oh gosh, I don't think I can remember. John, maybe? Drew? I don't know. Something short. Ben? No, that doesn't sound right." Thomas suddenly grabs her necklace, a diamond cross on a silver chain, and tugs. "That's Mommy's necklace, baby." To us, she adds, "I should probably get going. He really will get fussy soon."

"Real quick," I say, "can you think of anyone who was interested in her that summer? A customer or someone who worked nearby? At Mesquite maybe? The police always said the person we're looking for wouldn't have known Kasey well. He probably crossed her path a handful of times and she caught his eye."

"Well," Lauren says, "Detective Wyler asked me more or less the same thing back then, and I gave him the name of someone, but it never amounted to anything, so it must've not been anything."

My heart starts thumping hard. "Who?"

"My old boss at Mesquite. He was"—she glances over her shoulder, but the nearest church goers are a good ten feet away—"pretty sleazy. Always staring at the girls' chests and saying gross stuff. Whenever someone would call him out on it, he'd laugh and say they needed to learn how to take a joke. There was an alley behind the restaurant where a handful of the places shared a dumpster. It was the one we used at the record store too. And all the girls who worked on the strip knew not to take out the trash alone, because sometimes he'd be out there smoking and . . . you know. You wouldn't want to get stuck in a back alley with him at night. I guess you could say that about a lot of guys though."

"What was this guy's name?" Jenna says.

"Steve McLean. But we all called him Skeevy Steve."

"And you gave his name to Wyler?"

She nods.

"His full name? You said Steve McLean?"

"Yeah."

Jenna glances at me, and I can see the unspoken question in her eyes. This was a solid lead. What had Wyler done with it? She looks back to Lauren. "Do you know how long he'd been working there by the time you started?"

"I'm not sure exactly, but he was the manager, and from the way people talked, it seemed like he'd been around a while. A few years at least. Oh," Lauren adds with a look at Jenna, "I guess that means he was there the same time your sister was."

CHAPTER ELEVEN

We walk back to Jenna's truck. "Shit," I say when she turns the engine on and the dashboard clock illuminates. "I'm going to be late for work. I'll have to change in the car."

She pulls out onto the road. "I'll drive fast."

I lean over to unzip my backpack and pull out my thick black work pants. But just as I'm about to kick off my Converse so I can tug them on, I stop. What Lauren just told us hits me all over again. "I can't believe we have a name," I say. It pulses in the air around me: *Steve McLean*. "I mean, I know that's what we wanted, what we were looking for, but . . . I don't know, I guess I didn't actually think we were gonna get one."

"I know," Jenna says.

"You don't recognize his name, do you?" I have to ask, even though I already know the answer. I would've seen it in her eyes if she had.

"It's not ringing any bells, but that doesn't mean Jules never said it. If they worked together, it would've been ten, eleven years ago. What about you? Do you remember Kasey ever mentioning him?"

"No," I say, then add bitterly, "Not that that means anything." I hear Lauren in my head, *Kasey never told you.* "Apparently, she didn't even mention her best friend quitting the job where they worked together."

Jenna looks over at me. "Hey, all this happened a long time ago. Kasey could've told you and you just forgot. It doesn't mean you and your sister weren't close. I've misremembered things about Jules— like, a lot. And even if she didn't tell you, it doesn't mean anything. It's not like that would've been this big, earth-shattering news."

"Yeah," I say. "You're probably right." But I don't really mean it. It would have been big news to Kasey that summer—at least I think it would have—which means she would've told me about it and I wouldn't have forgotten. I feel like I'm not seeing something right in front of my face.

Jenna reaches into her purse on the bench seat beside her. "Here."

I look over to see her holding an unopened bag of peanut M&M's. "Did you . . . get these for me?"

She shrugs. "I'm still feeling bad about, you know, the whole lying thing. I'm trying to make it up to you."

I feel a tug at the corner of my lips. "Thanks." I open the bag and pop an M&M into my mouth. "I want to track this guy down, Jenna."

"I do too. But we need to get some history on him first, dig around online. I can do that. And after everything Lauren told us, I think we should talk to Wyler too. If she's telling the truth and she gave McLean's name to the police, why the hell have you never heard it before?"

"I'll call him," I say as I tug my pants on under my dress. "During the investigation, he made this whole big deal about giving me and my parents his cell, promised to answer if we ever called."

"You sure?" Jenna's eyes slide from the road to look at me. "I don't mind."

I pull my dress over my head, then put on my shirt. "It's one phone call, Jenna. I can handle it."

"It's just, I know you have a lot going on right now."

Suddenly, I understand what she's doing. She's seen my apartment full of unwashed dishes and unfinished projects. If she doesn't expect anything from me, she can't be disappointed. I hear Pam from the animal shelter in my head: *When you say you're gonna do something, please just do it.*

"I'll call Wyler," I say.

"Okay." We pull into the Funland parking lot. "But just ask for a meeting. I want to be there when you talk to him."

"Yeah, no shit. Jesus, your faith in me is overwhelming." I lean over to tie my shoes and look at the clock. I'm twelve minutes late. "I gotta go. Thanks for the M&M's." I hand them over, but Jenna shakes her head.

"They're yours."

"Right," I say, opening the door and hopping out. "I forgot. Guilt candy."

"Hey, it's better than a guilt tomato."

I pop one into my mouth. "Mm. The taste of regret. My favorite."

Jenna laughs and my chest swells. I can't remember the last time I made someone laugh.

At the end of my shift nine hours later, I'm walking by Brad's open office door when I hear my name. I turn to see him sitting behind his desk.

"Hey," he says. "You have a minute?"

I step into his office. "What's up?"

"You mind closing the door?"

I close it and then sit in one of the chairs facing his desk. Like Funland itself, Brad's office is a relic of the past. The faux-wood-paneled walls and the rough gray carpet are fading to a monochromatic beige. His desk is a mess of papers, and boxes of files line the floorboards. A grinning decal of Rocky the raccoon, our Funland mascot, peels from the wall over Brad's head. Rocky's dressed in the same colors as my uniform, a red-and-yellow-striped shirt with a matching cap.

"I noticed you come in for your shift earlier," Brad begins.

"Oh. Shit. Yeah, sorry I was late. The bus took longer than usual."

He waves a hand. "No, no, that's not what I meant. I, um, I'm sorry, Nic, but I happened to overhear you on the phone."

"Oh." It would've been when I called Wyler. It was the first thing I did when I got out of Jenna's truck. He didn't answer, so I left a message.

"I could be making this up—I seem to be losing my hearing in my old age—but I thought I heard you say Detective Wyler's name."

When Kasey went missing, my parents all but disappeared with her. My mom into her drinking and then eventually into her new family in Florida. My dad into denial, silence. In those crucial first few weeks, Brad and his wife Sandy were the scaffolds holding up my crumbling family. The two of them organized search parties and printed flyers with Kasey's face, posting them on every telephone pole between Mishawaka and Grand Rapids. And unlike the rest of our friends and neighbors, who stopped coming by and calling around the six-month point, Brad and Sandy never did. The Andrewses are the closest thing I have to family outside my own blood.

Still, I hadn't meant for anyone to overhear me.

"Nic?" he says. "Is everything okay?"

"Yeah, yeah." If he's already heard Wyler's name, it won't take much for him to put the rest together. Plus, it has suddenly occurred to me that Brad could be a resource. He and Sandy were there throughout it all. Sandy was in and out of our house every day, delivering food from the meal train she'd organized. Brad spent almost every evening in the garage with my dad, drinking beer and talking about the investigation. He would've had more wherewithal throughout the whole thing than me or my parents. He might remember things we don't.

Finally, I say, "I've been looking into Kasey's disappearance."

"Oh. Jesus, Nic, I don't know what to say." Brad studies my face. "Do you think this is—I don't wanna sound, you know—but do you think this is the best idea, with everything you've got going on?"

"I'm fine," I say. I can't look directly at him. His expression of sympathy is too much to bear.

"Does your dad know?"

"No. And please don't tell him. This may all amount to nothing, and, well, you know how he is."

Since Kasey's disappearance, my dad's adopted a confounding

mix of sentimentality and denial. The home where she and I grew up, the one where only he now lives, has hardly changed at all over the years. He hasn't gotten one new piece of furniture or swapped out one picture from the wall. I avoid going there because it's like walking back in time. And yet, he can't even say her name. I let it slip during Christmas dinner one year and his eyes blurred over. "It's been another cold one," he'd said, as if he hadn't even heard.

Brad lifts his palms. "I get it. I won't. But you know, Nic, I care about you too. Sandy and I've known you since you were three hours old. I worry about you. You've had a rough few years topped off by a rough few months. Are you sure this is the smartest thing for you to be doing right now?"

"No offense, Brad," I say, "but I'm doing it whether you think it's smart or not."

He lets out a small rueful laugh. "Understood. In that case, then, is there anything I can do to help?"

I fill with a stunned sort of gratitude. If I'd known this conversation was coming, I could've predicted the pitying smiles and words of caution. His support is a nice surprise. "Actually, yeah. You know how the police always said whoever took Kasey would have known her?"

Brad clears his throat. After the investigation fizzled, we never did this, never dissected what happened that summer. He's wide open compared to my dad, but even so, our tragedy is a heavy thing to hold. "I remember they said it would be someone on the outskirts of her life. He would've known her, but not necessarily the other way around."

"Do you remember the police ever mentioning any names in particular?" I say. "Anyone they were looking into?"

"I don't think so. Not that I can remember. Why do you ask?"

"I learned there was a man that summer, someone who worked nearby the record store and . . ." The words turn to stone in my mouth. It's unbearable to say the rest out loud, and by the look on Brad's face, I know I don't have to. "Does the name Steve McLean mean anything to you?"

For a moment, he's so still, I'm not sure he's heard me.

"Brad?"

"Sorry, I—" He lets out a ragged breath, runs a hand down his face. "I know Kasey was your family, but we loved her too. Me and Sandy." It's the first time in a long time that I've seen his cheerful façade drop. It's the most I've liked him in years. "This is all just . . . unexpected. What's the name again?"

"Steve McLean."

"I . . . I don't know. It doesn't sound familiar."

"The police knew about him."

Brad's chin juts back. "They did?"

I nod.

"They had his name?"

"Yeah."

"I didn't know," he says. "Not that I would. Your dad was the one who kept me in the loop, so I only knew what he told me. But you talked to Wyler about it?"

"I got his voicemail. I'm going to."

He frowns. "How'd you get McLean's name, then?"

"I talked to Kasey's friend from high school, Lauren Perkins. They worked together in the record store that summer. Apparently, she gave Wyler McLean's name during the investigation."

"She's Joe and Bitsy's kid?"

"Yeah."

"Well," he says, "if she gave them his name, they must've looked into him, right?"

"Then why wouldn't they have told us about him?"

Brad shrugs. "Maybe it was a dead end?"

"But even if it was, shouldn't they have told us about leads like that? I mean, they basically just kept us in the dark the whole time."

"I know." His voice is thick with pity. "Maybe they were trying to spare your family if they didn't think it was a good lead? To be honest, Nic, I never got the feeling the police were hiding anything. I always thought their lack of updates was because they just had so little to go on. You know, they had her car a hundred and fifty miles away. They didn't have prints or anything stolen. It was like she disappeared into thin air."

That's what people always say about my sister—hell, it's what I always say—and for years it's what I've let myself believe, because it's easier to swallow than the truth. If the impossible happened, it would've been equally impossible to prevent. But though she may have gone missing without a trace, one thing I know for sure is that bodies don't just disappear. Kasey is out in the world somewhere, waiting to be found.

There's a knock behind me, and I jump, turning to see the door already opening.

"Brad?" I recognize the voice before I see its owner. "Oh, sorry to interrupt—" Sandy begins when she sees that Brad isn't alone, but then her eyes land on me. "Nic!"

Her warm smile melts something inside my chest, the way it always does. When it was clear Kasey wasn't coming home, my mom left, and Sandy slipped seamlessly into the role. Tonight, she's wearing black leggings and a blue T-shirt, her honey-colored hair pulled back into a ponytail. In her hands is a Tupperware filled with what looks like brownies.

"Hey, Sandy."

She walks over and pulls me into a hug.

"Hey, hon," Brad says. "Am I late?" Then, to me: "My car's in the shop so Sandy's been driving me to and from work. I was supposed to be outside waiting." He gives me an exaggerated look: *oops.*

"I figured you lost track of time," Sandy says. "So I decided I'd come in and get you. I wanted to get rid of these anyway." She lifts the Tupperware in her hands. "Thought I'd leave them here for the staff. I don't know why I still make brownies when there's just the two of us to eat them . . . What are you guys chatting about that has you both here late?"

I'm opening my mouth to tell her—I can ask her about McLean too—when Brad says, "Oh, just work stuff. Nothing exciting."

Sandy looks from him to me. Over her shoulder, I catch his eye, and he gives me a pleading look that I understand. Kasey's disappearance isn't a topic that's easy for any of us. "Yeah." I nod. "Work stuff."

"Well, I'm glad I'm seeing you, Nic. I've been meaning to have you over for dinner. It's been too long."

"That sounds great." Sandy's meals are the only home-cooked ones I get.

"Good. We'll get something on the calendar, then. In the meantime, take these." She hands me the Tupperware. "The staff won't know what they're missing."

"For real?" There have to be a dozen brownies inside, but I'm not about to refuse.

She smiles. "They're rocky road."

Her rocky road brownies have been a favorite of mine since I was a kid, and because neither she nor Brad likes marshmallows, I understand that she made them with me in mind. "Thanks." I pull out my phone to check the time—I must be running late for the bus—but I'm distracted by a flurry of texts from Jenna.

"Everything okay?" Sandy says.

I look up, startled. "Yeah. Fine. I just—I have to go. Sorry."

"Of course," she says lightly, though her expression is shadowed with concern. She pulls me into another hug that I return too briefly.

"See you tomorrow, Nic," Brad says, but I'm already slipping out the door.

The moment I'm alone, I click on Jenna's messages and our text thread fills my screen.

Holy Shit, the first one reads.

Steve McLean is all over the internet. Lauren only knew the tip of the iceberg.

Call me!

CHAPTER TWELVE

The Grand Rapids police station hasn't changed much over the years, and walking into it is like walking into an old forgotten nightmare. Around every corner is another memory I'd prefer to keep buried. That's the room where I sat, a cup of weak tea in my hands, as Detective Wyler took down my statement about the day Kasey went missing. That's where some uniformed officer got my fingerprints so they could compare them to the prints found in our car. That's the door to the bathroom where I once ran to throw up in the middle of an interview. Wyler and I had been talking about something relatively benign when it happened. I'd been telling him how Kasey always took care of me when we were kids, making me breakfast on the weekends when our mom was asleep, too hungover to remember to feed us, and suddenly my stomach lurched. When I came back, there was a soda and vending machine chips on the little table, which he slid over to me. Adrenaline, he said, was a fickle thing.

Wyler did eventually call me back, though it took two more voice-mails to get his attention. When he did, two days after I first reached out to him, I told him Jenna Connor and I were looking into our sisters' cases and we had a few questions. Would he mind sitting down with us sometime within the next week? It was obvious he was surprised to hear from me, and he seemed skeptical about the visit, but he agreed. "I have a window this Friday afternoon," he said. "You can swing by the station then."

Jenna had to use a sick day, and I asked Brad if I could come in this weekend instead and, as I knew he would, he said yes. So, here I am again, in a place teeming with bad memories. But this time, I'm not alone. I have Jenna by my side now, and we have ammunition in our pockets.

Jenna did her due diligence when researching Steve McLean, and what she found makes Lauren's account of him seem almost juvenile. According to the internet, McLean has racked up a hefty list of offenses over the years. He was charged with intimidation and multiple instances of domestic violence against his ex-wife, and there are protection orders against him filed by two other women. Most disturbingly, he was charged with rape but took a plea deal before it ever went to trial. That seems to be his legal MO: In almost every case, he took some kind of plea that lowered the charges to misdemeanors. Jenna says the offenses are the kind police and judges chalk up to an inability to have decent relations with a woman, nothing criminal. But the implications are clear.

And these are just the things for which he's gotten caught. Which makes me wonder: What else has he done that he's gotten away with?

On top of all this, Jenna found that McLean's family owns a small piece of land in Kentucky. I wouldn't have thought anything of this if it weren't for what Wyler told my family all those years ago: that the man the police were looking for most likely owns or is familiar with some sort of property where he brought Kasey after the abduction.

I've never been in Detective Wyler's office. Back when I came to the station during Kasey's investigation, he didn't have one, and I was always led to the conference rooms. But he's the sergeant in charge now, and an office came with the promotion, though it's dinkier than I would've imagined. It's not that different from Brad's, actually, just a small, run-down room drowning in files.

"Sorry I wasn't able to meet earlier," Wyler says after he shakes hands with me and Jenna. "Things around here have been busy. In fact, I'm feeling a bit guilty you girls came all this way. A new case fell into my lap the other day, so I'm afraid I don't have much time."

Once, Kasey had been his number one priority, and a phone call from me would have made him drop everything. I know I shouldn't blame him for not still working on a seven-year-old cold case, but I do. I resent waiting days for an audience with the man who did nothing but let us down. Briefly, I think about the family in Wyler's "new case," the people he doesn't wait to respond to. I envy the hope they undoubtedly have. I pity them for what's coming.

"And as I mentioned over the phone," he continues, "I'm no longer the lead on your sister's case. It was passed on to another detective a few years ago when I took the promotion."

"We know," Jenna says. "But it's you we wanted to see."

He nods. "I also feel it's prudent to add, since both of you are here, that while we always theorized Kasey's disappearance was connected to Jules Connor's, Jules's case was not within my jurisdiction, so I can't speak to it with any authority."

"It's Kasey we're here to talk about."

Jenna offered to spearhead this interview, which was fine with me. She was going to ask open-ended questions, she said, let Wyler do most of the talking. Most important, she—we—were not going to mention Steve McLean's name until we had to. McLean is our trump card, the only card we have.

"Well," Wyler says, "you have my attention."

"We understand that the police have to keep some things under wraps during an active investigation, but now that it's been so long, we were wondering . . . were there any leads you didn't tell Nic's family about?"

Although it was Jenna who asked the question, Wyler looks at me. "In most cases we can't share every lead with the families. We have to protect the integrity of the investigation. But in this case, we didn't hold anything back. Because there was nothing to hold back."

"But you never told us anything," I say. "All you ever said was that you were looking for a guy."

"A man on the periphery of Kasey's life, yes. That was our theory."

"That's not a theory. That's a fucking line."

"Nic—"

"No, really. I can count all the words of your entire *theory* on two hands. A-man-on-the-periphery," I say, punctuating each word with a finger, "of-Kasey's-life. That's eight words."

Wyler stares passively at me. I think back to the day I smashed that mug on the driveway as he pulled out, one of many times I'd snapped that year. Perhaps, by now, he's used to me. My gaze flicks to a glass bowl on his desk. It's filled with those hard candies wrapped to look like strawberries. I grab one, unwrap it, and pop it into my mouth.

"Help yourself," he says. I glower at him.

"Can you tell us," Jenna says to Wyler, "when you were looking for this man, what avenues did you go down?"

"We spoke with people in Kasey's life. Her family, for instance. Her friends. We asked them if they knew where she was going that night, why she was on the road. We asked if they'd seen any shift in her behavior and you, Nic, told us before she disappeared, she'd been stressed with school. We asked if they could think of anyone in Kasey's life who would've been motivated to take her. We asked if they knew of any man who showed a little too much interest, anyone who kept coming around the house or the store where she worked. That kind of thing."

"And? Did that get you any names to look into?"

"Unfortunately, it didn't produce any viable suspects."

"But were there names?" Jenna says, and I hear the smallest crack in her calm exterior. Wyler's diplomacy is edging into caginess. "You did look into people. Right?"

"We looked into many people. We just didn't find any viable suspects."

"You keep saying *viable* suspects," I say. "But what about unviable ones?"

"Well, in that case, Nic, we would consider them unviable."

Jenna and I exchange a look. My question was dumb, for sure, but it feels like he's dancing around something.

"During your investigation," Jenna says, "did you ever talk to Lauren Perkins?"

Wyler shakes his head. "You're gonna have to refresh my memory."

"Lauren was Kasey's friend from high school. They worked at the record store together that summer. Or at least most of that summer, before Lauren got a job at the restaurant next door."

"Of course," Wyler says. "We spoke with Lauren, yes."

"So did we." Jenna lets the words hang in the air.

"If you have a specific question, I'd be happy to answer it."

"Lauren gave us a name. Of a man who worked at the barbecue place right by the record store where Kasey worked that summer. He had a reputation for harassing women. Steve McLean. She told us she gave you his name too."

Wyler leans back in his chair. Again, even though it was Jenna who said it, he looks at me. "Nic, I'm sorry Ms. Perkins got your hopes up, but we looked into McLean. He wasn't our guy."

"Why?" I say.

"For starters, take a look at the crime scene—Kasey's car abandoned on the side of the road. When we got there, it was immaculate. No sign of a struggle, no blood, no fingerprints aside from your family's, which we'd expect to be there, not a dollar bill taken from her wallet. It was clean, self-contained. Steve McLean is not that kind of guy. He's the type who gets heated and slaps a woman when he thinks she's out of line, or grabs someone's backside when no one's looking. He doesn't premeditate his crimes, he improvises them. Plus, he's not a rich guy and he's greedy. If McLean had abducted your sister, at the very least, her wallet would've been taken too."

"So, wait," I say. "You're ruling out McLean because the crime wasn't his *style*?"

"Profiling goes a long way in these cases, Nic."

"That's such bullshit. You can't rule somebody out because you don't think that's the way he would've done it. Maybe you didn't understand Lauren when she told you, but this guy is a predator. We looked him up online. He has protection orders against him. Charges of domestic violence. Of rape."

Wyler frowns. "Those must be recent. Seven years ago, he didn't have all that."

"That's not true," Jenna says. "The dates are online. In 2012, he had a charge of intimidation from his ex-wife and one of domestic violence."

"You're right. I didn't mean he didn't have any charges, but those were specific to his ex-wife. The two of them clearly weren't capable of maintaining a healthy relationship."

My eyes go wide. "Excuse me? Did you just blame McLean's ex-wife for his violence?"

Wyler is quiet for a moment, then says, "It was bad phrasing. All I was trying to point out is that at the time we were looking at him, he hadn't racked up the kind of charges you mentioned."

"So," I say. "He's just gotten worse."

"Look." His voice is curt. He's getting flustered. "I'm not defending McLean. I'm telling you he wasn't our guy."

"Because you had him fill out an online personality test? And you just don't think a Gemini has that much foresight?"

Jenna shoots me a warning look. I know I'm not doing us any favors here, but my skin is hot with resentment. For all these years, this man has hidden the name of a potential suspect from me and my parents—for what?

"His family owns land in Kentucky," I say.

Wyler narrows his eyes. "I'm not following . . ."

"You told us that the man who abducted Kasey would've had a property where he took her."

"A lot of people own property, Nic. It's circumstantial. McLean also had an alibi."

"What was it?" Jenna says.

"He spent that night at a friend's house. They hung out till the early hours of the morning and then McLean crashed on his couch. He was there all night. And before you ask, I honestly can't remember the friend's name, but take me at my word when I say we looked into it. It checked out."

"But—"

"I'm not sure what else to tell you, girls. McLean doesn't fit the profile and his alibi is solid." He makes a show of looking at his watch, then stands. "Now, I'm sorry, but I have a briefing to get to. It was good to see you again, Nic. Jenna. I'm sorry I couldn't be more help."

Jenna and I walk across the police station parking lot to her truck. She's probably half a foot taller than I am, and I have to jog to keep up with her.

"You gotta get better at this, Nic," she says. "You can't snap every time someone pisses you off."

"Jenna, he knew about McLean. This entire time." I reach into my pocket and pull out a strawberry hard candy. Just before we left Wyler's office, I grabbed a handful. The pettiest revenge.

"I know. But Wyler's one of the few resources we have. We can't burn that bridge, even if he is a dick."

"Such a dick," I say.

Jenna lets out an incredulous little laugh. "He really was. I think we should reach out to the detective who inherited your sister's case when Wyler got promoted. They might not know as much, but maybe whoever it is won't be as condescending."

"Okay," I say. "I'll do that."

She nods. "God, Wyler. And here I was always so jealous of your family getting Grand Rapids PD. But, Jesus, victim blaming McLean's ex-wife? Acting like an alibi from a friend and a personality profile are irrefutable proof of innocence?"

"Yeah." The candy clicks against my teeth. "And it just backfired. I suspect McLean now more than ever."

I'm expecting Jenna to respond with her usual level-headedness, to tell me we need to pause, do our research, get our ducks in a row, blah blah blah. But instead, she stops and turns to face me. "Oh, absolutely. Screw everything Wyler just said. We're finding Steve McLean."

CHAPTER THIRTEEN

Mesquite Barbecue is loud and crowded. Silverware scrapes against plates, ice clinks in glasses, voices ricochet off the walls. Jenna and I slide into the seats of a booth across from each other, and the red vinyl sticks to the backs of my thighs.

It's Saturday evening, just over twenty-four hours since Wyler did his best to tell us Steve McLean wasn't our guy, and I've had a long day. I spent two hours at the animal shelter this morning, where I tried and failed to hang with Banksy because Pam was following me around like some court-appointed babysitter, then nine hours at Funland—burning my fingertips from lighting so many birthday candles, going hoarse from all the singing. I smell like wet dog and pizza grease and now, on top of it all, meat.

Jenna hadn't been able to find McLean on social media during her online search, so we're doing things the old-fashioned way and trying to track him down here, the last place we know he worked. Between his rap sheet and the high turnover rates of restaurants, we assume he hasn't worked here in years and that anyone he used to work with is long gone too. But asking around is the only shot we have.

A waiter around my age sidles up to our booth. He's got floppy hair and an amused-looking smile. He introduces himself as Matty, then asks if we know what we'd like to drink.

"I'll take a—" I almost finish the sentence with *glass of red wine.* I could, no doubt, get away with it. The odds of running into one of the few people who know about the parameters of my intervention program are minuscule. But then I hear the screeching tires and crunching metal as I hit that tree. I see the red-and-blue lights of the officer pulling up behind me. Guilt, like fire, burns me from the inside out. "I'll just take a water."

Jenna asks for the same, and Matty leaves, then reappears a few minutes later to deliver them. "You two know what you'd like to eat?"

"Actually," I say, "we were wondering—" Jenna kicks my shin beneath the table.

Matty looks back and forth between us, that amused smile on his lips. "You were wondering . . . ?"

"If there are any specials," Jenna finishes.

"Uh, no, sorry. But the steak is good tonight."

"Great. I'll take that. With a salad and baked potato on the side."

I hesitate, looking over the menu, wondering if I should get the cheapest thing I can find or just nothing at all. Before I can decide, Jenna says, "She'll have the same." I open my mouth to protest, but she waves it off and Matty turns to leave. "It's on me."

My throat tightens. People are always taking care of me—Brad, my lawyer, my probation officer—but they seem to do it more out of obligation than affection. I haven't experienced Jenna's kind of generosity since before Kasey went missing. "Thank you."

She shrugs. "You should really eat something other than candy every once in a while, Nic."

A smile pulls at my mouth. "Hey, why'd you cut me off earlier? I was gonna ask him if he knew this fucking pervert we're looking for."

"That's why," she says.

"Oh, come on. I wouldn't have used those exact words."

"We have to come up with a plan. Think about it. If we come out swinging and we're talking to someone who knows McLean, someone who may actually *like* the guy, they probably won't want to talk to us."

"All right, all right," I say. "What's the plan, then?"

"I think our best bet is to talk to the employees who've been here the longest, find someone who knew someone who knew him."

"Right. Okay."

"And I was thinking we should ask a female employee. We don't want to say why we're looking for him off the bat, but if it comes to that, a woman may have more empathy for what we're doing."

But I'm no longer listening. Something just behind Jenna's shoulder has caught my eye. "Holy shit."

"What?" Jenna turns, looking into the dining room, a sea of red-and-white-checkered tablecloths and fatty meat glistening on plates.

"Oh, you've got to be fucking kidding me," I say.

Jenna spins around to face me. "What're you talking about? And what are you looking at?" Again, she looks at the room of people.

"Not there. There." I point to a plaque on the wall just behind her shoulder. It reads, in bold letters, EMPLOYEE OF THE YEAR, STEVE MCLEAN. It's from last year.

"Oh, screw that," Jenna says acidly. "You've got to be—"

But just then Matty returns, placing two side salads in front of us. "Is there anything else I can get for you guys at the moment?"

"Actually, yeah. Just a quick question." Jenna points at the plaque. "Is that guy working tonight by chance?"

Matty gazes at it. "Oh, Stevie?" he says with a grin. "Yeah, he's here. He's working the bar."

He juts a thumb over his shoulder. I turn to look at the bar and see a man behind it, his back to us, shaking a cocktail shaker. He has short brown hair, average build, average height. There's nothing remarkable about him.

"Stevie's a great guy," Matty says, waggling his eyebrows. It's clear he thinks he's in on whatever game we're playing, acting like cupid for the table of cute girls. "Here, let me get him for you."

"Oh, no, that's okay—"

But it's too late. Matty has already called out his name. Steve McLean turns around, and at first his gaze lands on Matty, then Jenna, then slowly, almost leisurely, it moves to me. Across the room, our eyes lock, and a grin spreads across his face. Spiders crawl up my spine.

CHAPTER FOURTEEN

Thank God it's a Saturday night. McLean's attention is pulled quickly to a patron at the bar, then another, and even though he keeps looking over at our table, it's obvious he's too busy making drinks to break away. The moment Matty brings our food, Jenna asks for the bill.

"We can't approach him here," she says after he's swiped her card. "If what we're asking gets out, it could jeopardize his job, and then he'll never talk to us."

"I wasn't planning on it."

For the first time, Jenna and I are on the same page about our next step. But not because I give a shit about Steve McLean losing his job. Or because, like she's always telling me, I think we need to strategize our approach. Being in the same room as my sister's possible killer has the walls closing in around me. I can feel his gaze on my face, my neck, my mouth. It makes me want to crawl out of my own skin.

"I wanna eat fast and get the fuck out of here," I say.

We do, and it's only outside the restaurant, sitting shotgun in Jenna's truck, the doors closed and locked, that I can finally relax. For a moment, we sit in silence, the hot summer air a relief from the prickling chill of Mesquite.

"We can talk to him another time," Jenna says. "It doesn't have to be tonight."

"No. I wanna do it. We can wait in the car till he's off work."

"We shouldn't talk to him here."

"Fine," I say. "Then we'll follow him home."

I feel Jenna looking at me from the corner of her eye. "Are you sure? We can take a day or two to regroup. He's not going anywhere."

"No. If we wait, between both our jobs and my community service, we won't be able to do it for another week." The truth is though, I just don't want to wait. I want to confront this man who harasses the women around him and manages to still charm his way to employee of the year. I want to talk to the man who worked alongside Jules and close to my sister. If he had anything to do with their disappearances, I need to know.

Jenna glances at the clock. "Okay. If he's bartending, he'll stay till closing, which means we probably have an hour or two."

I slump back against the seat. "God, the world can be so fucked up. Here our sisters were murdered all because they were women, alone on the road at night. Then this asshole is groping girls in a back alley and he still gets his name on a goddam plaque."

"I know," Jenna says. "Meanwhile, the media literally commodify Jules and Kasey for being young women who died."

"Fucking exactly." I wipe angry tears from my eyes. "And they all got it so wrong, you know? All of them."

Jenna looks over at me but doesn't say anything.

"Watching the news talk about Kasey was, like, beyond surreal. And not because what was happening was so hard to believe. I mean, it was, but it was more than that. They made her out to be someone I didn't recognize, a total stranger. When the police came to us for a photo, they told us to choose one that didn't have much significance, because by the time everything was over, we'd never be able to look at it in the same way again. But we had no idea how much the media would fabricate Kasey's entire personality based on one fucking picture of her. In the one my mom picked out, Kasey was wearing her favorite jean jacket and her hair was pulled over one shoulder. It looked like her, yeah, but it was such a specific look, like she was a cheerleader who got straight As. And when people talked about her on the news, you could literally hear in their voices that they felt sad she'd disappeared because she was, like, pretty and did well in school. I think one anchor actually used the words *all-American*."

I've never said this much to anyone before, not to my parents or any of my friends, not to Brad or Sandy. It makes me feel naked, but also lighter too, so I continue. "They painted this whole portrait of her that—you know, it wasn't wrong, but it wasn't even close to the full picture. They made her seem boring. Kasey was so much more than that. And people bought it too. I used to get all this mail from strangers telling me to have faith, to not give up on God's plan, blah blah blah. And they would write all these things about Kasey . . ."

I think back to a card some grandmotherly type had sent, in which she'd handwritten this saccharine poem titled "Nic and Kasey, Sisters Forever." Somehow it weaseled its way into my brain and I've had it memorized ever since:

Two branches of the same tree,
two pieces of a soul.
Where one sister goes, the other will be,
for she is but half of the whole.

"I could just tell," I continue, "that they thought they knew Kasey because they'd heard about her on the news. But she would've hated all that shit."

"She was lucky," Jenna says.

"Excuse me?"

She turns in her seat. Her eyes had been unfocused, staring through the windshield, but now they're sharp. "Sorry. Never mind."

"No. What did you mean?"

She hesitates.

"Jenna."

"Fine," she says. "Do you remember the news talking about Jules's disappearance before Kasey went missing?"

"Yeah, of course."

She gives me a look. "Not when they covered the cases together. *Before* Kasey went missing."

"Um . . ." I squish up my face, trying to think back. "I don't know. I can't remember."

"Exactly. Because her disappearance wasn't on the news. At least, not really. A handful of local stations covered it for a few days, but even they just did it in passing. It was only when Kasey went missing that the media started talking about their cases together. And even then, they'd always have Kasey's photo really big and Jules's really small, if they showed it at all. Do you remember the picture of her they used? She looks like a girl from no money who grew up to be a bartender, which she was. She wasn't beautiful like Kasey, she never had braces, she looked like a smoker, which, again, she was. But nobody cares about that girl. Whenever the TV anchors mentioned her, they had this tone—it was so messed up—like they were all surprised Kasey was taken, but Jules, you know, that was kind of to be expected."

Had I noticed this back then? It feels vaguely familiar, like a dredged-up memory, but I can't be sure. That year I was so blurry from grief that I only had one word, one name in my brain: *Kasey, Kasey, Kasey.* Now that makes me feel insensitive, narcissistic.

"I'm sorry."

"No," Jenna says quickly. "No, no, no. I don't want an apology—at least, not from you. I hated how the media made our sisters compete in death. I'm not gonna do it with you now. You're not the one I blame."

There's a painful swelling in my chest and I have the urge to grab her hand, to hold it in mine, but I don't.

"Plus," Jenna says. "Jules just got a head start. The media eventually tore Kasey down too."

I haven't listened to every news story or read every blog about our sisters like Jenna has, but I know what she's talking about. It happened fast, only a month or two after Kasey disappeared. One day, she was America's favorite missing girl; the next, she was a specimen to be examined and picked over. Somehow, the media discovered the names of the two boys Kasey slept with in high school and suddenly she was a slut. What was she wearing the night she'd been taken? they asked. Could she have gotten herself into a bad situation with a man? Some podcaster without a single relevant credential called her a nymphomaniac. Then, when he found out she shoplifted a bottle of nail polish once upon a time, she was suddenly that *and* a sociopath.

That story was the worst because my sister had only done it to protect me, like she had so many other times in her life. She was with me in the drugstore when I slipped the little bottle into my back pocket. Kasey told me it was obvious and to hand it over. "We can't get this," she said. "Mom would be so mad if we spent five ninety-nine on something called"—she flipped the bottle over and laughed—"*rendez-blue*." But then she looked into my face and sighed. "Oh, all right. But let me." She tucked it into her jean jacket.

"Yeah," I say to Jenna. "The ironic part is that I was so much worse than my sister ever was. She was always picking me up from parties, holding my hair back when I got sick from drinking too much. Yet she's the one who gets crucified because she had the bad luck of getting taken. She was only nineteen. *Nineteen.* And still the entire fucking country raked her over the coals for every mistake she ever made. They didn't seem to understand that everybody's an idiot when they're a teenager. Most people just have the good luck to stay alive long enough to grow out of it." Not me though, I guess.

"Jules was twenty-four," Jenna says. "She was finally growing up, you know. I could literally see her future start to expand, to brighten. Like, she discovered she loved to draw and did that all the time. She never talked about doing it professionally or anything, but I could see her start to think about it, start to dream. And then she was taken and all that was erased."

She reaches across me into the glove compartment and grabs a bag of peanut M&M's. This time she pours some into her own palm before handing it over to me. We eat in silence, and the minutes tick by. Thirty minutes turn to sixty, then to ninety. We watch people exit the restaurant and drive away until there are only a handful of cars left.

Eventually, Jenna breaks the silence. "What would you do?" she says. "You know, if Steve McLean is the one who took them?"

"What would I do to him, you mean?"

"Yeah."

I've thought about it over the years—of course I have. But whenever my daydreams get vindictive, the man who took Kasey is always faceless, and the violence I wreak on him sort of fades to black. Now, despite knowing Steve McLean is a bad man, inserting his face into this scene stops me in my tracks.

"I don't know," I say. "We're not sure he did it."

"Take McLean out of the equation, then. Let's say it's just some guy. But you know with absolute certainty that he did it. He took and killed your sister. What would you do then?"

The faceless man is easier to imagine. In my mind, the two of us are in an empty room with a metal chair. I tie his hands to the legs as a lightbulb swings slightly over our heads. I punch him in the jaw, and when he falls over, I kick him in the ribs until he cries out. But what happens after that, when he's bleeding from the lip and pleading for his life? Maybe I turn him in to Wyler. Though none of that feels quite right. "I don't know," I say. "What would you do?"

Jenna doesn't hesitate. "I'd buy a gun. I'd drive to his house and shoot him in the head."

I look over at her, but she doesn't look back. She just stares through the windshield. "Oh, hey," she says after a moment. "There he is."

I follow her gaze to the front door of the restaurant. It's open, and Steve McLean is walking through.

CHAPTER FIFTEEN

Through the windshield, we watch McLean cross the parking lot, unlock his car, and sink into the driver's seat. My heartbeat quickens. It's one thing to talk through a theory from the comfort of Jenna's living room. It's another to follow Steve McLean home. I feel better with Jenna by my side, and she's put her pepper spray in the top pocket of her purse, but seeking out the presence of the man who may have taken Kasey feels like lighting a match to test the heat of its flame.

Jenna waits as he pulls out of the parking lot, then turns her key in the ignition. Grape Road is almost empty, and she follows at a distance. We're anticipating the trip to his house to take at least fifteen minutes, but after only traveling a few blocks south, he turns. Not into a residential area but into the parking lot of O'Reilly's, an Irish pub off Grape Road. Jenna pulls into a spot a few down from his, and we look at each other.

"What d'you think?" I say.

She shrugs. "It's definitely safer to do it in public."

"Yeah, but will he talk?" My hesitation is half-hearted. We've come this far. I want to see it through.

We give McLean a few minutes' head start to curb any unlikely suspicions he may have that someone is following him, then we head in.

The bar is dark and bustling. There's a muffled roar of voices and the clinking sounds of the bartender making drinks.

"Hey," Jenna says beside me. Her eyes are locked on the far end of the bar. I follow her gaze to find McLean, sitting alone in a booth, an already half-empty glass of beer in front of him.

We walk over, my heartbeat thumping in my stomach, my ears, my armpits. When McLean's eyes catch on us, he looks surprised, then a grin spreads across his face. "Well, well," he says. "If it isn't you two."

"Hi." Jenna's voice is friendly. She's a much better actor than I am. "Mind if we join you?"

He can't believe his luck. "By all means." He waves a hand to the seat across from him and we slide in. I'm on the inside, between Jenna and the wall. It makes me itchy, claustrophobic.

"I'm Jenna." When I don't say anything, she adds, "This is my friend Nic."

McLean looks from her to me, and I see him clock my standoff-ishness, but it doesn't seem to faze him. He's clearly pleased with the turn his night has taken.

"Steve. You ladies want something to drink?" He waves at a waiter who's already walking our way.

I order a club soda with lime and Jenna orders a glass of white wine. I know she's doing it for the pretense. One sober woman is a coincidence, two looks fishy. McLean orders another beer. My loathing for this guy is so strong that it's reorienting his features into something deformed and monstrous. But up close, even I can see an objective sort of attractiveness in his face. He has a sharp jaw, bright blue eyes. I can see how he's lured women in. But there's something else just beneath the surface that gives him away, a too-eager glint in his eyes. Would Kasey have pulled over if she recognized him on the road? I like to think she wouldn't have, but that feels wishful.

"Actually," I say as the waiter turns to leave. "Make mine a red wine."

Jenna's eyes flick over my face, but she stays quiet. "You know,

Steve," she says, "you look so familiar to me. I feel like I've seen you before tonight."

"Oh yeah?" He seems to be interpreting her easy tone for flirting, and maybe that's what she's going for.

"Yeah. How long have you worked at the restaurant?"

"Long fucking time. Maybe I've made you a drink before."

"Maybe. Have you always been the bartender?"

"Used to be the manager, but it wasn't my bag. Making drinks is just so much sexier."

I force myself not to roll my eyes.

"Wasn't it called something else back in the day?" Jenna says. "The restaurant, I mean. Something like—" She snaps her fingers. "Oh, I can't remember."

"Famous Jake's," McLean says.

"That's right! You know, my baby sister actually used to work there." She's never used the word *baby* to describe Jules, and it crawls up my skin even though I know she's baiting the hook for him. Again, I realize just how good Jenna is at talking her way into getting what she wants.

"No shit?"

"Her name was Jules." She uses the past tense. We're not hiding anymore. "Jules Connor."

"Huh." He leans back into the booth, gazing at his beer as he makes lines in the condensation with his fingertips. "I don't know. Doesn't ring a bell."

"Really? She worked there for a few years."

"Nah, can't seem to place her."

"You don't even recognize the name?" I say. "It was pretty well-known there for a while."

McLean doesn't respond.

"Back in 2012, she was all over the news. Jules Connor was one of the girls who went missing from the side of the road. Not far from here, actually."

He pulls his phone from his back pocket, glances at the screen. "Shoot. Ladies, I'm sorry, but I have to get this." He slides out of the booth.

Jenna and I lock eyes. It's a phony call, it has to be, and we can't lose him now. But just as I'm turning around in the booth to make sure McLean doesn't walk out on us, he's back. He sits, tucking his phone into his back pocket, and takes a sip of beer. When he puts it down, it seems he's found his footing, like he knows how he's going to play this.

"Sorry about that," he says. "Now, where were we? Oh, that's right, the Missing Mishawaka Girls. I remember that story." He looks at Jenna. "One of those girls was your sister? I'm sorry to hear that."

"Thank you." Jenna pulls her phone out of her bag, taps the screen, and holds it out over the table. "This is her."

McLean shoots the screen a fleeting glance. "Huh."

"Do you remember her now? You were probably her manager when she was there, right?"

"How long ago are we talking?"

"Ten years," Jenna says. "She worked there for three years and left in 2009."

"Ah, Jesus." He chuckles. "I can't remember what I had for breakfast today let alone some girl I worked with a decade ago."

I know he's lying. I can see it in every line on his face. I want to hurl myself across the table at him, use my fingernails as claws. "It's weird, because women you work with definitely remember you."

I expect him to bristle at this, but instead he barks out a laugh. "Oh, I get it. You two got my name from some touchy little chick I used to work with and you tracked me down, huh? You fancy yourselves a couple of Nancy Drews." He has the bravado of a man who's gotten away with a lot over his life, and it's unnerving to sit across from him. Pepper spray or not, Jenna and I can't force him to tell us the truth if he doesn't want to. We can't force him to do anything. "Who did you talk to?" he says. "What is this said woman's name?"

Jenna and I are quiet. Our drinks finally arrive, and the moment my wine touches the table, I grab it and gulp half of it down.

"Ah, come on, Nancy Drew," McLean says when the waiter walks away. "You're not gonna tell me who I made such a lasting impression on?"

"I can't remember," I say. "But I do have another name for you."

He lifts his eyebrows, his mouth quirking upward. "Consider me intrigued."

"Kasey Monroe."

"Kasey Monroe . . . Kasey Monroe . . . Oh shit! Yeah, I do remember her." I'm expecting him to say he remembers her from the news, the other missing girl, but he doesn't. "She used to work at that little record store by the restaurant. Oh my god, yeah. That name is like a goddamn bell in my head."

I feel Jenna look over at me. "What do you mean?" I say.

"That name, Kasey, Kasey, Kasey."

I'm enraged by the flippant way he's saying my sister's name, but more than anything, I'm confused.

"I used to work with this uptight little bitch, right? And this chick would not shut up about Kasey Monroe. Name was always in her mouth." He takes a sip of beer, clearly enjoying the rapt audience. "Those two were—oh, what do you call them nowadays?—frenemies! That's it. Best friends who hate each other. She would just talk and talk about how she was so sick of her friend, Kasey. How Kasey was ruining her life. How annoyed she was by Kasey. My god, it went on and on. Finally, I had to bring her into the office and tell her nobody gave a shit."

I open my mouth, close it again.

"Who was this?" Jenna says.

He cocks his head. "You know what? I can't actually remember her name. She wasn't bad to look at though. Petite little thing. Long blond hair she always wore in a ponytail. Freckles on her nose and cheeks. Cute, you know, but uptight. Not very fuckable."

My stomach twists even though I'd seen it coming. He's describing Lauren Tate née Perkins. Kasey's best friend.

CHAPTER SIXTEEN

My world tips. I glare across the table at Steve McLean.

"You're lying." He has to be. Other than me, Lauren was Kasey's closest friend. She may have turned into someone I don't recognize, but that doesn't negate what she meant to my sister.

"Uh-oh," he says with a grin. "Struck a nerve, did I? No, but it's all true. My hand to God. I don't know why, but that chick hated Kasey." Despite loathing this man, despite knowing he's a liar and a misogynist, I don't believe he's lying now. He hardly seems to be thinking before he speaks, let alone using artifice. "Maybe that's who you guys should be talking to, you know, if you're looking into Kasey's disappearance."

"We—" But I stop when what McLean said sinks in. *Kasey's disappearance.* He's been acting like he only knew who Kasey was because of Lauren, but he knows exactly who she is and why we're here. "You knew her, didn't you?" I say. "Not knew *of* her. Knew her."

"She was so feisty, you know? That kind of thing tends to leave an impression."

"What—what're you talking about?"

"I saw her one day in the parking lot outside the restaurant, crying and waving her arms around. It was quite the show. If I'd thought to sell tickets, I could've made a boatload."

None of what he's saying makes any sense. Kasey was the calm one, the one who always talked me down from my moods. And yet there's still that look of guilelessness in his eyes. "Who was she talking to?" I say. "Was it Lauren?"

McLean shrugs. "Beats me. Whoever it was was standing behind a car. It was a shame though. The crying, I mean. Really fucked up her face, made her look all puffy and shit. Normally, she had such a pretty face." He sips his beer, then licks his lips. "You look a little like her, you know? Thought so the minute you sat down."

I shrink away from him. Has he known who I am this entire time? I think of that phony call earlier. He could've easily googled Jules and linked her to Kasey, linked Kasey to me. I did the family press conferences. My face is online. Or maybe he didn't need the reminder. Maybe he knew my face, because my sister's is branded into his memory—the face of the girl he took from the side of the road, the girl he killed.

"What did you do to her?" I say, my voice trembling with rage. "What did you do to my sister?"

McLean claps a hand over his chest, gives me a look of mock horror. "Don't tell me you suspect *me*, Nic. I haven't done a thing."

I lurch up from my seat, my thighs bumping roughly into the table. Our glasses shake, our drinks threatening to spill. McLean laughs.

Jenna leaps to her feet, grabs me by the shoulders. "Nic, calm down. Let's go."

"What did you do to her?" I shout again, as Jenna pulls me from the booth. "I swear to god, if you touched her—"

This makes McLean laugh harder, and something inside me breaks.

"You should be in fucking prison," I say. Then I spit in his face.

Jenna is shoving me toward the door, but just before she turns me around, I see the moment my saliva hits McLean's skin. His laugh dies in his throat. His eyes turn cold.

"What the fuck, Nic?" Jenna says once we've slid into her truck and slammed the doors behind us. "What were you thinking?"

"He deserved it."

She lets out a little shout of frustration. "You can't do that. You can't just do stuff like that."

"Sorry," I say, but I'm far from it. I wish that table hadn't been between me and McLean, wish Jenna hadn't been there to hold me back.

"Jesus, two weeks ago you didn't even want to talk about our sisters' disappearances and now you're attacking someone because you think he might have been involved?"

"Two weeks ago, I didn't think we had a chance at figuring out what happened to them. I didn't think we had a fucking prayer. But I do now."

"Fine," she says. "I'm glad you're finally invested, but what's the endgame here, huh? If McLean is the one who took our sisters—"

"You don't think he is?"

"I don't know, but if he is, what did you just gain us? A target on our backs, for sure. Anything else?"

"I . . ." I turn to look at her, my ragged breathing beginning to slow. I imagine McLean following Jenna to her house, slinking in the shadows of the trees in her yard, stepping quietly to her bedroom window. "I—I'm sorry."

She sighs. "Let's just get out of here before he comes outside."

It's past midnight now, the sky black. As we drive, the stoplights blur to streaks of red and green. My adrenaline slowly fades, leaving shame in its wake. Jenna trusted me to do this with her, and all I've done is put her at risk by pissing off a dangerous man. For the millionth time in my life, I wish I were a different kind of person. A better kind.

When I meet people who've heard of Kasey, I always get the feeling that they think seven years is enough time to have moved on.

Losing her is sad, of course, a tragedy, they're so sorry for my loss. But before I can even finish thanking them, they've already switched topics. *So, what do you do now?* they ask with amnesiac smiles. These are the people who don't know what real loss is, don't understand how it worms into your brain and infects your blood. They wouldn't understand how sometimes, even now, I pick up my phone to call Kasey, and when I remember, it feels like a hole being blown through my chest. They wouldn't understand how nighttime turns every stranger into a stalker, a predator, someone to both fear and despise. Even now, I'm a hornet's nest of anxiety, a knife's slash of pain.

Jenna and I have been driving in silence for so long that when she speaks, it makes me jump. "Here we are."

I look around and realize she's pulling up to my apartment. "Right," I say. "Thanks for the ride. And listen, Jenna. I really am sorry—"

She holds up a hand. "I know."

I grab my bag, but don't get out. "So, do you think what McLean said about—"

"Hey, Nic. I know we have a lot to talk about, but I'm exhausted. Can we just take a beat and go over it in the morning? Tomorrow's Sunday. You're not working, right?"

How could she possibly want to wait that long? Questions and suspicions are pinging so violently around my mind, I feel electric. "Sure," I say. "Fine."

I open the truck door. It's isolated out here, in the southeast corner of town. Beyond my apartment complex is nothing but fields. Moonlight glints off a nearby power line tower. Overhead is a star-studded night sky.

I'm closing the door behind me when I stop, turn to face her. "Just one thing."

Jenna sighs, but nods.

"Do you remember the way Wyler talked about McLean yesterday? He said, like, *He's the kind of guy who gets heated and slaps a woman when he thinks she's out of line.*" I'm mimicking Wyler's low voice. "*He doesn't think this stuff up in advance, he just acts.*"

"Yeah . . ." she says.

"That was Wyler's big reveal about why McLean wasn't 'their guy.' But McLean knew who I was back there. He knew what we were doing. And he let us. He toyed with us a little, then dropped a bomb and laughed when we reacted."

"I know," Jenna says. "I thought about that too."

The implication swirls in the silence around us: Steve McLean is way savvier than the police are giving him credit for.

CHAPTER SEVENTEEN

Pam is sitting at the front desk of the animal shelter when Jenna and I walk in the next morning.

"Nic? What're you doing here? You're not on the schedule today, are you?" Her obvious horror at the idea is almost laughable.

"I'm just visiting," I say. "I wanted to bring my friend."

The first thing I did when I woke up this morning was call Jenna. I'd given her the time she'd asked for, but still, it seemed she wasn't quite ready.

"Hang on," she said. "Lemme wake up first. I need coffee. And let's do this in person, okay? I'll come pick you up and we can go somewhere. Is there anywhere that makes you—I don't know—calm? We have a lot to talk about, and I'd prefer to do it with nice, normal Nic, not spit-in-a-bad-man's-face Nic."

The first thing that popped into my head was Banksy.

"I see," Pam says, her smile tight. "Welcome."

"We'll just head to the cat room," I say. "Always good to see you, Pam."

Five minutes later, I've taken Banksy out of his cage and brought him to the room designated for interacting with the cats, which is mercifully empty. Jenna and I sit on the floor, our backs against adjacent walls, our legs out in front of us. The tips of our shoes almost touch.

"I can see why you like him," Jenna says with a nod at Banksy. "He's just like you." Banksy hasn't quite taken to Jenna and sits curled in the far corner. His crooked tail is wrapped around his body, and his one eye glares lazily in her direction. "Are you thinking about adopting him?"

I haven't been able to articulate that plan yet, not even to myself. After all, I couldn't take care of my first cat, so why would I think this one would be any different? Still, every time I walk through the doors of the shelter, my eyes find the sign on the far wall: LOOKING TO ADOPT? LOOK NO FURTHER! and I feel a little ache of longing.

"No," I say. "Can we talk about last night now?"

Jenna nods. "We can talk."

"The way McLean reacted to our sisters' names . . . It was so fucking creepy. He had to have done something, right? He has to be involved." I say this as if McLean's individual reactions to hearing Jules's name and Kasey's name were the same, even though they weren't. When he talked about Kasey, he was crude, careless, mocking. But when Jenna brought up Jules, he got quiet, and for some reason, this was the reaction that sent a chill up my spine. But if Jenna didn't pick up on this, I'm not sure I want to point it out.

"I don't know what it means," she says. "But yes, it was definitely creepy." Her voice is soft, and I think perhaps she got the same read I did.

"What do you think about what McLean said about Lauren? Do you think it's true? That for some reason that summer she was annoyed with my sister?"

"I don't know," Jenna says. "I have no idea why she would lie about that, but it does kind of add up, doesn't it? Maybe that's why she stopped working at the record store. To put some space between her and Kasey."

"I thought about that too. Changing jobs for the last month of summer seems like a lot of work just for tips. Especially for Lauren. Her family wasn't super well-off or anything, but they had more money than we did. I don't think she would've been that desperate for cash. But I just can't wrap my head around them fighting. I mean, I remember that summer. Kasey spent the night at Lauren's all the time."

"Even at the end?" Jenna says. "In August?"

I squeeze my eyes shut, trying to remember the timeline of that summer, but my memories don't work like that. I can conjure flashes—Kasey and me painting each other's nails, Kasey and me sneaking vodka from the liquor cabinet, Kasey snapping at me for monopolizing the car—but I can't put anything in order. I let out a frustrated groan. "I don't know."

From his corner in the room, Banksy blinks open his one eye. He yawns, stretches, saunters over to me, and curls into my lap. I put a hand on his warm little body, feel his rib cage slowly rise and fall.

"If Lauren and your sister did have a falling out," Jenna says, "that could have had something to do with why Kasey was acting off. And it would explain the argument in the parking lot too. Kasey worked at the record shop and Lauren worked next door. It'd make sense that if they had some sort of confrontation, it'd be there."

"Maybe. I mean, yes, it could explain a few things, but it's hard for me to believe McLean over Lauren. I think we just need to talk to her again."

"I agree. But how are we gonna find her? She probably went to church again this morning, but"—Jenna checks the time on her phone—"yeah, she's got to already be home by now. Not that having this conversation surrounded by a bunch of church people would be the best strategy anyway."

"I already figured that part out," I say. "When we said goodbye to her last weekend, she told me to give her love to my parents, and I realized I know her family. I mean, I don't know them well or any-thing, but if I call, they'd probably give me her address. I feel like an idiot for not thinking of it the first time around."

"Well," Jenna says. "I think bumping into her at church was a less threatening way to start, but I'm all for showing up on her doorstep now. Do you have their number?"

"No. But I can get it."

I pull out my phone and tap on my dad's contact. A bubble of dread fills my chest. I love my dad, but I don't love talking to him. The line rings and rings. I'm about to hang up when I hear his voice.

"Nic?" He sounds surprised, as he always seems to be when he's reminded of my existence. This is why things between us are hard. He can't say Kasey's name, but she's the only thing that fills his brain. I understand—in this, I am my father's daughter—but his grief is so big and unruly, it leaves no room for me. It's as if the moment Kasey disappeared, I vanished with her. "Hey. Uh . . . How are you?"

"I'm fine." I feel Jenna watching me, but I keep my eyes on Banksy, asleep in my lap.

"Good, good . . . Brad tells me things at work are going well." I can tell by the way he says it that Brad has not mentioned me looking into Kasey's disappearance. Good.

"Yep," I say. "Things are fine. I don't actually have that much time though. I was calling for a favor. Do you have a number for the Perkinses?"

"As in Joe and Bitsy?"

"Yeah."

"I'm sure I have it somewhere . . . Let me put the phone down for a minute." I'm relieved but not surprised when he doesn't ask why I want it. A few moments later, he comes back on the line. "Okay. I found a few here in the Rolodex. I'm guessing this first is their landline, if they still have one. The other two are for their cells."

"Perfect." I look at Jenna and nod.

My dad reads the numbers aloud on speaker, and I type them into my phone. When he finishes, there's a moment of silence, which he fills by clearing his throat. "You should stop by the house sometime. I could fix us dinner or something."

"That sounds great. Why don't you text me some dates?" We both know the invitation will die here, but sometimes I can't help but make it harder. *You still have me,* I want to say. *You still have one daughter left.*

"Will do. Take care now."

After I hang up, Jenna says, "Do you know what you're gonna say? To the Perkinses?"

"I was thinking I'd tell them I ran into Lauren at church. Say she was really nice to talk through some things with me and I want to send her a thank-you, but I don't have her address."

"That's good," Jenna says. "I think you might be getting better at this."

"Well." I scratch Banksy behind the ears. "I'm learning from the best."

Jenna needed to swing by her mom's place to drop off some medicine, but even with the errand, it's less than an hour later when we pull up to the address Mrs. Perkins gave me over the phone. Lauren's house is a two-story red brick with an American flag flapping out front and one of those green, summery wreaths on the door.

Jenna and I are out of the truck and walking up the front path when the garage door rumbles open and a white SUV pulls into the driveway. I see Lauren behind the wheel. She parks in the garage, gets out of her car, and slams the door behind her. She looks like an almost different person today, so unlike the pristine woman we saw last week at church. Her hair is pulled into a limp ponytail, unwashed strands falling around her face. She's wearing jeans and an oversized button-down with a smear of what I imagine is spit-up on her shoulder.

"No!" she calls as she starts walking toward us. "I cannot talk to you. How did you even find me?"

I knew Lauren wasn't going to be happy to see us again so soon, but this reaction is a shock. "I-I'm sorry if this is a bad time," I stammer. "We—"

"Bad time? Bad time? My husband's out of town and I'm taking care of two kids on my own, who are in the car right now and—" She waves a hand. "You know what? It doesn't matter. I need to get my kids in the house, and you two need to leave." She turns and starts striding back to her car.

I give Jenna a confused look that she mirrors back at me. Maybe we went a little far by getting Lauren's address from her mom, but surely that isn't what has elicited this extreme of a response.

"Lauren," Jenna says. "Is everything okay? What's happened?"

Lauren whirls around. "Look, Nic, I talked to you because Kasey was my friend. But I am not getting wrapped up in whatever it is you guys are doing. I have two kids, and I am not putting them in any more danger. We were doing fine, and then the moment you came along—" She stops short. "Please just leave." She presses a series of buttons on a little pad on the wall and the garage door starts to close.

"Wait!" I call out to her. "The moment we came along, what?"

But she's already disappeared from view.

"What the fuck?" I say, turning to Jenna. "'Any more danger'? What the hell is that supposed to mean?"

"I don't know," Jenna says. But I can tell she does. We both do: Sometime in the last week, something scared Lauren into not wanting to talk about my sister.

CHAPTER EIGHTEEN

It's the middle of the day, hot and sunshiny, and Lauren's neighborhood is alive with summertime. Kids laugh and shout in the distance, the sprinklers in a nearby yard make a rhythmic beat, and somewhere a few blocks away, I can hear the tinkling song of an ice cream truck. Despite all this, I feel a chill of fear.

Jenna looks around. "Let's talk in the truck."

"What do you think happened?" I say once we've climbed in and closed the doors. "Do you think someone talked to her?"

"Or did something else," Jenna says. "But, yeah, I think someone tried to scare her. And it obviously worked."

"Jesus. This is because of us. Just like Lauren said. I mean, what're the odds that we approach her about all this and then less than seven days later, someone else just happens to do the same fucking thing?"

"But how would anyone know what we've been doing?" Jenna says. "I haven't told anyone. Have you?"

"No. But, I mean, we've talked to people. Wyler, McLean—McLean! It could've been him."

"Maybe, yeah." Jenna screws up her face. "But Lauren already gave us his name. If it were him, why wouldn't she just say it?"

"Maybe she didn't know it was him. He could've called or left a note or something."

"And you're sure you haven't told anyone else?"

"Yes, of course I'm . . ." My voice fades.

"What?" Jenna says.

"Nothing. I just realized I mentioned it to Brad too, but—"

"Who's Brad?"

"I've told you about him," I say. "He's a family friend. He gave me my job at Funland."

"And you told him you were looking into Kasey's disappearance?"

Beneath her casual tone, I feel an edge of accusation and let out an incredulous little laugh. "He has nothing to do with this," I say, thinking of the way Brad so carefully tucks his Funland polo into his khaki slacks, how he kisses Sandy goodbye on the cheek. "Believe me."

"But what did you tell him?"

I shrug. "He heard me leaving a voicemail for Wyler. He was there for the entire investigation, so he knows Wyler, knew what it meant that I was calling him. I asked him if he recognized McLean's name."

"What about Lauren? Did you mention Lauren's name to him?"

"No. I don't know. But it doesn't matter. The idea that Brad has anything to do with this is, like, absurd. You just gotta take my word on this one."

"Hang on, Nic," Jenna says. "Think for a second. Did you mention Lauren's name or not?"

I roll my eyes. I'm about to say no again when it occurs to me. "Yeah, I did. I told him she gave us McLean's name."

"Shit."

"Jenna, stop. Listen to me. I trust this guy. He's been like a second dad to me since I was born." Brad, with his good-natured check-ins and gentle reminders. Brad, the man my dad has gone fishing with dozens of times over the years. Brad, the man we've vacationed with, the father of the boys with whom we grew up, the mild-mannered boss who's let me get away with so much over the years. "He's not the one who scared Lauren. I promise you."

"Okay . . . but somebody got to her, and our options are pretty limited. The list of people who know what we're doing is, like, three."

"That doesn't mean it was him," I say. "Jesus. It was probably fucking McLean. You met that guy. We didn't give him Lauren's name, but he got there in the end."

"That's true." But she looks skeptical.

For a moment, we're quiet, lost in our thoughts. Eventually, Jenna says, "What if . . ."

"What?"

"I don't know if it'll work, but I just got an idea."

"Okay . . ." I say.

"What if we knock on Lauren's door and tell her we know about Brad. If he was the one who scared her, she'll think we already know about what happened, and she might talk."

"That's your idea?"

Jenna shrugs. "If it doesn't work, we're no worse off than we are now."

"Why use Brad's name?" I say. "Why not McLean's?"

"Because we've already talked to Lauren about him. I know that was before whatever happened happened, but she seemed perfectly fine talking about him at the time. There are three people who know what we're doing—Wyler, McLean, and Brad—and the only one out of the three we haven't spoken with her about is Brad."

"I mean, sure," I say, "but there's a good chance whoever got to her did it anonymously and Lauren doesn't even know who it was. If our theory that someone scared her is even right in the first place." But the real reason I'm pushing back is because a bad, frenetic energy is building inside me. I don't usually think of Brad sentimentally, but with Jenna pointing fingers at him, I realize that he and Sandy are the only people I really have left in the world. I need Jenna to believe me when I say he's innocent.

As if reading my mind, Jenna says, "If you believe Brad had nothing to do with this, this'll be the first step toward proving it."

I close my eyes. I don't have much faith in the plan, but I want

Jenna to be able to cross Brad off her list. I want to move on. "Fine," I say eventually. "But I'll do the talking."

Jenna lifts her palms. "Be my guest."

Once again, we get out of the truck and walk up Lauren's front path. When I press my finger into the doorbell, there's a sudden explosion of activity at the sound of the chime: a patter of feet, an excited exclamation from Beth Anne, then a sharp one from Lauren, telling her, I imagine, not to answer the door.

Through one of the tall, narrow windows that frame the door, I see Lauren approach. When she locks eyes with mine, her face goes hard. "Nic," she says from behind the glass. "I told you I can't talk." Her words are muffled but distinguishable.

"I know, but—"

"Just go away." Her plea screws into my chest. I may not like the person she's become, but I can tell she's genuinely afraid.

"Lauren, we—"

"Nic, please."

I shoot a sideways glance at Jenna, then force out the words. "We know about Brad!"

Silence. For a long moment, there's nothing. Then the slide of a lock, the twist of a knob. The door creaks open a few inches to reveal a sliver of Lauren's face.

"You know about him and Kasey?"

CHAPTER NINETEEN

Everything inside me drops. Angry tears sting my eyes. I've been mad for years, mad at the man who took Kasey, mad at God or the universe or random fucking chance for allowing the person he chose to be my sister. But I've also spent that time thinking I knew everything there was to know about her. Whatever this "Kasey and Brad" thing is—it knocks me out at the knees. I may not know the details yet, but I know it is bad. It is wrong.

I can't seem to speak, so Jenna does. "We don't know everything, but we do know about them."

Lauren scans the street behind us, then says, "Fine. You can come in. Just—hurry." The moment we're through the door, she closes it and twists the deadbolt. "Here. Come into the living room."

We follow her, and somewhere beyond my haze of shock and confusion, I register eggshell-colored walls, dark wood furniture, family photos framed in silver. The Tates clearly have more money than Kasey and I ever did, but it's sterilized, cookie-cutter. As if it were intentionally designed to be the set of some wholesome, universally appealing Midwest sitcom. *The Tates: America's Favorite Family.* A clamor of little footsteps reverberates around the house like a tiny storm. Beth Anne. Lauren said Matthew was out of town. I wonder vaguely where Thomas is.

In the living room, bright plastic toys are strewn across the rug and crumbs litter the coffee table. Lauren goes to the window, peers out, and twists the blinds tightly shut. There's so much we need to ask her, so much I don't understand.

"How did you find out?" she says once we're all sitting down, Jenna and me on the couch, Lauren across from us in an armchair. Her back is rigid, fingers jittery. "About the affair?"

Affair. The word slices through me. It doesn't fit, not when it comes to Kasey and Brad. Kasey, who spent her last summer alive reading textbooks and lying curled up in bed with me on weekend mornings. Kasey, who was only nineteen when she was taken. And Brad who is our dad's age, who is a dad himself. Something floats into my mind, a memory of Kasey and me lying tangled in her quilt. "They're such boys," she would always say when she talked about the guys we hung out with that summer. "I need a man, Nic. A real fucking man."

"It doesn't matter how we know," Jenna says. "But that's basically all we do know. Can you tell us the details?"

Before Lauren can respond, Beth Anne launches herself into the room.

"Mama!" She's in gingham shorts and white T-shirt with frills on the shoulders, her blond hair in unruly curls. "Time for pool now."

"Beth Anne," Lauren says. "We're supposed to be having down-time. Why aren't you watching your movie?"

"Because I wanna go pool!"

"We can't go to the pool right now. I just put your brother down for a nap."

"But I wanna," Beth Anne says with a dramatic wobble in her voice. "I wanna play fishy."

"We're not doing that right now. We're not going outside. Do you hear me? If you don't wanna watch your movie, why don't I get you a cookie and you can color in the kitchen while Mama talks for a minute, okay?" She stands, steers Beth Anne into the kitchen, and reappears a few minutes later alone.

Without her daughter there, it's easier to hang on to my anger, which is what all my incredulity and bewilderment are turning into. How could Lauren have known this and kept it a secret for all these years? "Tell us what happened between them," I say.

She twists her wedding band around her finger, her eyes darting anxiously around the room. "If I tell you, that's it. You can't come back, and you can't tell anyone I talked to you."

Jenna and I both nod.

Lauren sighs. "Brad and Kasey were sleeping together that summer, the summer she went missing. I don't know exactly how it started. I mean, I know your families were friends, but other than that . . ." She hitches a shoulder. "Anyway, I caught them one day in her car. She was on a break. I was taking the trash out in the alley behind the shop, and I saw her in the back seat with him. I was so shocked I almost didn't realize it was Brad."

"How did you know him?" Jenna says.

Lauren looks surprised at the question. "Just from around town. My parents knew him and his wife. And their boys were a little older than us, but before they graduated, I saw Brad and Sandy every once in a while at school functions and stuff. When I confronted Kasey about it, she denied it. But then I told her I'd seen them together, her and Brad—actually, I probably called him Mr. Andrews."

She lets out a sad laugh, then says, "Anyway, that's when she finally opened up. She told me they'd been seeing each other basically since the beginning of summer. He worked at Funland, obviously, which was near the record store, and on his lunch break, he'd come over and the two of them would sit in her car and . . . I don't know. Talk. Hook up.

"She made me promise never to tell anyone," Lauren continues. "And I said something like 'If you have to keep it a secret, it's probably not a good idea to be doing in the first place.' She was being reckless. Stupid. If anyone found out, it could destroy his family. But also, you know how it is. If word got out that she was involved with someone like that, people would make it her fault. She'd be a home-wrecker. She didn't exactly take it well."

"So that's why you guys were fighting that summer," I say.

"Who told you we were fighting?" It's me she asks, but it's Jenna who responds.

"We tracked down Steve McLean, Skeevy Steve. He told us he remembers you from that summer, said when you started working with him at the barbecue place, you talked a lot about Kasey. He got the impression you guys were —he used the word 'frenemies.'"

"Oh," Lauren says with a little frown. "Well, I was the only person who knew, and I didn't know how to handle it. For weeks, we fought about it, and finally I just gave up. I didn't want to deal with it anymore. That's why I got the job at Mesquite. I don't actually remember talking about Kasey that much, but I was really worked up about the whole thing, so I guess I could have."

It explains why Kasey didn't say anything about Lauren changing jobs. If anyone had pried, their questions would lead to a truth that, as Lauren put it, could destroy lives. I understand now why it was a secret, but I still don't understand why it was a secret from *me*.

"Did you and Kasey ever fight in the parking lot?" Jenna says.

"The parking lot outside the restaurant, you mean?"

Jenna nods.

"Um . . . no? At least I don't think. Why?"

Jenna opens her mouth to answer, but I cut her off. I don't give a shit about explaining anything to Lauren, not now. "You made it seem like you and my sister were super tight that summer," I say.

"I'm sorry. I was trying to protect her. That's why I didn't tell you. I've never told anyone."

Beside me, Jenna leans forward. "Didn't you think that Kasey having an affair with an older, married man was incredibly relevant to an investigation into her disappearance?"

Lauren holds up her hands. "Yes, of course I did. Well, actually, when I first heard she went missing, I thought she'd just run away with him. Not forever but, like, for a few days. She did that a lot that summer. Spent nights away with him. So, that's why—"

"Wait," I say. "Kasey spent all those nights with you. At your house."

"That's just what she said. Which was another reason we were fighting. I was sick of being her excuse, being complicit or whatever."

All of Kasey's lies are spinning into one enormous tornado in my head. And the same, single question is its eye: Why didn't she trust me with the truth?

"So, that's why I didn't say anything when it first happened," Lauren continues. "There was all this confusion about the circumstances of her disappearance, and the details about her car and wallet and all that didn't make it to me for a while, so I thought the whole thing was far more innocuous than it was. And I didn't want to get Kasey in trouble or ruin her life. I don't know what your parents would've done if they found out about the affair, but I knew it would be bad. And to be honest, Brad might've been a jerk for cheating on his wife, but I know how close your families were. I didn't want to ruin everyone's life if he had nothing to do with it."

"But what about after that?" Jenna says. "When it was obvious Kasey hadn't just run away. Why didn't you say anything then?"

"I was going to. I swear. When I learned the details of her disappearance, I thought maybe Brad wanted out and had done something to her. But I was scared. I was nineteen. The police hadn't even talked to me yet, so I was trying to figure out how to approach them when I ran into Brad's wife. It was during one of the first searches we all went to, in Grand Rapids around where Kasey's car had been found. The two of us started talking, and Sandy told me she wished she and Brad could've been there for your parents earlier, the moment they found out Kasey went missing, but her family had been out of town. It was completely unprompted. Without even knowing I was suspicious of him, she gave me Brad's alibi. He'd been on vacation with his family when Kasey was taken."

I open my mouth, then close it. My head is too crammed full of shock and confusion and resentment to shape any of it into a logical question.

"Back then," Jenna says, "in 2012, did Brad know that you'd found out about their affair?"

Lauren shakes her head. "I don't know. If he did, Kasey never told me. Why?"

"Well, what you said earlier, outside. You made it seem like . . . Did something happen to you since we talked last week? Did somebody threaten you or try to get you to stop talking to us?"

Lauren's eyes fill with tears as she nods.

"What happened?"

"It was terrible." She grabs a tissue from the side table to wipe her wet cheeks. "Two days ago, on Friday night, Matthew had already left town, so I was alone with the kids. I took them to this event at our church. It was, like, a potluck thing. They'd set up tables and chairs by the playground and there was a bouncy house and they hired someone to do face-painting. There were so many people there, there had to be over a hundred." She inhales a shaky breath. "God, I'm a terrible mother. I can't believe I let this happen."

"What?" Jenna says. "What happened?"

"Well, I fixed a few plates for me and the kids and we were sitting around with a bunch of the other moms, just talking. There's, like, a little group of us with kids all about the same age. After we ate, the big kids went to play on the playscape. I was keeping an eye on Beth Anne, but I had Thomas too, and eventually, I needed to change his diaper. It was a messy one, so I wanted to do it in the bathroom, and I asked my friends if they could watch Beth Anne while I went into the church and they said yes, of course. And I don't blame them for what happened. Really, I don't. Because Beth Anne would've only disappeared for a minute, max. She could've just walked behind the bouncy house or the slide and reappeared sixty seconds later and no one would've known."

I shoot a glance at Jenna, who has a look of dread on her face.

"Anyway," Lauren says, "I was walking out of the church with Thomas when Beth Anne ran up to me. She looked fine. Totally normal. She had her face painted like a fairy and she was smiling, you know. She was having fun. That's when she told me she had a secret and she could only tell me. But, you know, four-year-olds have secrets all the time. They saw a cute doggy and it's a secret, or they didn't brush one tooth. Whatever. So I was only half listening, but then she told it to me and my blood just ran cold."

"What was it?" I say.

"'Stop talking about Kasey Monroe.' That was my four-year-old's secret."

CHAPTER TWENTY

In the weeks after Kasey went missing, our house transformed. Where it had once been the quiet home of two parents who didn't quite love each other and two teenagers who spent more time outside the house than in, during the fall of 2012, it was a swarm of activity. A stream of local volunteers flowed through the front door at all hours of the day, collecting flyers and staple guns and bottles of water. Sandy organized a meal train and was constantly rearranging dishes in the fridge or packing homemade sandwiches into little plastic bags for people to eat on the go. Brad and my dad sprawled a huge map of Michiana over the dining room table and huddled around it as they strategized where to search next.

Thinking back on it now, our efforts seem dinky and useless. All it did was give us something to do with our hands while we slowly came to the realization that Kasey was never coming back.

One evening that September, after I got home from the day's search party, I walked straight through the dining room, where my parents were talking with Brad and Sandy, and into the kitchen to make myself a vodka Sprite. By then, I'd started drinking more brazenly and more often. I kept waiting to get caught, but my dad was too distracted to notice anything, and my mom seemed to think she was the one going through the alcohol so quickly. Whenever she got to the bottom of a bottle, she'd just sigh and go out for more.

I was screwing the top back on the vodka when Brad walked into the kitchen, and I froze. Surely this was going to be the moment I finally got caught. But with one look at his unfocused eyes, I could tell that he, like everybody else, was lost in his own world.

"Hey, Nic, I've been meaning to ask you—" He shot a glance over his shoulder. "This summer, did Kasey ever, you know, mention anything?"

I stepped in front of the bottle of vodka, blocking it from view. "Anything about what?"

"I don't know. Did she ever tell you what she was up to? How she was spending her time? I know you guys are close. She tells you things she doesn't tell other people."

In those days, this was the one thing everyone asked me: Had Kasey told me anything that could explain where she was?

"Brad, I told all of this to the police already."

"I know, I know. But I just want to make sure."

"Make sure what?"

"Just . . . that we've covered our bases. Did Kasey ever, I don't know, mention anything about work?"

By then, I was starting to get irritated. His questions were maddeningly vague, and like I'd said, I'd gone over this dozens of times already with Detective Wyler. "I mean, yeah, she talked to me about work sometimes."

"Really? Did she ever mention anybody coming by? Anybody specific?"

Before I could answer, Sandy walked in. "Brad," she said, placing a hand on his shoulder. Then, looking between the two of us, she added, "Oh. I'm sorry. Did I interrupt something?"

"We were just talking," Brad said.

I brought the vodka Sprite to my lips and drank deeply. For a moment, the kitchen was plunged into silence that felt awkward for reasons I didn't understand.

A strange, strangled noise cut through the quiet, so thick and watery, it was like a parody of a sob. I looked up to see that Brad's face was red and twisted and realized with a jolt that the sound had come from him.

"Honey?" Sandy said evenly. This was clearly not the first time he'd broken down that week. "Why don't you get some fresh air?" She gestured with her chin to the door that led to our backyard. When it closed behind him, she said, "I'm sorry. He's just scared. We all are."

I don't know what I said in response. My mind was on Kasey, and I was already starting to feel floaty from the alcohol, and none of Brad's behavior had struck me as odd. Sandy was right—we were all scared.

But now, sitting in Lauren's living room, knowing what I know about his affair with my sister, I wonder: Was Brad scared that night because Kasey had disappeared? Or was he scared because he thought their secret hadn't gone with her?

Jenna shifts beside me on the couch. "How did Beth Anne know to tell you?" she says to Lauren. "About the 'secret,' I mean."

Lauren wipes a tissue beneath both eyes. "A man told her he'd give her a piece of chocolate if she told her mom. She had it all over her face."

"Jesus . . . I'm sorry."

Lauren stares into her lap.

"Did you ask her what the man looked like?" I say.

"Of course I did. She said he was tall. Said he was wearing sunglasses and a hat, but that description could've fit almost every man there. I pushed for more but, you know, she's four."

"And did you do anything?" Jenna says.

"What do you mean?"

"I mean, did you tell anyone? Did you think about going to the police?"

"God no. I have nothing to do with any of this. All I wanted to do—what I still want to do—is exactly what that man said and never talk about it again." She seems to hear the harshness of her words, because she gives me a guilty look. "I'm sorry, Nic. Kasey was the closest thing I had to a sister, so I get why you're doing this. I really do. But please don't come to my house again. I can't put my family in any more danger."

I hear Jenna asking one more time if Lauren knows any other information she didn't tell the police and Lauren murmuring no, nothing, but I'm too troubled by what she's just told us to absorb much of anything. I need to get out of here. Finally, we say our goodbyes, then Lauren deadbolts the front door behind us, and Jenna and I walk quickly to her truck.

"That was Brad at the playground last week," she says once we're inside. "It had to have been."

"We don't know that for sure."

Only an hour ago, the idea that Brad was capable of using a four-year-old girl to threaten Lauren into silence would have struck me as absurd—the man I know wouldn't do that, he couldn't. But after everything we just learned, I'm not so sure. Still, Lauren was right. Beth Anne's description was so vague, it could've been anyone at the church last Friday. McLean or someone else.

"Nic," Jenna says. "Look at the evidence. Lauren was the only one who knew about the affair, and Brad has enormous incentive to keep her quiet about it." She hesitates. "I think we should go to the police."

"What?"

"Someone is actively trying to prevent us from learning the truth. If approaching a four-year-old on a playground is this guy's opening move, what's he gonna do next?" Her eyes dart around, looking through the windows. "We should probably get out of here." She turns her key in the ignition and pulls away from the curb. "I say we go to the police. Tell them about the affair and what happened to Beth Anne."

"No." I shake my head. "We can't do that."

"Why not? What happened at Lauren's church is relevant to the case. This is the kind of thing that could make the police reopen the investigation."

But that's exactly what I'm afraid of.

That summer, Brad was—what? Late forties, early fifties. More than twenty years older than Kasey. More disturbing though is that he truly was an uncle to us. The man who, when we were kids, slicked countless Band-Aids onto our scraped knees, got us juice boxes when our parents had their hands full. He held us when we were babies, carried us as toddlers, took photos while we played naked in the mud.

The idea that the hands that tied my shoes when I was a kid were the same ones that took Kasey's clothes off fifteen years later makes me sick. Then there's Sandy. It's not like I ever believed she and Brad were some storybook romance, but the idea of him betraying her so cruelly infuriates me.

And yet, no matter how much I hate him right now, I don't want to destroy his and Sandy's and my dad's lives by making him the target of an investigation. And that's exactly what would happen if we go to the police with the affair. They would reopen the case and only look at Brad.

"If Brad was the one at the playground the other day," I start to say, and Jenna gives me a look. "If he was, he only would've been trying to hide the affair. Nothing else. He didn't have anything to do with Kasey going missing. You heard Lauren. He has an alibi."

"Yeah. One we heard secondhand seven years after the fact. It's not exactly airtight," Jenna says, but her voice has softened slightly. "Maybe you're right. Maybe he had nothing to do with Kasey's disappearance, but he knows a hell of a lot more about her and that summer than he ever let on. At a minimum, the police need to interview him about that."

My eyes rove around the truck, desperate for any sort of argument or leverage. "Lauren doesn't want to tell anyone. If we go to the police with the story of what happened to Beth Anne, she may not even corroborate it."

"Nic, this affair is a huge piece of the puzzle that no one knew about until now. We have to tell the police."

Something inside me snaps. "It's not a puzzle, Jenna! It's my goddamn life. Brad is—" The word *family* turns sour in my mouth. Brad is not my family. He never was.

"Brad cheated on his wife with a nineteen-year-old girl," Jenna says slowly. "What he is is a piece of shit."

I'm quiet for a moment. She's right. Of course she is. And yet. "What about Jules?"

Jenna's gaze flicks from the road to me and back again. "What do you mean?"

"Brad's affair with Kasey has nothing to do with Jules. If we bring it to the police, they're just going to focus on that. They may not look into your sister's case at all. I say we take a few days. See if we can find any connection between the affair and Kasey and Jules going missing."

Maybe it's shitty of me to use Jules as bait, but what I said was true. And I know Brad had nothing to do with my sister's disappearance— I just need time to prove it.

Jenna is quiet as she drives. An electrical tower outside my window catches my eye, and I realize we're already at my apartment complex, taking the winding road to my building. "Fine," she says eventually. "Let's take a beat. Digest all this and talk in a few days."

"Thank you."

We pull up to my door and she puts the car in park. "But, Nic, be careful. Okay? Someone out there knows what we're doing and doesn't like it. I know you don't want to believe Brad was the one who got to Lauren or took our sisters, but if he was, your relationship with him is not going to keep you safe."

CHAPTER TWENTY-ONE

The Funland kitchen is loud and bustling. Pans clatter onto stovetops, rubber-soled shoes squeak against the linoleum floor, grease sizzles in pans. I'm standing by the service station waiting to run an order when I feel a hand press gently into my shoulder blade. I turn toward it and have to force myself not to flinch. Brad. It's been barely twenty-four hours since Jenna and I spoke to Lauren, and I'm still feeling jumpy and betrayed. I've avoided direct contact with Brad throughout my shift so far, but I knew this moment was coming. Still, I can't meet his eye.

"You all right, Nic?" he says.

"I'm fine."

I can tell he doesn't believe me, but he just nods toward the food prep station where José, one of our cooks, is slicing a pizza on a round silver tray. "Would you mind running that to table thirteen for me? Aubrey just went on break."

"Sure."

José slides the tray onto the service station and I grab it, then turn to leave. I'm two steps from the door when Brad calls my name.

"When you get a second," he says, "swing by my office, okay?"

I see him in sunglasses and a hat, hiding in the shadows of a playground waiting for Beth Anne to skip by. I see him in the back of Kasey's car, his fingers frantic on the button of her jeans, his mouth too hard against hers. I see him driving slowly on that road outside Grand Rapids, see him stalking through the darkness to Kasey's driver's side door.

Stop, I think. This is Brad. He may be a creep, but he's not a murderer. I believe it. I do.

And yet, as I look over my shoulder and flash him the most casual smile I can, my mouth is dry as bone. "Sure," I say. "No problem."

I don't swing by his office. The idea of sitting across from him in that little windowless room, pretending he didn't have an illicit affair with my sister, makes me claustrophobic. I know if I want to prove his innocence, I'll have to talk to him sometime, but I'm not ready yet. I avoid crossing paths with him all day until nine o'clock rolls around and, finally, I can leave.

In the employee locker room, I grab my backpack and head to the back door that leads to the west-side parking lot. I don't normally leave this way—it almost doubles my walk to the bike rack out front—but I don't want to pass by Brad's office. I push my palms into the metal bar and am stepping into the fading dusk light when I hear my name. Brad's voice is unmistakable. A knot tightens in my chest as I turn to face him.

"You never paid me that visit," he says.

"Oh, right. Sorry. I forgot."

"No biggie. Let's talk now."

"I can't, actually," I say. "I have to catch the—"

He waves a hand, cutting me off. "Don't worry about the bus. My car's out of the shop. I'll give you a ride. We can talk on the way home."

I don't want to be alone in a car with him right now, but what could I possibly say to get out of it? "Okay, then. Thanks."

Brad has an SUV, and once he's pushed the seats down, my bike fits easily inside. I climb into shotgun, throwing my backpack in the space by my feet.

"So," he says once he's pulled out of the parking lot and onto the street. He knows the apartment complex where I live, so I don't have to give him directions. "I just wanted to check in with you. See how things are going. I know you have a lot going on right now."

"Things are fine," I say.

"Geez, Nic," he chuckles. "Getting information out of you is like pulling teeth. How's the community service going?"

"Yeah, it's not bad." Because this is safe territory and I want to stay in it, I elaborate. "It can be fun, actually. I like being with the animals. They're less complicated than humans."

"Good. Good." But he sounds distracted. "And what about all the legal stuff? I know you had a court date at some point. That happen yet?"

Shit, he's right. I do have that coming up. I need to find out when. "Not yet."

For a few minutes we drive in silence. "You must be busy though," he says. "Between all that and work, do you have time for anything else? What about what we talked about last week? Are you still looking into Kasey's disappearance?"

Questions and accusations churn inside my chest, but until I can confront him, they'll be trapped there like moths with frenzied wings. I need time. To process, to dig deeper. To talk through everything with Jenna so I have her calm and analytical mind to balance my own frenetic one. "Not really," I say. "Like you said, I have a lot going on."

"That's too bad." Another long beat of silence. "And what about the Perkins girl? The one you told me you talked to. What's her name again?" His voice is oh so casual.

"Who, Lauren?"

"That's it. Did you ever talk to her after that first time?"

"No." If Brad *was* the one who threatened Lauren, I'm not about to put a target on her back by letting him know it didn't work. "After we talked that one time, I reached out again over Facebook, but she never got back to me. I don't wanna push it."

He turns into my apartment complex. "Well, she probably told you everything she had to say the first time anyway."

"Probably. By the way, do you remember which building I'm in?" He's driven me home a handful of times since my license was suspended, but my complex is huge, and I pray to a god I don't believe in that he's forgotten. I'm trying to hang on to my belief that he has nothing to do with any of this, but the truth is I don't know what he's capable of. If he doesn't remember my building number, I'll give him a fake one and bike from there.

"Of course I do," he says. "This thing's a steel trap." He taps a finger to his temple as he navigates to my building and puts the car in park. "I even remember which apartment you're in. That one right there." He leans over me to gesture at it, and I turn my head to look: He's pointing straight at my front door.

It's only when I'm in my apartment with the deadbolt locked behind me that I can exhale. I walk to the kitchen and twist off the top of a bottle of wine. I pour myself a glass, take a sip, then top it off, replaying the drive home with Brad in my mind, trying to see it objectively.

But I'm at war with myself, defensiveness and suspicion clawing their way over each other like rabid animals. Did Brad instigate that conversation to check on my emotional well-being, or is he keeping tabs on my progress in the investigation? Did he bring up Lauren out of innocent curiosity or because he was trying to see if his message had gotten through to her? And most unnerving of all, was that joke about his mind being a steel trap just Brad being Brad, with his lame attempt at humor? Or was it a reminder that he knows where I live?

If I could just understand what happened between him and Kasey that summer, I could prove he had nothing to do with her going missing. But how? Where do I start?

As I gaze into my glass of wine, I realize with a jolt that I'm supposed to be at my weekly AA meeting right now. I was supposed to go after work today, but Brad wiped it from my mind. "Shit." I'm going to have to find another meeting this week so I don't break my probation.

At the thought of AA my mind flashes, as it always does, to the accident that put me there—and that's when it hits me. An idea of where to go next. It's a long shot, I know, but at this point, it's all I've got.

CHAPTER TWENTY-TWO

After the police found my sister's car on the side of the road and declared it a crime scene, they taped it off, investigated it, and a mere day and a half later, they packed everything up and told us the car was ours again. They seemed to think they were doing my family a favor, expediting the process so we could have the vehicle back. What they didn't understand was that none of us would be able to drive it ever again.

My mom wanted to sell it, but my dad put his foot down. Kasey would need something to drive when she came back. I wasn't going to drive around the crime scene of my sister's abduction, so I took every penny I'd ever made and bought the world's cheapest car on Craigslist. To free up space in the garage for it, my dad got a storage unit to store Kasey's old car, and that's where it's been ever since.

That car, I realized, is at the center of everything. It was the last place Kasey was before she was taken, and apparently, it was where she and Brad hooked up on their lunch breaks. The police combed through it years ago, but what if they missed something?

It's a little before nine in the morning when I pedal up to the storage facility on my bike. Last night, I called my dad to ask how to get into our unit, inventing a feeble lie about wanting to store some boxes. He pretended to believe me, then tracked down the two codes I'd need. I enter the first into the box by the gate. It shudders open and I pedal through. The facility is small, with no more than forty or so units, and I find ours easily. I enter the second code into the lockbox, use the key inside to unlock the metal door, then tug it open.

And there it is, our old car. It's a black Honda Civic with the one bumper sticker Kasey snuck onto the back before our mom saw and told us not to put on any more. It was tacky, she said, and would decrease the resale value. The sticker is big and white, stark against the dark metal, printed with that song lyric Kasey loved so much: *We are not two, we are one.*

The unit is just big enough for me to walk around the car, open the driver's side door, and slip into that old familiar seat. The air inside is sweltering. Suddenly, I feel as if I'm back in the summer of 2012, on my way to pick Kasey up from the record store and drive us home with the stereo blaring and the windows down. But just as longing starts to fill my chest, I replace it with numbness.

I came here to investigate. I don't want to feel.

Looking around the dark interior, I find the key nestled in the cupholder. I turn it in the ignition, but the engine only kicks over a few times. In the foot space on the passenger side, I see a smattering of receipts, a tube of lip gloss. I envision Kasey on the night she was taken, running the little brush over her lips, checking her reflection in the overhead mirror. I reach for it, imagining the ghost of my sister's hands, the whorls of her old fingerprints interweaving with my new ones.

"Stop," I say aloud.

I pull from my backpack one of the plastic bags I brought to collect everything I found, toss the lip gloss in unceremoniously, then grab the receipts. The first is from Wendy's, the price of a couple Frosties. The next is from Sonic, the next from a gas station. I look at the dates, study the prices, but I feel like an idiot. These aren't clues. These are meaningless slips of paper.

I twist in my seat to look into the back and spot the big black CD case where Kasey and I used to store our music. "No way," I breathe, reaching for it. Once we were in high school, we were mainly using our iPods and those tape adapters, but every once in a while, we'd pull out this binder and play some of our old stuff.

I tug the binder onto my lap and unzip it. At the first page of CDs, I can't help but laugh. There's the Killers, Destiny's Child, Green Day, Spice Girls. I think back to our middle school years, to this one month of time when Kasey and I played "Wannabe" from the CD player in her room on repeat every day until we knew every word. I flip through the binder, each subsequent album dredging up a new memory. Kasey and me riding our bikes, singing "We Go To-gether" from *Grease* as we pedaled around the neighborhood, Kasey and me sunbathing in the backyard, holding invisible microphones while we sing-shouted the Backstreet Boys' "I Want It That Way," Kasey and me painting our toenails in her room, dancing to "Semi-Charmed Life" by Third Eye Blind. Kasey and me, Kasey and me, Kasey and me.

Finally, I get to the end and the golden bubble of memory pops. Kasey is gone. I am alone. Suddenly, the car seems to shrink around me, and I buzz with the need to get out of here. I shove the binder into my backpack, crawl over the center console, and dig around the back seats. I find some loose bits of paper, an old bottle of nail polish, the liquid crusted along the edge. I chuck it all into the plastic bag, then clamber back into the driver's seat, where I pull out my phone and photograph the entirety of the car's interior—the seats, the dash, the roof, the floors.

When I'm done, I glance at the time on my phone and groan. This took longer than I thought, and now I only have thirty minutes to get to work. Thirty minutes till I have to pretend Brad is my family friend and amiable boss instead of what he really is—a lying, cheating prick.

I'm home from work and finishing one of Sandy's brownies when there's a knock on my front door. It makes me jump even though I know it's Jenna. It's been three and a half days since we saw each other, and although I'm no closer to understanding how Brad fits into what happened to our sisters, she's given me the time I asked for. I've been dreading this all day. I know she's going to push for us to talk to Brad or to go to police, but I'm still not ready for either. The thought of what he did turns my stomach, and I wanted to punch him in the face so badly today at work my fingers twitched with it. But I can't get myself to believe he's a killer.

"You've been okay?" Jenna says once we've settled into my living room, she on the couch, me on the floor. "You still haven't gotten any threats, right? No one's approached you or sent you any messages or anything?"

I shake my head. "I would've told you if they had. You?"

"No. And same. I hope that means whoever got to Lauren doesn't know she talked to us again." Just as I'm feeling grateful she said *whoever* instead of *Brad,* she adds, "Have you spent any time looking into him? Brad, I mean?"

"I searched around our old car this morning," I say. "The one Kasey was driving the night she was taken. The one she and Brad . . . you know. It hasn't been touched since that day, and there was a ton of stuff in it. I brought it all home to go through."

"I didn't realize you guys still had it," Jenna says. "Jules's car was so old when it died, we never brought it home from the impound lot. I can help you go through whatever you found."

"Thanks," I say. "I've been thinking more about the alibi Lauren told us too, that Brad and his family were out of town when Kasey went missing. I didn't realize it at first, but I know where they were. They have a reunion at their lake house the same time every summer in August. I've heard about it for years. They have dozens of people crammed into a handful of houses for almost a week. The alibi holds up. Brad couldn't have left in the middle of all that without someone noticing."

"Where's their lake house?" Jenna says.

"On Nyona Lake. Near Macy, if you know where that is." I've been there many times. It's where our two families used to vacation together. "I looked up the drive Brad would've had to do if he'd taken Kasey—it's three hours from Nyona to Grand Rapids. And he would've had to do it twice in one night to make it back unnoticed. That's six hours."

"That is pretty far," she says.

"Exactly!"

"I said it's far, Nic, not impossible."

But now I'm on a roll. "When did Jules go missing, again?" I know the date is somewhere in the back of my mind, but it isn't branded into my memory the way August 17 is.

"August 4th."

"Hang on." I pull out my phone and open my calendar app. At the top, I navigate from the month display to the year, scroll all the way back to 2012 and find August 4. "That was the first weekend of August."

"Yeah?" Jenna says. "So?"

"My dad goes on a fishing trip with Brad the first weekend of August every year. They have for decades, since before I was born."

"Where do they go?"

"Same as the reunion. The Andrewses' place in Nyona Lake. When Jules was taken, Brad would've been over an hour away." I sit up onto my heels. This is the evidence I've been looking for.

"Hang on," Jenna says. "Are you sure they went that weekend? I mean, what're the odds they go the exact same weekend every year?"

"They have it blocked off, always have. My dad used to joke about how it's the one nonnegotiable he ever had." My voice is getting louder, faster. Finally, I feel as if the evidence is lining up with what I've known to be true all along.

"Slow down," she says. "You said this lake house is only an hour outside town? That's hardly iron-clad proof of anything. Jules was taken in the middle of the night. He could've left the lake, driven to Mishawaka, killed her, and come back."

"That would've taken—what—four, five hours? At a minimum. My dad would've noticed if Brad had disappeared in the middle of the night for that long."

"Nic," Jenna says wearily. "That's not necessarily true."

"You're just looking for ways he could've done it because you think he's guilty."

"And you're looking for ways he couldn't have because you think he's innocent." She huffs out a frustrated breath. "We need to talk to him. That's the only way we're gonna find anything out."

"I know," I say. "I just . . . I need more time."

"For what?"

"Let me talk to my dad first. Let me ask him about the family reunion and his fishing trip with Brad that year." If my dad figures out that I'm digging into Kasey's disappearance, the conversation isn't going to go well—if it goes at all. "After that, I promise we can talk to Brad. But this way, when we do, we'll be ready."

Jenna studies my face. "Fine," she says eventually. "But I'm coming with you."

"Obviously."

She lets out a half laugh, half groan. "Why does everything have to be so hard with you?"

"I'm being thorough!" I give her my best innocent look. "You taught me that."

She rolls her eyes. "God, sometimes you can have serious little-sister energy." The words swell inside me, warm and golden. But there's something beneath the feeling too, something like an ache. Before I can look at it too closely, Jenna grabs one of my couch pillows and tosses it at my head, and then we're both laughing. After a moment, it fades. "By the way," she says. "I've been meaning to ask. Did you ever reach out to that detective? The one who inherited your sister's case after Wyler's promotion?"

For a moment, I have no idea what she's talking about. Then my mind flashes to the other week, after we met with Wyler. Jenna suggested we reach out to his successor, and I said I'd do it. But then we'd met with McLean and Lauren, and I'd been so distracted by all this Brad stuff that it fell right out of my head. "Shit," I say. "I totally forgot."

"Do you just want me to do it?"

"No, no, no. I'll do it tonight."

"Okay," she says with a little grin. "So stubborn. Hey, do you wanna go through the stuff you found in your car now?"

"Yeah." I grab my backpack and pull out the plastic bag. I put the CD case on the coffee table, followed by the nail polish and lip gloss, then turn the bag over and let the rest fall out in a rain of junk.

Jenna plucks one of the receipts from the pile. "Mind if I take pictures?"

I don't know how a fast-food receipt could possibly solve the disappearances of our sisters, but I just say, "Go for it." She snaps a photo while I take another from the pile.

"What's this?" she asks. "Does it mean anything to you?"

I glance over to see her holding a business card, something I hadn't noticed this morning. I lean over to read the finely printed words: O'NEIL'S AUTO—OIL, TIRES, AND BODY.

"I don't know," I say. "Maybe it's the last place we got our oil changed? I took pictures of the car's interior, so I can check." I pick up my phone, navigate to the photo I'd taken of the windshield, then zoom in to view the oil change sticker. "No, never mind. They don't match."

"Hmm." Jenna takes another picture while I start scanning the rest of the photos on my phone. "Oh my god," she says, reaching for the big black binder. "Is this all your old music?"

I grin. "Yeah, I had so many flashbacks when I went through it this morning."

She unzips it and a laugh bubbles out of her. "Spice Girls, of course, classic. And the Killers. God, I loved 'Mr. Brightside.'"

"Who didn't?"

She flips through the pages slowly, a small smile on her lips. I go back to the pictures on my phone. A few minutes pass in silence until it is broken by an odd, constricted sound like a moan caught in the back of a throat. I glance over and see Jenna's smile has vanished.

"Jenna?"

She looks up quickly as if she's been caught shoplifting.

"Are you okay?"

She glances down at the binder and then up again. "Yeah. Sorry, I just— What is this?"

She points at one of our mix CDs, one of the ones Kasey decorated with a marker. In her neat, loopy handwriting are the words *We are not two, we are one.* Around them are little multicolored dots, yellow stars, pink hearts.

"Kasey burned that one," I say. "With stuff from the seventies and eighties. She loved all that kind of music. That's a lyric from one of her favorite songs."

"'Strangers,'" Jenna says. "By the Kinks."

"You know it?"

"I . . ." Jenna clears her throat. "It reminds me of Jules."

I realize then what's happening. I know because it happened to me only a few hours earlier. A memory of her sister has knocked her out at the knees, like walking along a sidewalk and falling into a pothole she didn't see coming.

"Kasey liked it too," I say. "Loved it, actually. She wrote out the lyrics to it all the time. On her homework, her binders, everywhere." I hesitate. "The one that got me earlier was 'I Want It That Way' by the Backstreet Boys."

I was trying to make her laugh, but Jenna's face remains stony. Then, abruptly, she says, "Where's your bathroom?"

"Oh, uh, it's through there." I nod toward my bedroom.

She stands and disappears through the doorway.

"Shit," I mutter, slumping back against the couch. Had I been narcissistic, talking about Kasey, who felt like an extension of me, when Jenna was lost in thoughts of Jules? Or had I sounded flippant when I mentioned the Backstreet Boys? Despite how our relationship started, Jenna is the closest thing I have to a friend right now, but I don't know how to behave in the face of her grief. Probably because I've never dealt with my own.

I stand up and walk to the kitchen to open a bottle of wine. I was trying not to drink tonight, but Jenna could obviously use a glass, and this investigation has a way of chipping through my willpower. I take my phone with me, continuing to scroll through the photos of our car's interior as I go. As I'm screwing off the wine top, I study the picture of our oil change sticker, then swipe to the next, a photo of our odometer. I'm about to flip to the next when something catches my eye, and I set the bottle of wine down halfway through my pour.

"Wait a second." I squint at the photo, then flick back to the previous one. "Jenna!" I call.

I hear my bathroom door open, and a moment later she walks back into the living room. She still looks rattled, but her eyes are dry. "What?"

I tap my phone's screen. "According to this sticker, the last time we got our oil changed was August 2nd. At the time, our car's mileage—the mileage on this sticker—was 164,021 miles."

"Okay . . ."

"In the picture of our odometer"—I swipe to the other photo—"the one that stopped clocking miles the night Kasey went missing, the night of August 17th, the car has 164,589." I look up at her. "That's a difference of over five hundred miles in, like, two weeks."

She hesitates. "Well, a hundred and fifty of those are from driving to Grand Rapids that night . . ."

"Which leaves . . ." I look around the room. "Three hundred and fifty miles?"

"That doesn't sound right?" she says.

"That doesn't sound possible. There's no way Kasey and I drove that much in two weeks. Especially because those were the weeks when she was refusing to go out and studying alone in her room most nights. We were going to work and stuff, and I mean, I was still going out some, but I got a ride most of the time. Which means . . ."

Jenna finishes my thought. "Kasey went somewhere else that night."

"Or," I say, "in the two weeks leading up to her disappearance, without telling anyone, she was sneaking off enough to put over three hundred miles on our car."

But where had she gone?

CHAPTER TWENTY-THREE

A little after six the following Saturday evening, I pedal up to my old childhood home, drop my feet to the pavement, and pull my phone from my backpack. When I see there are no notifications from Jenna, a small bubble of exasperation swells inside me.

The past few days since I last saw her have been a blur. The end of summer is fast approaching, and Funland is getting its usual surge of parties before all the kids go back to school. And because I missed my regular AA meeting that night Brad gave me a ride home, I had to track down another in South Bend to make up for it. Throughout it all, I haven't been able to stop thinking about Kasey and Brad and those unexplained miles on our odometer. I've hardly had time to scarf food down before I fall asleep at night, let alone make time to touch base with Jenna. So I suppose I can't blame her for her radio silence when I'm doing the same.

And really, I don't need a confirmation text to know she'll be here. We made the plan to talk to my dad before she left my apartment on Tuesday night, and she's more eager to ask him questions than I am.

Because I couldn't come up with a single believable explanation for randomly introducing a new friend to my dad, we had to think of another way to spring Jenna on him. We decided that I'd show up alone for dinner, then after an hour, I'd say my friend was swinging by to give me a ride home. If my dad didn't invite Jenna in, she'd ask to use the bathroom and we'd go from there.

I walk my bike to the stairs leading to the porch and lean it against them. I called my dad earlier in the week, so he's expecting me, but he doesn't know the real reason I'm here, and my dread builds with every step I take closer to the front door. When I reach it, I hesitate, as if the air in front of me has calcified. My relationship with my dad has grown distant, and barging in seems intrusive somehow. But it feels awkward to ring the doorbell of the home where I grew up, so I do what I always do and split the difference, knocking as I enter.

"Hello!" I call. "Dad? It's me."

He appears in the doorway that leads to the kitchen. "Nic," he says with a genuine smile that cracks me open a little. "Come on in. You hungry? I just got out stuff to make sandwiches."

We walk through the living room and into the kitchen, and like I do every time I'm here, I marvel at how little has changed. There's the old plaid couch where Kasey and I used to sit till late into the night, watching movies and sharing a package of Oreos. There's the ring on the coffee table where my dad left a beer one time, and my mom, when she discovered it, yelled for a full ten minutes. There's the dining room table that was never used till Kasey went missing and then was transformed into the central hub of our search.

"Ham and cheese okay with you?" my dad says.

"Sure." I sit at the little kitchen table while he piles slices of ham and provolone onto two pieces of white bread. Once the sandwiches are plated, he spoons some store-bought potato salad next to each.

"Thanks," I say as he sets a plate in front of me. "This looks great."

"Well, it's not exactly gourmet, but it does the trick." He opens the refrigerator door. "You want something to drink? I have water, orange juice, beer—" His voice cuts out suddenly and he clears his throat.

With his back turned to me, I don't have to hide my eye roll. Just like Kasey's disappearance, the DWI is something my dad insists on pretending never happened. "Water's fine," I say, then, when I see his hand hovering over the row of beers, I add, "You can drink, Dad. I don't mind."

He brings our drinks over and we begin to eat. "So," he says between bites. "How're things going?"

So much between us feels like a conversational landmine, and I scour my mind for something safe to talk about, eventually telling him about Banksy and the animal shelter, without ever mentioning the reason we both know I'm clocking so many hours there. I ask him about work at the fish hatchery, and he tells me all about his new boss. During a lull in the conversation, I pull out my phone and check the time. It's almost seven. Jenna should be here any minute. I make sure my ringer's on, then tuck it back into my pocket.

But five minutes pass, then ten, and when Jenna still hasn't called, that bubble of exasperation turns to irritation. Has she forgotten? Did her plans change and she didn't tell me?

"So . . ." my dad says. Outside of Thanksgiving and Christmas, we don't normally spend one-on-one time together, and I can feel him reaching for ways to pass it. "Brad tells me things at work are going well."

My heartbeat quickens at the sound of Brad's name, and I shoot another glance at my phone. Jenna is now officially twenty minutes late. The prospect of interviewing my dad alone makes me jittery with nerves, but at this point, I'm starting to think Jenna's not coming, and here he is, handing me the perfect opening.

"Work's fine," I say. "Busy, but good." I take a sip of water, going for casual. "When did you and Brad hang out last?"

"Well, he would've come over last night. We still do our weekly beers, you know. But he was heading down to Nyona with Sandy for their reunion."

"It's nice you guys still do that. See each other every week, I mean."

I hesitate, running the tines of my fork through the dregs of potato salad on my plate. The main thing Jenna and I planned to ask about tonight was Brad's whereabouts on the nights of Kasey's and Jules's disappearances. If he was at his family reunion during the former and on the fishing trip during the latter like I assume he was, those will be the pieces of evidence I can give Jenna to finally get her off this Brad thing. They're not irrefutable proof that he wasn't involved, but they're as close as we're going to get.

"What about that fishing trip the two of you used to go on?" I say. My instinct is to poke at his alibi for Kasey's disappearance first, but I'm not sure how to broach that without my dad getting suspicious, so I start with this instead—where he was when Jules was taken. "You guys still do that every summer?"

"Course we do, you know that."

"How many years have you been going, again?"

"Since before you were even born." He searches the ceiling. "Our first year was probably 1988 or so?" He grins, proud of the tradition. Meanwhile, all I can think is *Your best friend is a liar and a cheater and a piece of shit.* And also, *Please let him be innocent.*

"Wow . . ." I say. "And you go the same weekend every year, right?"

"First weekend in August. You know what I always say. That's the one nonnegotiable I have."

My body slackens in relief. I'm not done asking questions, but this is what I was hoping for—my dad's confident corroboration of Brad's alibi, without him ever knowing I was looking for it in the first place. His best friend may be an asshole, but he didn't kidnap Jules. And if everything Wyler and the police and every reporter and media outlet have said is right, that Jules was taken by the same man who took Kasey, that means Brad didn't kidnap my sister either.

"Actually," my dad says, "you know what? That's not true."

My eyes dart to his face. He's staring at a spot on the table, a small frown between his eyes.

"What's not true?" I ask.

"We did miss one year."

"What—what happened?"

"Brad couldn't make it," he says with a shrug. "I can't remember why . . . That's the only time either of us has ever canceled though, so it must've been something important. Something big."

"And . . . what year was that?" *Don't say 2012,* I think furiously.

My dad stands, grabbing our plates and putting them in the sink.

He turns on the tap and sprays the dishes with water. Then he turns to face me. "It would've been 2012. I remember because it was right before—" His voice cuts out and he clears his throat to cover it, but I know what he almost said. He almost said, *Right before Kasey went missing.*

CHAPTER TWENTY-FOUR

My dad's words twist in my gut. It's impossible to think that the man I once considered an uncle had anything to do with the disappearances of Jules or Kasey. And yet Brad was not out of town on the night Jules went missing after all.

"Nic?" I hear my dad's voice as if I'm underwater. "Are you okay?"

On Tuesday night, I warned Jenna that we'd need to be subtle, tactful, when we talked to my dad. If we bombarded him with all our questions at once, I said, he'd shut down. And so far, even without calm, methodical Jenna by my side, that's exactly how I've been playing it. But in the wake of this revelation, all my tact slips away. Recklessness fills its place, a machete tearing through a field.

"Just thinking about Brad," I say. My voice is unrecognizable even to myself. It's cold, needling. "I know you two are friends, but— I don't know—I'm not sure he's really all that great of a guy."

"What?" My poor dad obviously has no idea why I've turned from benign daughter to acerbic monster, and guilt twinges inside me. It's not him I'm feeling rageful toward, but the rage swallows me nonetheless. "What on earth is that supposed to mean? Did something happen at work?"

"No. He—" I almost say it. The word *affair* is on the tip of my tongue. But I can't. It would destroy my dad. I think instead of Brad's alibi for Kasey's disappearance. "He goes on fishing trips with you and comes over for weekly beers, but when you actually needed him, he wasn't there." I'm talking around it like my dad does, but he knows exactly what I mean. I can tell from the way he's watching me, as if I'm a bomb that may explode.

"Brad was there for me when nobody else was," he says. "He was there for this family. From day one."

"Well, not actually day one. He was out of town, wasn't he? At his family reunion with Sandy and the boys. The day we needed him most he was on vacation at the lake."

"No, he wasn't," my dad says. "Sandy took the kids a few days earlier, but Brad stayed in town for a work thing. Who do you think organized the search party that first day after Wyler told us Kasey—"

The words that had been tumbling out of his mouth cut off. He stiffens then turns around to face the sink.

So, Brad hadn't gone to the family reunion with Sandy and the boys. At the search party that day, when Sandy told Lauren that her family had been out of town, she must've been referring to herself and their kids, not Brad. Which means that on the night Kasey went missing from Grand Rapids, Brad was an hour closer to her than we originally thought. And he was alone.

In the span of five minutes, my dad has destroyed the only two alibis Brad had.

"Dad," I say. "Can we talk about what happened to her? Please?" This is the first time I've ever asked, and I know he will resent me for it, but I can't stop.

My dad stands with his back to me, quiet. As if I said nothing at all.

"Do you remember the weeks before Kasey went missing?" I continue. "Do you remember how strange she was acting?" Brad may now be a clear suspect, but there are still things that don't add up. Why was Kasey scared that night she told me to be careful? Why was she driving through Grand Rapids before she was taken? Where else did she go that accounted for all those miles? And how does Brad fit into any of it? Maybe my dad won't know the answers, but I have to ask.

He yanks the sink faucet to high and the rushing sound of water fills the kitchen. "I'm glad you came over, Nic. It's always good to see you."

"Dad," I say. "Please. Just talk to me. Something was going on with Kasey before she went missing. I used to think she was just stressed, but now I think she was scared."

I know he can hear me. I'm practically shouting over the sound of the water, but he just grabs a sponge and begins to scrub the plates like he's scouring year-old stains.

"Did you ever notice Kasey going anywhere during that time?" I say. "Did you or Mom ever catch her sneaking out at night?"

"You should come back again soon."

Tears sting my eyes, but he could know more than he thinks he does. "I looked around our old car the other day," I say. "We got our oil changed two weeks before Kasey was taken. There was a difference of over—"

An enormous crash cuts me off—the plates shattering in the sink. My dad turns, and I see that his hands are soaking wet, a stream of blood and water running down his wrist. But it's his expression that unnerves me most. It's a stone façade about to lose its hold.

"Nic." His voice trembles. "There's a baseball game on right now. I was thinking about watching it."

I like to pretend I'm nothing like my parents, but that's far from the truth. I drink like my mom, and for seven years, I've been just like my dad too: content to hide my wounds from myself so long as it meant I never had to examine the pain. But all that does, I realize now, is make the sores fester and grow.

"Right," I say. "I guess I'll just use the bathroom, and then I'll take off."

The moment I turn the corner out of the kitchen, I drop my hands to my knees. It feels as if the confrontation cleaved me in two. As I catch my breath, I hear my dad tear off a paper towel—I assume to mop up the blood. Then he cracks open another beer, and there's the sudden murmur of voices as the TV comes to life. I straighten and head to the bathroom.

The door I find myself in front of though is the one to Kasey's old room. I haven't been in it since she vanished, but it is a flame and I a moth, and I can't stop my hand from twisting the knob. Then, for the first time in almost a decade, I open the door and step inside.

My parents left the room exactly as it was the day Kasey went missing. Her closet gapes open, clothes spilling out. There's a bunched spaghetti-strap shirt on the floor near her hamper, aimed but missed. On her desk, a textbook lies open, a highlighter on top, uncapped and long since gone dry. My eyes flick to her unmade bed, to the indentation in her pillow the size of a skull, where one of her long auburn hairs still clings to the fabric. I walk over and dip my palm into it, careful not to touch the pillowcase, because it feels too precious to disrupt.

As I straighten, I spot Kasey's favorite jean jacket, the one that was immortalized in her missing poster, hanging in her closet. I walk over and run a fingertip along the seam at the shoulder. The jacket is so quintessentially Kasey, I get a pang of sorrow that she didn't have it with her when she was taken. The thought makes me envision her decomposing body underground somewhere, shreds of T-shirt clinging to bone. I tug the jacket off the hanger and pull it on, wishing I could absorb it into my skin and take it—take her—with me.

As I turn to go, my eyes catch on something pinned to Kasey's bulletin board, and I walk over to look at it. I remember most of the stuff there: a photo from one of our road trips to Dayton, Kasey and me sticking our tongues out at the camera in the back seat of our family's car. There's a picture of her and Lauren in tank tops and chokers, and my favorite of Kasey holding me as a baby. But the one that caught my eye I don't recognize.

In it, Kasey is alone, the same age she was when she went missing, only months or maybe weeks before. Her body's turned away from the camera, but she's looking over her shoulder as if someone just called out her name. Around her, leaves are frozen midflutter, the sun low in the sky. Unlike the rest of the photos, this one is decorated with Kasey's telltale pink hearts, the same she used to decorate the mix CD Jenna found.

Past Kasey, I see water and the cut-off corner of a dock—Brad and Sandy's lake house. Lauren's words fill my head: *Kasey did that a lot with Brad that summer. Spent nights away with him.* It's obvious now where they went. I pull the photo from the board and flip it over. Blank. Still, it's evidence enough. I slip it into the pocket of Kasey's jean jacket, only to discover that the pocket isn't empty. Inside is a little slip of paper folded into a square the size of a quarter.

I unfold it and see that it's a receipt from a gas station. With all those miles she was putting on the car, she probably had a lot of these lying around. I skim it and see nothing to indicate the station's location. On the back though is something more interesting: an address, written in handwriting I don't recognize. I pull my phone from my back pocket and type it into my maps app. A pin pops up— the bait shop in Nyona. But who wrote the address? And why would Kasey have had it in her pocket? I flip the receipt over, and my breath catches in my throat.

I was so preoccupied searching for the location of the gas station, I missed the date she visited it. Printed in ink that's faded but clear, it reads, August 17. The day Kasey disappeared. If she went to the bait shop that day, it means that sometime in the twenty-four hours before she was taken, she was less than a mile from Brad's lake house.

The last shred of loyalty I had to Brad disappears, sloughing off me like dead skin. In its place I feel nothing but a seething, burning rage. I've been delusional, ignoring evidence that the man is a monster because once upon a time he put a Band-Aid on my knee. Jenna has been right all along.

I close out the maps app and pull up my call history, tapping on Jenna's name at the top of the list. It rings through to her voicemail, which is unusual. Normally, she answers my calls after the first ring. I pull up our text thread and type, Found something. Ready to talk to Brad. Call me. Then, for good measure, I call again, not caring how desperate it looks. But like the first time, it just rings and rings.

I think suddenly of Lauren, her eyes wide in fear at the sight of us when we showed up at her house. I think of the man hiding behind the playscape waiting to tell Beth Anne his "secret." I think of Brad leaning over me to point at my front door.

When Jenna's voicemail clicks on, the realization hits me with a certainty as real and heavy as stone. She didn't miss tonight because her plans changed or she forgot. She didn't show up because something is wrong.

CHAPTER TWENTY-FIVE

U rgency tidal-waves through me, but it is so belated, I want to scream. I haven't heard from Jenna since she walked out of my apartment on Tuesday night—five days ago. So much could have happened between then and now. I pray that I'm just being paranoid, that revisiting Kasey's disappearance is fucking with my head, but I feel in my bones that something more is going on. Jenna's words from the other week echo in my mind: *Someone out there knows what we're doing and doesn't like it.*

I stride to the door, my hand pausing on the knob. I need to get to Jenna's house, but how? I biked to my dad's, but it'll be dark soon. Plus, biking to Osceola will take far longer than I'm willing to wait. My dad's been drinking, so I can't ask him to drive. And with my license suspended, he won't let me borrow his car.

My fingers feel maddeningly slow as I pull up my Uber app. There's no filter for cars with bike racks, so I click on the last option, cars with wheelchair access, hoping I'll be able to contort my bike into the space meant for the chair. I balk at the estimated price of the trip—rideshares are a luxury I can't afford—but that doesn't matter right now. I order the car.

"Dad?" I call, walking through the house.

He's in the living room, in his recliner, hand wrapped around a beer. On the TV is a baseball game.

"I have to go," I say. "Thanks again for dinner."

"Sure." He doesn't take his eyes off the TV. "Talk to you soon." No *Let's do it again* or *Come over anytime.* Not that I was expecting it after our disastrous conversation, but still.

I pace for the entire six minutes it takes for my Uber to arrive. It's a white minivan driven by a guy named Gabe, and when it finally pulls up, I yank open the sliding side door and am relieved to find one of the bucket seats has been removed.

"Can I put my bike in here?" I say before Gabe, a twenty-something guy with acne, has a chance to say hi.

"Oh, um . . ." He glances from me to the bike.

"Come on, dude. You have plenty of space. I'll give you five stars if you let me." The pettiest bribe. When he hesitates, I add, "One if you don't."

He rolls his eyes. "Sure. Whatever."

I heave my bike into his car, then jump into shotgun.

"I have that you're going to 200 Erie Street, Osceola," Gabe says. "That right?"

"Yes."

It's not Jenna's address. I've only been to her house once, and her neighborhood was a goddamn maze, so when Uber's map popped up, I typed in Osceola, zoomed in on the area of town where she lives, and chose an address at random. Once I get there, I'll have to hop on my bike and pray I can find it.

As we pull away from the curb, I call Jenna again, but again it rings through. I glance at the map on Gabe's phone. Ten minutes to our destination. My knee jitters.

The moment we hit Osceola's main road, I say, "This is good. You can just drop me off here." I remember turning right into the neighborhood somewhere around where we are now, and I don't want to risk losing my sense of direction.

"You sure?" Gabe says. "We're still a few blocks away."

"I'm sure."

"All right, then."

Before he's even come to a complete stop, I fling open the door and jump out. I hear him mutter, "Jesus, lady," as I tug open the sliding side door and lug my bike out of the back. A sudden pain shoots up my leg like a knife. I look down to see that one of my pedals has sliced my calf, and a line of blood is running down my leg.

I lift my head to ask Gabe if he has a napkin or something, but the automatic sliding door is already closing. "You know," he calls through the shrinking gap, "those ratings go both ways." And then the door is closed and he's driving away.

I swing my bleeding leg over my bike, and as the air catches the cut, it stings all over again. I pedal off in the direction where I think Jenna's house is, my calf throbbing as my bike lurches over the train tracks and into the residential area beyond.

The sun has set now, and what little light lingers on the horizon is quickly fading. The endless chirp of crickets joins the deafening buzz of cicadas, but otherwise the town feels still and quiet. Almost preternaturally so. I bike past dark houses and empty lots, the grass overgrown and wild. The streetlights flicker above me, casting an eerie yellow glow over everything I pass.

I've been riding for about five minutes when I notice the same rundown church I passed by a few minutes earlier. The same white steeple, the same peeling red paint. I'm going in circles. I pedal past, then take a right. It's little more than a blind guess, and I pray I'm headed on a path I haven't explored yet.

And then, after another few minutes, I spot something I recognize from the time Jenna drove me here—a dense copse of trees she mentioned she liked because it made her feel surrounded by nature. I take a right at the next street then turn left into the neighborhood behind it. It's hard to tell in the dark, but I think this looks right.

"Come on," I mutter as I pass by house after house. "Where are you?"

And then I see it. The little white house with the towering tree out front. I skid my bike to a stop, the rubber tires squealing against the pavement. But my excitement is short-lived. There's not a single light on in the house, and the driveway is empty. The garage door is closed, so Jenna's truck could be inside, but there's no way to tell.

I launch myself off my bike, letting it crash into the yard, and race to the front door. For a fleeting moment, I think how Jenna would hate this plan—or rather, lack thereof. I haven't thought through anything. But there's no time to worry about that now. I lift a fist to the door and pound.

Nothing. No lights turn on. There's no noise beyond the door.

"Shit," I hiss.

I knock again, louder this time, but again there's only silence.

There's a hedge on both sides of the door, lining the outside walls beneath two symmetrical windows. I step off the concrete stoop to the right and squeeze my body between the plant and the side of the house, the stiff twigs scraping my bare thighs as I inch toward the window.

Suddenly, a light flicks on, and I freeze. I hear the sound of a deadbolt and turn to see Jenna's front door creaking open.

"Nic?"

I hear her voice before I see her. Then, from the sliver of darkness in the doorway, Jenna steps onto the stoop and into the light.

"What're you doing?" she says.

"Jenna?" She looks . . . fine. She's wearing a robe over pajama pants and a T-shirt, her hair dripping against the worn terrycloth. She hadn't been kidnapped. She wasn't being held prisoner in her own home. She was in the shower. "Jesus," I breathe. "You scared the shit out of me."

Her gaze flicks around the shadowed yard. "What're you doing here?"

"You didn't show up at my dad's tonight." I inch my way around the hedge and step back onto the stoop. "You haven't responded to any of my texts or answered a single one of my calls. I'm making sure you're still alive, that's what. Now, can I come in, or are you gonna make me stand here all night?"

She hesitates, and I notice a look in her eye I can't quite place. Wariness, maybe. Or fear. And that's when I realize that, although she is safe and unharmed, I wasn't wrong to worry. Something's happened.

"Jenna? What the fuck's going on?"

"Nothing," she says a little too quickly. "Sorry. Of course you can come in."

I slip through the doorway and into her dark house. She closes the front door behind me and flips on the light. I catch a glimpse of that wall covered in research as I turn to face her. Jenna doesn't normally wear much makeup, but now her face is completely bare, and it makes her look older, tired.

"What happened?" I say. "Why didn't you show up tonight?"

She starts to respond, but then she glances down and stops. "Whoa. Nic, you're bleeding."

I look at my leg to see the cut looks far worse in her bright house than it did in the dark. It's about two inches long and deep. Luckily, it's stopped bleeding, but a long swath of skin, from my calf to my ankle, is painted in sticky-looking blood, and it's pooled in the top of my sock.

"It's fine," I say, even though the sight of it has made it start throbbing again. "I'm more worried about you. What happened tonight?"

"You need to get that cleaned. Let me go get some stuff."

I start to protest, but she's already walking out of the room.

"Jenna," I say when she reappears a moment later, holding a wet, folded paper towel in one hand and a plastic caddy with gauze, Band-Aids, and a bottle of hydrogen peroxide in the other. "Forget about my fucking leg. Why didn't you meet me at my dad's earlier?"

She sighs, not quite meeting my eye.

"Did someone threaten you?" I say. "Like they did to Lauren?"

"No."

"Well, I can tell something happened. So, please, just—"

She lifts a hand. "It's my mom. It's the cancer."

"Oh." It's so unexpected, for a moment, my brain can't process it, as if she spoke the words in a foreign language. "Oh, Jenna. I'm sorry."

"I've been so wrapped up in it all, I've just been letting everything else fall by the wayside. But I'm sorry for not texting you back. And about tonight . . . with everything going on, I honestly just forgot."

"Oh. No. Of course. That's okay."

"With the cancer, you know, she has good days and bad days. But recently there've been more and more bad ones, and this past week has been the worst I've seen."

I don't know what to say. "Is she in the hospital?"

Jenna shakes her head. "She refuses to go. I don't blame her, really. She's been through a lot these past few months."

"Is there anything I can do? You know, to help?"

"No. But thank you."

I nod. Hesitate. Eventually, I say, "You were right. About Brad. I talked to my dad earlier and his alibis are worthless. Both of them. And I found something else too. In Kasey's old room." I feel like an asshole bringing up all of this right now, but I think Jenna would want to know what I discovered tonight no matter what else is going on in her life.

It must be true, because she says, "What'd you find?"

I tell her about the picture of Kasey at Nyona and the receipt from the day she went missing with the address scrawled on the back.

"You were right," I say again. "I was being delusional because, you know, Brad's like an uncle to me. At least he was. But he's a bad guy, whether he was the one who took our sisters or not. And I'm finally ready to talk to him. He's at the lake right now for that reunion they do every summer." As I say this, the coincidence of the timing strikes me. Almost seven years ago to the day, Kasey was taken. "I think we should go."

"Nic, it's almost nine at night. We can't go now."

"In the morning, then."

"I need to go to my mom's tomorrow," she says.

"Okay. No problem." But I get the feeling that there's something I'm missing, something she's not telling me. "We can go after you're done."

"Nic," she says. "Maybe it'd be best if we put a pin in all of this for a bit."

"Wait—what?"

"With everything going on with my mom, this just doesn't feel like the best timing."

I study her face. Three weeks ago, Jenna would have given an organ for answers about Jules's disappearance. Now she doesn't want to talk to the man who could be responsible for it? Something has to have happened this week that changed that—something other than her mom's cancer.

"Jenna," I say. "If something else is going on, you can tell me."

"Look, I'd be lying if I said what happened to Lauren didn't rattle me. I mean, approaching a kid on a playground is a pretty messed up thing to do to get someone to stop talking. So, yeah, I'm also worried that we don't know what we're getting ourselves into."

Something's still not adding up. We were both unnerved by Lauren's story, but afterwards, Jenna was nearly rabid to confront Brad.

"I get that," I say. "But it also means we're getting closer to the truth. I think we just need to talk to Brad. We've come this far. We need to find out what happened between him and my sister."

"You're not listening, Nic. I don't have time right now. So . . ." She hesitates. "If you're dead set on talking to Brad anytime soon, you're just gonna have to do it on your own."

My chin jerks back. "But—Jenna. I mean, I know how much you want to be there. Why don't I just wait for you? It'll be better with the two of us."

It's true, but the other truth is that I don't want to do this on my own. If someone had told me three weeks ago, when Jenna first approached me in the Funland parking lot, that my friendship with her would turn into the best part of my life, I wouldn't have believed it. But sometime when I wasn't looking, that's exactly what happened.

She sighs. "I don't know how long this rough patch with my mom is gonna last. This one's bad, and she has no one else. I can't just leave her alone. So, like I said, if you wanna talk to Brad, that's fine, but I'm not going to be able to do it with you."

It occurs to me then that she might be bluffing. After all, I haven't done a single thing on our sisters' cases without her. Maybe she's counting on me not taking her up on it.

"I'll go to the lake alone, then," I say. "Talk to him myself."

She looks taken aback at this, which makes me think I read her right, but after a moment's hesitation, she nods. "Just . . . be careful. Okay?"

"I'll be fine."

"I'm serious, Nic. If it was Brad who threatened Lauren, we don't know what else he's capable of."

"I'll be careful," I say. "Promise."

"All right, well, I have a lot to do tomorrow, so I should probably get some sleep. How'd you get here? Do you need a ride home?"

"I biked, but I can just—"

"No," she says with a wry smile. "You can't just. I'll give you a ride. But first, you need to put a bandage on that leg. I don't want you gushing blood all over my truck."

I live closer to Jenna's place than my dad does, and there's hardly any traffic now, so the drive goes fast. Before I know it, we're pulling up to my building. I'm about to open the door and hop out when I turn to face Jenna.

"Hey," I say. "Will you be honest? Did something else happen this week? Did someone try to scare you?"

"Nic—"

"Because," I continue over her, "you can tell me. I get that you're used to taking care of people. You did it with Jules, you're doing it with your mom, and Jesus, did you see yourself tonight with my leg and the hydrogen peroxide? Sometimes you can have real big-sister energy." I grin and she returns it, but it doesn't quite reach her eyes. "But if you're trying to protect me," I say, "don't."

"Nic, my mom has cancer and she's not doing well right now. We may not have the best relationship, but I'm all she's got. I'm not just gonna leave her to fend for herself when she can hardly get out of bed."

"You didn't answer my question."

Jenna sighs. "No one threatened me. Okay? I swear."

I stare at her for a long moment. Then, I nod and tell her I'm sorry about her mom, to call if she needs anything. But as I slide out of the truck and walk through the dark night, I remember how afraid she looked when she answered the door earlier, and my suspicion solidifies: Despite all her denials, I think someone tried to scare her. And just like it did with Lauren, whatever the threat was, it worked.

CHAPTER TWENTY-SIX

I wake the next morning alert and buzzing. Brad, I think. After all my stalling, and prevaricating, and clinging to the hope that he is blameless in Kasey's disappearance, we're finally going to talk to Brad.

I fling back the covers, but my feet pause just as they touch the old beige carpet of my bedroom floor. *We're* not going to talk to Brad. I am. Alone. On top of the dread this sends prickling up my spine, there's also the problem of how I'm actually going to get to the lake an hour away. I'd been so discouraged by Jenna's news last night, I'd completely forgotten she was supposed to be my ride.

In my oversized T-shirt and underwear, I pad into the kitchen to make a pot of coffee, pour myself a cup, then open my maps app. According to its directions, one way on a bike would take five hours, and it doesn't look like I can get that far using public transit. After yesterday, my dad's not going to drive me, and I can't think of a single other person I'd feel comfortable asking. I switch over to my Uber app, but the estimated price for a two-hour round trip actually takes my breath away. I can't justify it.

I think of my car, which has been sitting untouched in my apartment's designated parking space since my dad drove it home from the impound lot almost five months ago. But with my license suspended, driving it would be breaking the law, and I'm in enough legal trouble as it is.

Unable to stand still any longer, I swallow a gulp of coffee and head to my closet to throw on some clothes. I move through my apartment packing my backpack, because no matter how I get there, I'll have to bring my wallet and phone. More important, I'm going to need the receipt I found in Kasey's jean jacket with the handwritten address on the back.

My car keys sit in a jewelry bowl on top of my dresser, eyeing me as I sit on the floor to tie my shoes. I shouldn't drive. I know I shouldn't. But then I think of Brad, the man who potentially took my sister and Jenna's too, enjoying a peaceful family vacation, and I find myself walking to the dresser. Without quite telling my hand to do it, I grab the keys.

I'm a swarm of nerves as I drive to the lake, going five under and shooting anxious glances into my rearview the entire way. The route is straight and monotonous. Cornfields laced with strips of woods pass by my window in a blur of gold and green. The sky is a cloudless, endless blue. To me, it all feels unnervingly vast. Every mile of land I pass represents a thousand places that could have swallowed Kasey and hidden her from sight.

When I turn onto the road that leads to the little lake town, flashes of the past flicker in my mind like bits of a movie on a broken projector. Sun glinting silver on the water. A deck of playing cards on a soda-sticky table. Fresh fish dinners. Noisy games of Yahtzee. The memories shine with the feeling of rightness, of belonging. Me, Kasey, our mom and dad, the two Andrews boys, and their parents. But as I get closer and closer to Brad and Sandy's house, the scenes turn gray and lifeless. One of our little group is now dead. One may have been her killer.

The house is smaller than I remember, a one-story with blue wooden siding, the lake shimmering behind it. I assumed the hour-long drive would dull my nerves about confronting Brad and temper my anger at him, but instead, it compounded them into a white-hot fury. By the time I pull up out front, my hands are shaking. I grab the receipt with the address on the back from my bag then fling open my car door.

I'm walking up the front path to the house when I hear voices from behind it. There's a child's shriek of laughter followed by a peal of giggles. Beneath is the hum of adults talking. I glance toward the front door, but the house looks dark and still, so I follow the sound around the side and stumble headfirst into the Andrews family reunion.

The backyard crawls with people. Kids sprint in every direction, shooting giddy, panicked looks over their shoulders as they run from a little boy with no front teeth who's clearly "it." Adults stand in clusters, red Solo cups and cans of beer in their hands. Two picnic tables form a cornucopia of food: open bags of chips, jars of pickles and condiments, Tupperware bowls full of macaroni and cheese and fruit salad. The hinges of a cooler squeak loudly as a woman opens it to dig around inside.

As I gaze around at all the people, my conviction wanes. No one seems to have noticed me yet. Maybe I should just go back to my car and wait until I can catch Brad on his own. But as I start to head back around the side of the house, I hear my name. I turn to see Sandy walking toward me, and my throat constricts with nerves. She's the last person I want to do this in front of.

"Sandy. Hi."

"What're you doing here?" she asks, her voice bright.

My eyes rove around the yard as my mind races to come up with some logical excuse for barging in on their vacation like this. And that's when I see Brad. Standing by an open grill with an apron wrapped around his waist and a spatula in his hand. He's nodding along to something the man across from him is saying, and when he smiles, something cracks open inside me, leaking out a bitter blackness, a malignant tar of rage. Suddenly, everything else is swept from my mind. I no longer care about Sandy or embarrassing Brad in front of his family. All I care about is Kasey and finally getting the truth.

"I'm here to talk to Brad," I say. Without waiting for a reaction, I stride toward him, leaving Sandy frozen in my wake. Heads turn in my direction, the collective gaze of the Andrews family heating my skin, but I don't care. When I'm about ten feet away, Brad's eyes catch mine over the other man's shoulder, and his smile drops. He opens his mouth, but I don't want to hear his voice.

"Kasey was here that night," I spit at him, my words trembling and loud. The man Brad was talking to turns to look at me and instinctively slinks to the side. I pull the receipt from my pocket, wave it in Brad's direction. "I have fucking proof."

He lifts his hands. "Nic—"

"Don't," I snap. "Don't lie to me."

"Hang on—"

"What did you do to her?" I shout, my eyes stinging with tears. "What did you do to my sister?"

Suddenly, Brad's hand is around my upper arm, his fingers so tight and unexpected that my voice cuts out. He's never touched me like this before, and Jenna's warning from last night flashes in my mind: *We don't know what he's capable of.* "This isn't the place, Nic," he says, and although he mutters the words beneath his breath, they are hard as steel. He isn't going to let me speak his secret here in front of his wife and family. He won't allow it. "Let's go inside, then we can talk."

I want to tell him I don't give a shit about the setting in which we have this conversation, but yet again, when it counts, all I can do is freeze.

Brad turns to face the yard of people, which is split between those watching us openly and those pretending not to. "Sorry, everyone," he says loudly. He's positioned my body slightly in front of his own so no one can see his grip on my arm. "This is just a misunderstanding. We're taking care of it inside. You good to take over the burgers, Larry?" He glances at the man he was talking to earlier, who nods and reaches out to take the spatula from Brad's outstretched hand. "Now, please, get drunk and try to forget any of this happened!"

Halting laughter breaks out over the yard, people slowly turn back to their conversations, and the kids' game of tag starts again.

Brad steers me toward the house, and as he does, I spot Sandy stand-ing alone in the middle of the yard, watching us with an unreadable expression on her face.

It's only when we're both inside and the door has closed behind us that I finally find my voice again. "That hurts," I say.

For a fleeting moment, Brad frowns down at me as if he doesn't understand. Then he looks at my arm and lets go, as if he suddenly realized he was touching a flame. "I'm sorry," he says, and to my surprise, he actually looks it. It unnerves me—the quiet normalcy after the burst of violence. "But you shouldn't have barged in like that—"

He's interrupted by the sound of the doorknob twisting, and we turn to see Sandy slipping through the doorway.

"Sandy." His eyes go round with fear. He wants his wife nowhere near me right now, and about this we can agree. I was reckless out-side, but it is Brad I want to hurt, not her. And while the force of his grip may have scared me, there's nothing he can do to me here, not with his entire family outside the door. "I've got this," he says. "Don't worry. Go back outside."

"No." Sandy's voice is cool. "We need to deal with this quickly and quietly."

Brad walks over to her, one hand reaching for the doorknob, the other ushering her out. "It's just a misunderstanding, hon. Like I said. Nic and I can hash this out together."

"It's true," I say. "I'm sorry for showing up like that. I was just . . . I just need to talk to Brad."

"I wish that were the case," Sandy says. "But it's not."

I don't understand what she means, and by the look on Brad's face, he doesn't either, but he just continues to guide her toward the doorway. "I'll be back out in a minute. I promise—"

"Oh, for heaven's sake!" Sandy suddenly shouts, her voice rever-berating around the little house. "Would the two of you just let me speak? Kasey didn't meet up with Brad here the night she went missing. I was the one she came to see."

CHAPTER TWENTY-SEVEN

For a moment, all I can do is stare at Sandy. Her confession is so unexpected, I think I must have misunderstood it.

"W-what do you mean?" I finally say, looking from her to Brad. I assumed he would be the only one who could answer my questions, but he looks almost as confused as I am, gaping at his wife with panicked anticipation.

"Can I see that?" Sandy says.

At first, I have no idea what she's talking about. Then she nods at my hand, and I look down to see the receipt I'd been waving in Brad's face. I'd forgotten I was holding it. Without thinking, I pass it to her. As she studies the handwritten address on the back, I suddenly realize that I've given her the one piece of evidence that places my sister here on the night of her disappearance, something Sandy would no doubt want torn to shreds. Just as I'm about to snatch it back though, she hands it to me.

"Like I said, I'm the one who saw Kasey that night. That handwriting is mine."

My body stills as a lifetime of affection curdles to anger inside me.

"Sandy," Brad says. In sharp contrast to earlier, he now looks like a chastened schoolboy who's been caught doing something bad. The apron he's wearing is a ridiculous sunny yellow. Loathing for him wafts off my skin like heat. "I don't think you—"

"No," Sandy says. "Nic's found out enough. It's clear from that little spectacle outside that we'd be better off if we tell her the truth rather than let her run with her assumptions."

"But I don't even—"

"Oh, goddammit, Brad. Stop pretending like you don't know what's going on here. I understand that you have no idea what I'm about to say, but you know exactly what we're talking about."

Brad's mouth snaps shut.

"W-wait," I stammer. "I don't understand. Sandy, why did you see Kasey that night? What was she doing here?"

"I'll tell you. But first, you need to understand what happened before that." She heaves a deep sigh. "I'm going to sit."

There's a smattering of sagging, mismatching furniture in the living room, pieces they cobbled together from garage sales. Sandy sits in the corner of a faded maroon couch and I perch myself on the edge of an old blue armchair, too keyed up to relax. Brad follows us over but remains standing, as if at any moment, he might turn and run.

"It was the middle of summer," Sandy says, "that year, 2012. I was running some errands on Grape Road. I'd gotten an iced coffee and the caffeine was going to my head, but I couldn't get myself to stop drinking it with it just sitting there in the cupholder beside me, so I decided to throw it out. There were no trashcans around, so I pulled into this back alley with a bunch of dumpsters, and I saw a car."

Brad lets out a sputtering little groan, but neither Sandy nor I look over at him.

"I recognized it immediately," she continues. "It was Kasey's car, the one the two of you shared. I realized I must've been behind the record store where she worked, but I didn't understand why her car was there. It was obvious you couldn't park in the alley, and the car looked empty, so I started walking over to take a look."

I know what's coming because I've heard it before. Lauren told us the same story.

"When I got closer," Sandy says, "I realized it wasn't empty after

THE MISSING HALF 159

all. There were two people in the back seat. Having sex. I was morti-fied. I assumed one of the people was Kasey, and I obviously didn't want her to see me, so I turned to leave. That's when I saw it—Brad's car. It was parked in the lot on the opposite side of the alley, in a spot so far from everything else. And I just knew."

"Sandy—" Brad's voice is a croak.

"Please," she says. "Just . . . let me get through this. I was devas-tated. Obviously. But more than that I was furious. With every pass-ing minute, I realized yet another way the two of them had destroyed my life. Kasey was nineteen. I didn't know when they'd started sleeping together, but, God, if it got out, you know people would as-sume the worst. And maybe they'd be right. I know if it were my daughter, I'd probably want the guy in jail."

"It wasn't like that," Brad says. "It started that summer. You have to believe me."

I may hate him, but I do believe he's telling the truth. That's what Lauren said as well.

Sandy angles her face toward her husband but doesn't look him in the eye. "Even so, you were old enough to be her father. Can you imagine how fast this town would have turned on us if it had gotten out? The boys would've been ostracized, and people would've eaten me alive. 'The wife.'" She says it like it's a slur. "Isn't it somehow al-ways her fault? She knows her husband's secret and keeps it for him. Or she lets herself go, doesn't keep him satisfied, and he has no choice but to look somewhere else."

In my periphery, I see Brad give an involuntary twitch, the old wooden floorboards creaking beneath his feet.

"Maybe I could've dealt with all of that," Sandy continues, looking at me, "but your parents—they were our best friends. If it got out, we'd lose them too. I did nothing wrong, and yet everything I loved in my life was on the line."

"I'm so sorry, Sandy," Brad says. "I had no idea you knew."

Sandy lets out a disdainful laugh. "Of course you didn't. Because I was a well-behaved, middle-aged, stay-at-home mom. I was invis-ible. Even to my own husband."

"Invisible? No, I—"

She lifts a hand, cutting him off. "Oh, please. I can't remember exactly when it started, but I woke up one morning, and suddenly you only seemed to notice me when the dishes went unwashed or dinner wasn't on the table on time. Nobody thinks housewives have lives or stories or feelings, let alone secrets."

Empathy blooms in my chest, but it quickly hardens. Sandy knew Kasey was having an illicit affair right before she went missing, and she said nothing to the police. "What did you do?" I say. "When you found out about them?"

I see her register the coldness in my voice, see it stiffen her shoulders, and I realize this is the end of us. The end of dinners at their place, the end of Sandy's long hugs and homemade brownies. Too much has happened, and we will never find our way back.

"I knew I had to keep it quiet," she says, "make it go away. And I didn't think confronting Brad was the way to do that. Even if I told him to stop, I wasn't sure he would. But I had a feeling Kasey might not be as infatuated with him as he was with her. I thought she might listen to reason. So the next week, I went to the record store and asked to talk to Kasey outside. It was obvious she knew exactly why I was there. And the look on her face . . . well, it was also obvious she'd forced herself to forget about me, convinced herself the affair was a victimless crime. Like I said—invisible. But, confronted with the wife of the man she was sleeping with, she started crying almost instantly."

McLean's story of Kasey in the parking lot finally clicks. I'd been so distracted by the affair, I'd nearly forgotten about it. "Hang on," I say. "Kasey was nineteen. Brad was more than twice her age. He was the one who was married, he was the one who cheated on you, and she's the one you blame?"

"I *blamed* both of them, Nic. He might have been the only one cheating, but Kasey wasn't some innocent victim."

It's obvious though, from Brad's shock at all of this, that the only person to ever be held accountable for what happened between the two of them was my sister.

"But," Sandy continues, "she clearly didn't understand the magnitude of what she was doing. Didn't understand how many people she would hurt if it got out. I told her to break things off with him. She didn't need to tell him why, just that it was over."

Brad is quiet, but I can feel the horror radiating off him like a smell.

"What'd she say?" I ask.

"She said she would. I believed her."

"When was this?"

"End of July? Beginning of August?"

Right around the time Kasey started acting off. "But I don't understand. If she ended things with him, what was she doing here the night she went missing?"

"I'm getting there," Sandy says. "Over the next few weeks, I kept an eye on them both. I went back to the alley behind the record store almost every day, but as far as I could tell, Brad was staying at Funland and Kasey at the shop. It seemed they'd stopped seeing each other."

"We did," Brad says. "That was the end of it. I swear."

She ignores him. "But then one day Kasey came over to the house."

"What?" he says. "Why?"

"Brad," Sandy snaps. "I'm reliving the worst few weeks of my life right now. And if I have to sit here and explain how my husband risked everything we built together because of his utter stupidity and a pair of perky breasts, the least you can do is not interrupt me."

He opens and closes his mouth like a fish.

"Kasey came over to our house one day," she says again. "When I opened the door and found her standing there, I could tell she was terrified."

That memory resurfaces: *Be careful tonight, okay?* Kasey told me just a few weeks before she disappeared, her eyes electric with fear. *Don't go anywhere alone.* So, I hadn't rewritten history after all. "Why was she scared?" I say. "Did she tell you?"

Sandy cocks her head, giving me an odd look. "She didn't need to tell me. It was obvious. She was scared about what she was there to do."

"What do you mean?"

"Well, it required quite the set of balls. Your sister told me if I wanted her to leave Brad alone, I was going to have to pay." Sandy gives me a bitter smirk. "Ten thousand dollars."

CHAPTER TWENTY-EIGHT

The living room is plunged into a stunned silence. Right before she disappeared, Kasey asked for $10,000? To me now, the amount feels as out of reach as a bar of gold. To Kasey back then, making $8.25 an hour, it would've been inconceivable. Although, of course, if she asked for it, I suppose it wouldn't have been.

Before I can form any of this into a question, Brad says, "She asked you for money to stay away from me? But we weren't even seeing each other anymore. We didn't get back together after she broke things off." He looks almost cartoonish in his distress, his hair standing on end, the lines on his face so deep they looked etched.

"Like I said," Sandy says, "the money was for her to keep it that way. Which I thought was worth it."

But I can't get myself to believe that. Kasey wouldn't have gone to Sandy for that kind of money out of spite or opportunity. She only would've done it out of desperation.

"Did you give it to her?" I ask.

"Well. I wasn't going to be able to withdraw that much cash without Brad noticing and asking questions. I just wanted him to think Kasey broke up with him on her own. So I told her to give me time to get it together. We had some cash around the house that I could replace later, before Brad found out. And I made a few smaller with-drawals that wouldn't attract that much attention. Still, I couldn't come up with ten thousand."

"So, what happened?"

"A few days later, I was out here at the lake with the boys for our reunion. Brad had to stay behind for a work thing, but he was plan-ning to join us later. Anyway, we were all at the pizza place for dinner one night, the entire family, when halfway through our meal, the bell chimes and I look up to see Kasey walking through the door. Obviously, I knew she was there for the money, and it made me livid. It was like she turned into a completely different person that sum-mer. I mean, when I think about how close we all used to be . . ." Sandy shakes her head. "I couldn't believe she'd barge into our fam-ily reunion like that."

She gives me a look—the girl who just did the exact same thing—but I hold her gaze. "How'd Kasey know you were here?" I say.

"I don't know. Brad? Did you tell her we were going to the lake that week?"

"Um." He clears his throat. "I-I don't know."

"Maybe one of your parents mentioned something," she says. "Or she could've just remembered. We do it the same week every year." She glances out the window, at all the members of their family be-yond it, laughing and drinking beer. "When I saw her, I got up and intercepted her before she could make a scene. I told her to meet me in an hour by the bait shop so she could, you know, extort me in private. She didn't know where the shop was, so I jotted down the address on the back of some receipt I found in my purse."

Absently, I slide my hand into the pocket where I've stored it, one of the last things my sister ever touched.

"I didn't have as much cash as she wanted," Sandy says, "but when we met up later, I gave her what I had—almost seven thousand dol-lars."

For a moment, I'm quiet. It's all so much. Then I think of those missing miles on our odometer. "Where was she going after that? Did she tell you?" Because I found the receipt in Kasey's bedroom, she had to have gone back home that night before she disappeared. A drive to and from Nyona and then another to Grand Rapids would've been—what, 250 miles? It's a big piece of the puzzle, but it still leaves another 250 unaccounted for.

"She didn't say," Sandy says.

"Well, what about the money? Did she say what she needed it for?"

"I was paying her to stop screwing my husband, Nic."

I shake my head irritably. "That may've been what it was for you, but I don't believe that's what it was for her—at least not totally. Something else had to have happened, something that made her desperate for cash. I mean, she disappeared hours after you gave her that money. *Hours.* That can't be a coincidence."

"Well, at first," Sandy says, "when she went missing, I assumed she just took the money and ran."

"No. Kasey wouldn't have done that. Is that really what you think happened? That she was trying to run away?"

"I said I did at first, but it seemed clear soon after that, that's not what happened. Even if she was using the money to run away—"

"She wasn't—"

"*Even* if she was, I don't think she would've disappeared into thin air like she did. She wouldn't have abandoned her car or left her wallet behind. And I don't think she would've stayed away this long either."

"How could you have hidden all of this from the police?" I say. "While my parents—your 'best friends'—were offering money they didn't have for any scrap of information about Kasey, you two were busy hiding evidence to protect yourselves." Something occurs to me then. "Wait a second. At one of the first search parties that summer, you ran into Lauren Perkins, Kasey's friend from school. You told her that Brad was at your family reunion on the night Kasey was taken, even though he wasn't. Were you . . . trying to give him an alibi for Kasey's disappearance?"

"I'm not sure what you're talking about," Sandy says slowly. "I may have had a conversation with Lauren at one of the search parties, though if I did, I honestly don't remember it." But I can tell she's lying, and a chill creeps over my skin. She is far more calculating than I ever realized. "But we never hid *evidence*, Nic. You need to understand that. What happened between your sister and Brad had nothing to do with her disappearance."

"How do you know that?" I nearly shout it. "He wasn't even with you that night—"

"Nic," Brad says. When I look at him, I'm startled to see tears glistening on his cheeks. "I'm an idiot. I'm a fucking schmuck. And I'm sorry. For everything. But I promise I had nothing to do with what happened to your sister. I"—he shoots an anxious glance at Sandy—"I cared for her."

"No," I say. "You don't get to say that. You stole the last summer of her life, and when she went missing, the only thing you cared about was yourself." He opens his mouth to respond, but I don't let him. "Where were you on the night she was taken? Why weren't you at the reunion?"

"I-I was at work. I had to do inventory and we'd just had two of the waitstaff quit, so I stayed behind a day. That's it. I swear."

"What about the fishing trip with my dad that year? Why did you cancel?"

Brad jerks his head back. "What does that have to do with anything?"

"Jules Connor went missing on August 4th," I say, "during your annual fishing trip with my dad, but he said you canceled at the last minute."

"Christ, Nic. Do you really think I—"

"Just answer the goddamn question, Brad."

"I don't know," he says. "I don't remember."

"I do," Sandy interjects. "We were in couples therapy, a sort of save-your-marriage retreat. After everything that happened, I said I wanted to go. I still didn't tell him I knew about the affair. I couldn't stomach the idea of him denying it, and I just wanted to move on. So I told him I hadn't been happy for a while and I knew he hadn't either. It was a version of the truth. I made it very clear how serious I was. It was a now-or-never kind of offer. The retreat was that weekend, two weeks before Kasey went missing. I remember because he made a big deal about having to cancel his fishing trip."

Brad reacts to this just as he has to everything else he's heard today, with a look of utter astonishment.

"What happened to Kasey," Sandy says, "and what happened to that other girl were tragedies. But we've told you the truth. And that's everything we know. I need you to believe me when I tell you neither one of us had anything to do with Kasey's disappearance."

I'm not sure what to think. My gut tells me to believe her, but how can I after everything I just learned?

"You could've helped," I say. "If you'd told the truth when she first went missing, Kasey might still be alive today." I mean it, yet here I am holding the truth in my hands, and I'm no closer to understanding what happened that night.

"All I did," Sandy says, "is protect my family. When you have one of your own one day, you'll understand."

The anger that has been building inside me suddenly ignites into a storm. "*Kasey* is my family. And you might not have killed her, but you sure as hell let her die."

I stand, my eyes stinging. I want nothing more than to get away from them both, to never see them again. That I ever considered them my surrogate family makes me sick, as if I've swallowed something rotten. I'm turning to leave when something hits me.

"Wait."

"What?" Sandy says.

But it's Brad I'm staring at.

"What happened to Lauren Perkins? Did you go to her church the other week? Are you the reason she's scared to talk?"

Sandy snaps her head sideways. "Brad? What's she talking about?"

I'm half expecting him to say he doesn't know what I mean. He hardly knows who Lauren Perkins is, he's innocent, blah blah blah.

Instead, he sighs. "She was the only one who knew about me and Kasey. When you told me you reached out to her to ask about that summer, I got scared. I just tried to keep her quiet, that's all."

"What did you do?" Sandy says.

Brad hesitates.

"He followed Lauren's four-year-old daughter onto a playground," I say. "He gave her chocolate to pass along a message. *Stop talking about Kasey Monroe.*"

"Jesus."

"It was dumb," Brad stammers. "I know. But if the affair got out, I thought . . . I don't know what I thought. I just didn't want to risk you or your dad learning the truth. I couldn't . . . I didn't think I could handle that."

"What about Jenna?" I say. "Did you try to keep her quiet too?"

"Who?"

"Jenna Connor. Jules's sister. She's the one I told you about, the one who's been looking into everything with me." I think back to the look in Jenna's eyes when she opened the door yesterday. It was the same look Kasey had seven years ago when she told me to be careful that night. Wary. Scared. "I think something happened that made her want to stop."

Brad shakes his head. "I'm sorry, Nic. I don't know what you're talking about."

"No," I say. "It was you. It had to have been."

"I didn't do anything to her. I remember you telling me about her, but I don't even really know who she is."

I study his face, searching it for any sign that he's lying, but I find none.

If Brad didn't scare Jenna, who did?

CHAPTER TWENTY-NINE

My tires churn up gravel as I pull out of the drive, and five minutes later I'm flinging open the door of the nearest gas station, heading straight to the wine-and-mixers aisle. My head feels hectic and disordered, as if someone cracked open my skull, dug their fingers into my brain, and jumbled everything I once knew. Despite all the answers I got today, I feel further from the truth than ever. Why did Kasey ask for all that money? Where was she going when she put those miles on our car? What happened to scare her back then, and what happened to Jenna now? With all this roiling in my mind, I suddenly don't give a shit about my probation. I find the cheapest brand of red, grab two bottles by the neck, and carry them to the register.

Back on the highway, I lean over to grab my phone from my backpack. I know Jenna's with her mom right now, but I want to tell her everything I learned from Sandy. More than that, I want to know the truth—the full truth—about why she skipped today, why, after weeks of driving our investigation, she's suddenly taking a step back. My fingers dig around my bag blindly, but the wine is taking up so much space I can't find anything else. I slide my hand lower and discover a partially crushed bag of peanut M&M's. I toss it into my lap because it's already one in the afternoon and I haven't eaten anything today, then go back to my backpack, but still, I don't feel my phone. I glance over to find the zipper of the front pocket and swerve slightly, my tires grating loudly against the rumble strip.

"Shit," I mutter, straightening the wheel.

That's when a movement in the rearview mirror catches my eye, and my stomach drops. The lights of a cop car are flashing behind me. And I'm driving without a license.

"No." I flip my blinker and pull onto the shoulder. "No, no, no."

I'd been so careful for so long.

I watch in my rearview as the police cruiser pulls up behind me and a male officer gets out. I channel my inner Jenna, rolling down my window and putting my hands on the wheel at ten and two. I just need to do what he wants to see and say what he wants to hear.

"Afternoon," he says when he appears at my window. He's older than me, but not by much. His nametag reads H. SULLIVAN.

"I'm so sorry. I know I swerved back there. I just got some bad news and was distracted." I'm going for angelic, contrite, and just a tiny bit flirty.

"So, you haven't been out drinking yet today?" He cracks a half smile: a joke.

I laugh indulgently, hoping he doesn't spot the alcohol in my backpack. None of it's open, but still. "Not yet, no. Usually I'm a very good driver. I swear."

"Well, you look sober enough to me."

"I am. Happy to prove it too if you want."

Another smile. "I'll settle for your license and registration."

I lean over to open my glove compartment and riffle through a mess of papers to find my registration.

"All right," he says after glancing at it briefly. "One down. One to go."

I toss the registration back in the glove compartment then pull out my wallet, making a show of looking through it. "Oh my god," I say, slapping a hand to my forehead. "I just remembered. I took my license out of my wallet last night because I was using a different purse, and I must've forgotten to put it back. I'm so sorry."

"You don't have your license on you?" He lets out a weary breath, and I can tell he's starting to regret pulling me over. "You know it's against the law to drive without one, don't you?"

"It was a dumb mistake. The first thing I'll do when I get home is put it back in my wallet." *Please let me go,* I think furiously.

"Let me see your registration again."

I hand it over. He tells me to sit tight, then walks back to his car, where I watch him anxiously in my rearview. I zip the top of my backpack, hiding the wine, then wait for what feels like far too long. Finally, he gets back out and walks over.

"Miss Monroe, could you please step out of your vehicle?" His voice is all business now.

"What? Why?"

"Because your driver's license isn't in another purse at home. It's in some judge's desk right now."

Shit. "I'm sorry. You're right. I'll—"

He holds up a hand. "That's not all. You also missed a court appointment a few weeks ago."

At first, I have no idea what he's talking about. Then a murky memory wheedles into my head. The appointment was one of the many legal logistics I had to deal with in the wake of my DWI. It was set for right around the time Jenna came into my life and flipped it upside down.

"I'm sorry. I'll take care of it—"

"You don't seem to understand," he says. "It's against the law in Indiana to drive with a suspended license. If it was just that, I could let you get away with a ticket, but with the missed court appointment, there's a warrant out for you. So, I'll ask you one more time. Please step out of your vehicle. You're under arrest."

CHAPTER THIRTY

For the second time in six months, I am locked in a jail cell. Everything about the booking process gives me déjà vu. The ink that leaves black stains on my fingers, the emotionless gaze of the man behind the camera as he takes my mug shots, the droning voice of the officer as he informs me the magistrate doesn't work on Sundays, so I'll have to get bonded out tomorrow morning. It's all mortifyingly, sickeningly reminiscent of the night I got my DWI last winter.

When I get the chance to use the phone, there's only one person I can think to call.

"Hello?" Jenna answers. Her voice is standoffish, ready for me to be a pushy telemarketer.

I squeeze my eyes shut, working up the courage to speak. "Hi, Jenna."

"Nic? What number are you calling from?"

Shame creeps over my skin like a rash. "I'm . . . at the police station. I drove to the lake to confront Brad and got pulled over on the way home." I explain about the suspended license, the missed court appointment.

Jenna is quiet. Then: "Shit."

"I know."

"What do you need?"

I wish, so badly it hurts, that the answer was "nothing." I wish I hadn't needed Kasey to take care of me so much when she was alive, wish I hadn't needed Jenna to coerce me into looking into her disappearance, wish I didn't need Brad breathing down my neck just so I could get a minute of work done. But I am the neediest person I know.

"Could you pick me up tomorrow morning? I need a ride back to my place." I tell her the name of the county jail, which is almost an hour drive from Mishawaka. To get my car back, I'll have to hire a tow.

"Sure." It comes out as a sigh.

"And . . . This is so shitty, but if you have cash, could you bring that too? For my bail. I don't know how much it'll be, but last time it was a thousand, so probably something close to that? I have my credit card, but they only accept cash and money orders. I'll pay you back, obviously."

I can't afford that kind of money right now, but I have a feeling that when I tell Brad what happened, he'll be pretty generous. The thought makes me hate myself.

"Yeah," Jenna says. "I'll go get some cash this afternoon."

I close my eyes, which are starting to sting with unwelcome tears. I want to turn the clock back to a time when my life wasn't so fucked up, when I wasn't so fucked up. But as I mentally rewind past today and the moment I decided to drive without my license, past the missed court appointment, past five months ago when I drank too much and then hit a tree, I realize that in order to get back to a time when I didn't feel so completely broken, I'd have to erase the past seven years. All the mess and meaninglessness are so deeply woven into my life, it's impossible to separate me from the wreckage. I suppose that makes us one and the same.

"Thank you," I manage to say.

"Nic? You okay?"

The sound of my name out of Jenna's mouth splits me open even more, but I don't want to talk about myself. I can't handle any more pain or humiliation. I focus instead on the two good things I have left: Jenna and the progress we've made on our sisters' cases.

I clear my throat, cupping my hand over the receiver. "Jenna, what happened last week? Why didn't you come talk to Brad with me?" There's a movement out of the corner of my eye. I look up to see the officer who escorted me to the phone making a wrap-it-up signal with his hand. I bow my head and pretend I didn't see.

"Come on, Nic," Jenna says. "I told you. I'm taking some time to be with my mom."

"I know. I know. But I feel like you're not telling me every—" I'm interrupted by the officer clearing his throat loudly. "I think something else is going on, and I think the reason you're not telling me is because you want to protect me from it, but you don't have to do that."

"Nic," she says. "I—"

But the officer starts talking so loudly I can't hear the rest. "Miss Monroe, this isn't a lunchroom gossip session. It's time for you to hang up the phone."

I'm so embarrassed about being picked up from jail that when I climb into Jenna's truck the next morning, I have to force myself to meet her eye.

"How are you?" she says.

"Not great."

It's a vast understatement. I have felt so much shame and self-loathing over the past twelve hours, it has sunk into my skin, into my bone. I've condemned myself to a life of more fees I can't afford, more begging for rides and racing to catch the bus, more lawyers who treat me like a delinquent child, more averting my gaze when people ask what's been going on lately. On top of all that, my eyes burn and my stomach roils from lack of sleep. Just when I'd started to feel I had some direction, some purpose, I'm reminded of what a fuckup I really am.

"I brought you coffee," Jenna says, nodding toward two to-go cups nestled in the holders between our knees. "And a breakfast sandwich. I was just gonna go with a bag of candy, but I thought you could use a real meal for once."

I give her a weak smile and grab the coffee. I'm not sure I can stomach any food at the moment. "Thank you."

We're silent as Jenna pulls out of the parking lot and onto the road. I take long sips of my coffee. With each inch we put between us and the police station, I feel a tiny bit more normal. "Do you wanna talk about it?" Jenna says.

"If by 'it' you mean my confrontation with Brad, then yes."

This was the only thing that got me through the night—the thought that if I could just get Jenna back on the investigation, we might be able to work out the implications of everything Brad and Sandy told me. Which makes me even more frustrated with Jenna's insistence that she only missed yesterday because of her mom. Maybe I'm wrong. Maybe that is the full truth, but my gut tells me something else is going on. And yet, as much as I want to push this angle, I heard the exasperation in Jenna's voice when I brought it up over the phone. I need to take a different approach now. I need to get her invested again.

"Okay," she says. "What about it?"

"For starters, we were both right and wrong about Brad. He *was* the one on the playground at Lauren's church the other week. He was trying to keep her quiet about the affair. But I don't think he had anything to do with our sisters' disappearances."

"Okay."

I snap my head sideways. "'Okay'?" Mere days ago, Jenna was like a freight train of determination to talk to Brad, to prove his guilt.

She sighs. "What? Do you not want me to believe you?"

I want you to tell me what the fuck happened, I think. Instead, I say, "There's more. There's a lot we didn't know about."

"Like what?"

So I tell her. I tell her about Sandy discovering Kasey and Brad in the alley, and about how Sandy confronted my sister at work. I tell her about Kasey asking for money and her trip to the lake the night she went missing, which still leaves 250 miles unaccounted for on the car.

"Something occurred to me last night," I say after I've given her every detail I can remember. There was so much to recount, we've already made it to my apartment. Jenna's put the car in park, but the engine's still running. "What if Kasey and Jules were wrapped up in something?"

"What d'you mean?" she says.

"Kasey wouldn't have asked for that kind of money unless she was desperate. Desperate why, I don't know. To get out of something, maybe, to pay somebody off. But it looks similar to what Jules did in 2009, doesn't it? She started acting off and withdrawn, then out of nowhere, she quits her job, moves her entire life, and never tells you why? It all points to something big, don't you think? Bigger than the two of them."

Jenna is quiet, so I keep going.

"What if we were right from the start? What if all of this has something to do with McLean? I mean, we got sidetracked with this whole Brad thing, but McLean's always been a suspect. We still need to look into him. I know the police believe his alibi, but what if they got it wrong? McLean knew both of our sisters, and he's definitely shady enough to be involved in something. The timeline is throwing me because all that stuff with your sister happened three years before she and Kasey went missing. But what if . . ."

I glance at Jenna, but she's staring at a spot on the steering wheel with a faraway glint in her eye.

"Jenna?"

"What?"

"I was talking about McLean. Was there anything that could've pointed to Jules being wrapped up in something with someone like that? Did she ever seem desperate for cash? In 2009 or 2012? I know we've gone over this a million times, but maybe we missed something."

Again, Jenna is quiet. A minute turns to two.

"Jenna?"

"Do you ever just imagine Kasey on a beach somewhere?"

I freeze, my coffee cup inches from my mouth. "Um. Sorry, what?"

"For years, whenever I'd think of Jules, I'd always think of the night she was taken. I'd picture her standing beside her car as some stranger creeps up to her in the dark. I'd think of the way he might've held a knife to her throat or slammed her head against the top of the car. I'd think of all the violence he could have done to her, of the pain and fear she would've felt and the casual way he would've taken her life."

I'm startled to see tears welling in Jenna's eyes. It's the first time I've seen her cry.

"But recently," she continues, "I've starting thinking about her somewhere else. Somewhere where she's free and happy. Somewhere where her body is her own. Jules always wanted to go to Thailand—that was her dream vacation. And recently, when I think of her, that's where I try to imagine her. I imagine her on the beach in cutoff shorts and an oversized T-shirt, her toes in the ocean. Sometimes, I put a piña colada in her hand. And the only reason she can't call is because the cell reception is shitty." She lets out a watery little laugh as she turns in her seat to face me. "Do you ever do that?"

When I think of my sister, the oldest she ever gets is nineteen. She's a teenager curled in her bed, playing with my hair as we laugh about some long-forgotten inside joke. Or she's in a strange room, duct-taped to a chair, bruises on her face. She's driving a car, singing with the windows down, or she's a pile of bones in the earth. I don't imagine her with a present and future, because that was taken from her a long time ago. "No," I say. "I don't do that."

"You should. It makes things easier."

"Fine. I will." I won't.

Jenna looks at me expectantly.

"What?" I say. "Now?"

"Yes. Close your eyes and picture Kasey somewhere safe. Somewhere she always wanted to go."

"Jenna. I don't want to do this right now."

"Just try it, Nic." Her voice is unusually forceful.

I stare at her for a moment, then finally, close my eyes. "Okay," I say. "I'm imagining her on a beach—"

"No. Don't use mine. It has to be specific to Kasey. Where did she always say she wanted to go?"

"I don't know," I say, but then suddenly I do. "Nashville, I guess? She always said it had one of the best music scenes in the world."

"Good," Jenna says. "Picture her there."

I envision Kasey in a piano bar. Not one of the big ones that only do covers of country songs but a dive that specializes in seventies rock. She's in ripped jeans and a T-shirt, nursing a glass of red wine. I imagine her singing softly beneath her breath while the man at the piano plays something by the Rolling Stones. For a moment, she looks happy. But then I think of her car pulled over on the side of the road, her door flung open, the overhead light flickering in the black night. I picture a man walking toward her, and the happy version of my sister vanishes.

"It's not working," I say. "I can't just imagine Kasey alive and force my brain to believe it. I want to find answers."

"Well, I don't," Jenna says. "It's too much. It's too hard. Between that and my mom—" Her voice cuts off. "I'm sorry, Nic. I know I pulled you into this."

"Wait. You're *giving up*?"

"I need to be there for my mom."

"And you can be," I say. "You can take as much time as you need. I know I'm not the most patient person in the world, but there's no deadline on this. Take a week with your mom. Take a month. I don't fucking care. But you can't just drop this. Not now."

"Look, I'm sorry. I really am. But maybe you should think about taking a break from all this too. It's obviously not helping with every-thing else you have going on."

"Wow. Thanks."

"I didn't mean—"

"I know what you meant," I say. "And I know why you said it too. You're trying to get me to stop. You're trying to shelter me. I just wish you'd tell me what you're trying to protect me from."

"I'm trying to protect you from the pain of it," she snaps. "Okay? The pain of continuing to look into our sisters' cases only to find nothing . . . Believe it or not, and despite how much of an asshole you can be most of the time, I've actually come to kind of like having you around. And I don't want to see you get hurt."

My throat tightens. I've always gotten the feeling that everyone who's showed up for me these past few years—my dad, Brad, Sandy—they've all done it out of a sense of obligation, a leftover love for the person I was before Kasey disappeared. But Jenna has only known the person I am today. And despite my impatience and bitterness and cynicism, she cares about me. I want to tell her that I like having her around too, that she's the first person I've let in in years. No one could ever fill the place that Kasey occupies in my heart, but during these past few weeks with Jenna, the enormous weight that settled onto me when my sister disappeared has begun to feel just the tiniest bit lighter.

But all I can say is "I'm not going to stop. I can't."

"Fine. In that case, you'll be okay without me. You're stronger than you think. I know you don't believe that yet, but you are."

"I'm really not. The first time I tried to talk to someone without you, I wound up in fucking jail." I shake my head. "The point is, we can work around whatever you need to do for your mom. Hell, I can help you."

"You're not listening to me," Jenna says. "It's too much. I can't do it anymore."

"You don't actually expect me to believe that, do you? I know you, Jenna. On the first day we met, you told me that when Jules didn't come home that night, you went looking for her. It's been seven years and you haven't once stopped searching—until now. So, what happened? Just tell me the truth."

"Nothing happened! How many times do I have to tell you that?"

"Then you're a fucking quitter."

"Says the woman who's never finished a single thing she's ever started."

The words crack against my cheek like a blow. Still, they just reinforce my belief that something else is going on here. Jenna wouldn't aim that low unless she was deliberately trying to push me away.

"I'm not quitting this," I say. "Because we are closer than we've ever been. When we started, I didn't think we'd learn a single thing the police hadn't already told us. But we did. You can't just drag me into this and then leave when the answers don't fall into our laps after a month."

Jenna smacks her palms against the steering wheel. "This is the end, Nic."

"It doesn't have to be—"

"For my mom," she says. "It's the end for my mom. I don't know how long it's gonna take, and I know I don't have the best relationship with her, but I'm not going to spend the last few weeks of her life chasing answers we're never going to get. I wish I could have given her some closure, but we're never gonna know what happened to Jules and Kasey. We never had a chance."

Her face is wet, tears slick against her lips. "So, please," she says, "don't call me or text me about it again. You can do whatever you want, but you're gonna have to do it alone."

CHAPTER THIRTY-ONE

I am numb. For days after that conversation with Jenna, I go through the motions of my life, mindless and blank. A puppet on strings. In the mornings, I call my lawyer and start the process of yet another legal entanglement, then I go to work, where I sling pizza and mop vomit and sing the birthday song. In the evenings, I drink.

I've given up on cutting back, and I can't seem to remember why I was trying to in the first place. It's not like I can drive anymore. I haven't picked up my car from the impound lot where it was towed, so I couldn't make that mistake again even if I tried. And without Jenna to push me in the case, I don't know where to go or what to do. On top of all of that, with everything that's happened over the past month, I don't want this numbness to pass. I don't want to feel whatever comes next. I want to disappear.

It's Friday night, five days since I last saw Jenna. When I walk into my apartment after work, the first thing I do is grab an open bottle of wine from the counter and pour some into a thrift-store mug, the closest clean thing I can find. My phone vibrates from my back pocket and I pull it out. I don't recognize the number, but I answer anyway.

"Nic?" a woman says. Her voice is familiar, but I can't place it.

"Who is this?"

"Pam." When I don't say anything, she adds in a slightly irritated tone, "From the animal shelter?"

"Oh." I give my phone a bewildered look. Pam has never called me and I wonder vaguely what I've done to deserve it. Did I accidentally skip my visit last weekend? Did I forge her signature on my hour sheet? But the days are a jumbled blur. "Hi."

"This may be silly," she says. "But, I don't know, I thought you may want a heads-up before you come in tomorrow."

"About what?"

"Well . . . Banksy was adopted today."

Pam continues talking, but I don't hear what she's saying. The only thing in my brain is Banksy. Banksy with his crooked tail and one eye. Banksy with his mottled fur and skinny neck, his surly moods interrupted by surprising bursts of sweetness. I think of the time Jenna and I visited him and, after glaring in our direction for half an hour, he tiptoed over and curled into my lap.

Pam is midsentence when I mumble something and hang up.

The moment the call disconnects, something inside me snaps. Everything that has happened these past few weeks—learning about Kasey's affair, my confrontation of Brad, getting arrested, Jenna abandoning me, now this—it all falls onto my shoulders, and I buckle beneath its weight. I slam the mug of wine into the sink, where it shatters, then bend over and let out a choked, silent scream. Tears spill onto the floor. A string of saliva falls from my mouth.

I didn't think there was a chance Banksy would get adopted. I thought I'd have time to work up the courage to do it myself. But, like always, I was too fearful, too weak. I don't bother to wipe the tears from my cheeks. I just grab the open bottle of wine by the neck and drink.

The next morning, my vomit is burgundy. The sight of it sloshing into the toilet bowl turns my stomach, and I retch again, which makes my aching head throb. I wipe the back of my wrist against my forehead and it comes back slick with sweat. My body is trying to turn itself inside out, to punish me for all my bad decisions, and I don't blame it.

I flush the toilet, then slowly, shakily get to my feet and pad into the kitchen, where I'm met by the scene of my self-destruction—the sink stained red, littered with pieces of the broken mug. Next to it are an oily baking sheet I used to make a frozen pizza for dinner and a plate of half-eaten crusts. Heaving a sigh, I walk to the sink and begin to pluck the pieces of ceramic out one by one, then toss them into the trash.

About halfway through, my phone chimes with an incoming email. I dig it out from the pocket of my sweatpants and click on the message, which I see with surprise is from Detective Aimes, the new missing-persons detective over at Grand Rapids, the one who inherited the case when Wyler got promoted. As I promised I would, I'd emailed her that night Jenna and I went through the stuff I found in Kasey's and my old car.

Hi Nic,

Apologies for the delay; our team was wrapping up an investigation. I'd be happy to speak to you about your sister's case. Can you come to the Grand Rapids station? Below are the days and times I'm available next week. Let me know if any work for you.

I stare at the message, taken aback. I'd all but forgotten I reached out to her, and my first instinct is to close my inbox, crawl back into bed, and respond to the email later—or, more realistically, ignore it until I've forgotten it was ever sent. I'm tired, and burned out from disappointment, and I don't know how to continue this investigation without Jenna to help me.

But just as I go to click out of the app, my last conversation with Jenna pops into my head. I realize now just how right she was— I never finish anything. I gave up on my first cat, and I lost Banksy because I was too scared to fail again. If not for Brad, I would've been fired from Funland years ago. I couldn't even get through probation without fucking it up. And if I'm being honest, totally and ruthlessly honest, despite what I told Jenna that day, I don't think I ever really intended to see our sisters' cases through. Not without her.

I can't keep living like this. I can't keep avoiding my pain by drinking myself to sleep and hoping someone else will come along and clean up after me. I can't keep bailing when something starts to get scary.

I look at the second bottle of wine I got into last night. Without letting myself rethink it, I grab the bottle by the neck, pull out its cork, and turn it upside down over the sink. The liquid pours out in loud glugs. There are two more bottles on the counter, both of which are unopened. I grab them too, twisting the corkscrew into one, then the other. Soon, they're empty. I turn on the faucet and watch as the water clears away the wine, and by the time the last red drop vanishes, I've made up my mind.

I'm going to make a pot of coffee, take a shower, and email Detective Aimes back. Because I am going to finish what Jenna started. I have to. Not for her or Jules or even Kasey, but for me.

CHAPTER THIRTY-TWO

Three days later, I walk through the front door of the Grand Rapids police station. It's quiet today, the lobby empty except for me and the receptionist behind glass. I give him my name, and he calls Detective Aimes to let her know I'm here. A moment later, a voice rings through the lobby.

"You must be Nic."

I turn to see a woman standing in the doorway that leads to the offices in the back. She looks to be in her midforties with brown eyes and matching hair, cut into a chin-length bob. She's wearing plain clothes, a white button-down and slacks, which puts me at ease. I know I've brought all my legal shit down upon myself, but still, I've had enough uniforms to last me a lifetime.

I step forward to take her hand.

"Nice to meet you," she says. "Why don't you come on back to my office."

Her office is a glorified cubicle, made up of one true wall and three partitions. Boxes and picture frames lay scattered around her computer. Folders of paper burst at the seams.

"It may look like I've just moved in," she says, settling behind her desk and gesturing at the chair opposite her for me to sit. "But this is the organized mess of four long years."

She smiles, and I return it. I'm determined to make a good impression. Without Jenna to smooth things over for me, I know I'll have to play nice.

"How can I help you, Nic?"

I've prepared for this—I had the weekend and a two-hour bus ride to think about what I want to ask—but without Jenna here, I feel jittery and unmoored. "Detective Wyler may have told you," I say, "but I've been looking into my sister's case."

"He mentioned it."

"And, well, I was wondering if you've uncovered anything new since you took over."

Detective Aimes stares at me for a moment. Then she leans back in her chair, clasping her hands across her middle. "Let me ask you something, Nic. What do you think happened to your sister?"

In all the years since Kasey went missing, I have been asked countless questions by countless members of law enforcement, yet never before have I been asked what I believe. The question is so unexpected, for a moment I think I must have misheard her. "I don't know," I say eventually.

"I'm not sure I believe that."

"Well, I guess I've always assumed what the police told us from the start. That whoever took Jules Connor took Kasey." I see Wyler sitting on our couch, telling us to give up hope that we'd ever find Kasey alive. Even after all this time, the memory still forms a lump in my throat. "And I think whoever took them killed them too."

Detective Aimes nods. "Any theories about why? Why the two of them, I mean."

My mind flashes to that conversation with Jenna in her truck last week. "I think there's a chance Jules and Kasey were involved in something that made them targets."

"Something like what?"

"I don't know exactly."

"What makes you think that, then?" she says.

I hadn't been planning on telling her any of what Jenna and I have discovered over the past month. I know I accused Brad and Sandy of complicity in murder for doing just that, so I suppose on top of everything else, I'm also a big fucking hypocrite, but after that conversation with Wyler, I lost my faith and trust in the police. And yet, Detective Aimes has already proven herself to be vastly different from him. Perhaps she'll continue to.

So I tell her. I tell her about how Jules and Kasey both went through periods of acting unusual. I tell her about Jules moving to Osceola and Kasey asking for money the night she disappeared. "I think it's possible," I say when I've finished, "that whatever they were wrapped up in could have involved Steve McLean. Jules worked with him right before she started acting off, and Kasey worked near him just before she did. Plus, I know he has a track record."

"Back up," Detective Aimes says. "How do you know your sister was asking for money? This is the first I'm hearing of that."

I hesitate. I don't have any lingering loyalty to Brad or Sandy at this point, but I can't quite get myself to believe that they're directly responsible for Kasey's disappearance, and I'm not ready to take away the only people my dad has left in his life. More important, I want Detective Aimes focused on why Kasey needed money, not the affair. So I tell her I know about the ten thousand because Kasey asked our family friend for it. When Detective Aimes asks for the family friend's name, I tell her the truth.

"And you think that this all points to Steve McLean?" she says.

"Well . . . it doesn't *not* point to him."

She cracks a half smile. "Wyler told me you'd bring him up. McLean."

"I know Wyler doesn't think it was him," I say, heat blistering my neck. "I know he thinks McLean's alibi is—"

"Nic—"

"I know he thinks it's solid," I continue over her. I realize that I'm no longer playing nice, but I don't care. I'm sick of the police not listening to what I have to say about McLean, sick of the way they defend him for seemingly the flimsiest of reasons. I don't know that he's the one who took Kasey and Jules, but I at least have the right to voice my suspicions about him. "I know Wyler ruled him out a long time ago—"

"Nic—" she says again.

But I barrel through. "If you'd just—"

Detective Aimes holds up a hand. "Nic. Please. Listen. Wyler may have ruled out McLean, but I haven't."

"Oh."

"As you know, all the evidence points to a man who knew Jules and Kasey both. And you're right. McLean fits. His alibi isn't airtight, but it's enough that in order to be sure of anything, in order to prove anything, we would need far more evidence against him. So I'll look into everything you've said. The money is a good lead. Thank you for sharing it with me."

"I . . . sure." This conversation is going so far in the direction opposite to the one I expected, I can't seem to find the words to keep up my side of it.

"And to answer the first thing you asked me," Detective Aimes says, "no, we haven't uncovered anything new since I inherited the case from Wyler."

"Oh. Right. Okay."

"However, there is one piece of evidence I don't believe he ever told you about. Now, before you get upset, he wasn't hiding it for the sake of hiding it. He was doing what he thought was best for the investigation. I probably would've done the same in those early days. But as you obviously know, a lot of time has passed, so I'm planning to release this piece of evidence to the public soon to get people talking again. If you can assure me that you'll keep it to yourself until we issue our press release, I'm happy to tell you now. Does that sound okay to you?"

My heart grows wings and starts to flap around my chest. A new piece of evidence? It's what I hoped for, of course, but it's far more than I ever expected. "I, yes, that sounds good. What is it?"

She leans forward, resting her forearms on her desk. "When they processed Kasey's car after she went missing, they found something. One of Jules Connor's hairs was in the driver's seat."

"I don't understand," I say slowly. "Jules was in Kasey's car that night?"

"Until we know one hundred percent what happened, anything's possible, but I don't think that's how it got there. More likely, it was there from some kind of transfer. As in, when whoever took Kasey actually took her, he was wearing an item of clothing he also wore on the night he took Jules. Jules's hair got caught in the fibers of a jacket or a T-shirt on August 4th, and it was still there on August 17th. It's why we've been so convinced all these years that the cases are connected."

I think of McLean and that lecherous smile he had as he talked about Kasey, the cagey way he spoke about Jules—he's the one person we've been able to connect to them both.

As if reading my mind, Detective Aimes says, "It doesn't point to anyone in particular, but it doesn't rule out McLean. I will look into him, Nic, I promise." She gives me a somber smile. "Is there anything else you'd like to ask me?"

I open my mouth instinctively, but realize I already got everything I came for. "No," I say. "I guess not."

"In that case, I'll do my best to keep you updated, but feel free to email me anytime. Now, why don't I walk you out?"

As if in a trance, I rise from my chair and sling my backpack over my shoulder. I'm so used to being disappointed, so used to my opinion being ignored, that I feel oddly whiplashed from the conversation. I thank her for meeting with me, and then together we retrace our steps back to the lobby and out the front door.

"By the way," she says after shaking my hand goodbye. "I meant to ask earlier but forgot. What happened between you and Jenna Connor?"

"What do you mean?"

"Well, your email made it seem like the two of you were working on your sisters' cases together, but you met with me separately."

"Wait," I say. "Jenna came to talk to you?"

She nods.

"When was this?"

"Let's see, it would've been . . . Saturday afternoon. Not this past Saturday but the previous. I told her what I told you, about the hair." Detective Aimes must see how much this throws me, because she says, "I didn't mean to overstep. I just hope everything's okay. I thought it was smart, the two of you teaming up like that."

I force a smile, tell her that everything's fine, but I feel as if she's reached forward and pushed me off the edge of a cliff. Saturday was the day Jenna bailed on me when I went to talk to my dad, the day she told me she wanted to step back from our investigation to take care of her mom. She made me feel so insensitive for accusing her of using that as an excuse, but now I know I was right. Jenna is lying to me—I just don't know if that should make me angry or scared.

CHAPTER THIRTY-THREE

On the two-hour bus ride back from Grand Rapids, I sit, my forehead pressed to the cool window, staring, unseeing, at the scenery passing by, thinking about a memory I haven't thought about in a very long time.

In elementary school, there was this night toward the end of the year when parents would come to school to see what their kids had been working on. The science teacher would display our three-panel poster boards on the solar system or tarantulas or the ocean tides. The English teacher would line her walls with our handwritten essays—biographies of our favorite historical figures accompanied by drawn portraits. All those Lincolns in top hats. The art teacher would prop our paintings on easels, put out a grocery-store cheese platter, and pretend her nine- and ten-year-old students were artists in a gallery. Spring Show-and-Tell, we called it. When I was in fourth grade, it was a very big deal.

For me, the art room show-and-tell was the pinnacle of the evening. I'd worked on my painting—a landscape of the woods—for what felt like ages, talked about nothing else at the dinner table in weeks. Two nights before the event, though, my dad told me he was going to miss it. He'd just taken a second job, which he did sometimes when money was tight. This one was selling shoes at the mall, and he couldn't rearrange his shift. I was devastated. Everybody else would have two parents there.

Despite this, I woke up on the day of the Spring Show-and-Tell hyper with excitement, and it only intensified as the day went on. Our art teacher had given us the option of staying after school to finalize our projects if we wanted, and I got the idea to add a moon to my landscape, so I stayed.

It took me the entire two hours between the end of school and the time my mom was due to arrive to paint my moon, taking pains to make sure the contours of the orb weren't all the same shade. I pictured my mom admiring it, holding it delicately by the edges, insisting it lie flat in the car on the ride home. She might even frame it, I thought. It really was that good. But my mom wasn't in the first round of parents to pass through the door, nor in the second. The minutes ticked by, and after almost an hour, she still hadn't showed. Her absence felt like a stone in my stomach getting heavier and heavier.

And then suddenly, I heard my sister say my name behind me. Her voice was so familiar, so uniquely soft and calming, that even though she was the last person I was expecting to be there, I knew it was her before I even turned around.

"Dang, Nic," she said, her eyes on my painting. "This one's yours? It's good. Like, really good."

"Where'd you come from?" Only in sixth grade herself, she wasn't much taller than the other fourth graders and she must've slipped in without me seeing. Without waiting for a response, I said, "Where's Mom?"

"She's sick. She told me to tell you she's sorry. She feels bad about missing."

"But . . ." I said, "she was fine this morning."

"I know. I think it's the flu or something, 'cause it happened really fast."

Kasey, it turned out, had taken the city bus to the stop nearest the elementary school. It wasn't a long ride, but it was the first either of us had ever used public transit, and to get us home, she had to navigate it all in reverse with a fourth grader by her side. When we walked through the door, the house smelled like vodka. It's obvious now, but it would take years for me to understand what happened that night, to understand that my sister had lied to spare my feelings.

The memory is softening my anger toward Jenna, turning my confused suspicion into something less ominous. Deep down, I still trust that she is trying to protect me, that, just like Kasey on the night of the show-and-tell, she is lying to keep me safe.

I just wish I knew what danger she thinks I'm in.

I've had an idea percolating on the ride home, and when the bus pulls into the station in South Bend, I make the snap decision to act upon it: I'm going to visit Jenna's mom.

I know she and Jenna have a complicated relationship, but during these past few weeks, Jenna has been a near constant by her side. They must be talking. And though it's morbid to admit, who could be a safer person to confide in than someone who's waiting to die? If Jenna has told anyone the truth about what's going on, I have to believe it would be her mom.

I unlock my bike from the rack outside the station and take the local bus back to Mishawaka. But instead of getting off at the stop nearest my apartment, I stay on for another three till we pass Memorial Park. I remember Jenna's mom's neighborhood from the time Jenna dropped medicine off there a few weeks ago, and unlike Jenna's place, surrounded by a maze of streets, her mom's is right off the main road. The idea of knocking on a dying woman's door to interrogate her feels icky, so I stop by a grocery store on the way to buy flowers. After I've paid for them though, I realize that showing up on her doorstep with a bouquet doesn't make me kinder, only more manipulative—I'm getting better at this. Maybe the thought should make me feel bad, but it doesn't. If the flowers get me even an inch closer to finding out what happened to Kasey, they're worth it. I stuff them into my backpack, then pedal the final quarter mile to Mrs. Connor's house.

When I reach the corner of her street, I slow, looking for Jenna's truck, but there's only one car in the driveway. Does it belong to Mrs. Connor? A hospice worker?

The house is just as I remember it, a small one-story with peeling gray paint and a sagging roof, as if its own weight is too much for it to bear. The yard is sparse in some places and overgrown in others, the effects of a dry summer on top of years of neglect. In the surrounding yards I spot a rusty tricycle, a deflating kiddie pool, Barbies stripped bare and limbs akimbo. Mrs. Connor's yard is empty.

Despite my conviction earlier, with every step I take closer to the screened front door, my sense of dread and impropriety grows. Here I am, a stranger, interrupting the last few weeks—possibly the last few days—this woman has left, and all I have to offer is a thirteen-dollar, plastic-wrapped bouquet of daisies. Nerves clench a cold fist around my neck. I imagine the inside of the house thick with the smell of decay, cluttered with pill bottles, an IV stand, all the other accoutrements of death I don't know about. I imagine a hospice worker leading me back to the bedroom, Mrs. Connor sunk in her bed, struggling for each breath.

I shoot a glance over my shoulder. Knowing Jenna, she won't be away for long, so it's now or never. I take a deep breath, lift a fist, and knock.

After a moment, the door cracks open, and a woman peers through, revealing nothing more than a sliver of her face—a narrow, watery eye; the pinched corner of a mouth. The house is dark and the screen door is shadowing her features, but even so, I know immediately this is not a hospice worker.

"Yeah?" the woman says. There's a burble of daytime television from the room beyond. "What d'you want?"

"Are you . . . Mrs. Connor?" Based on everything Jenna told me, I wasn't expecting her mom to be able to walk, let alone answer the door, but she also said the cancer was fickle. Good days and bad.

"Unless you got cigarettes, I'm not interested in buying."

"I—no. I'm not here to sell you anything."

The one eye I can see narrows. "You one of those bible beaters, then? I thought you guys dressed up more."

"Mrs. Connor, my name's Nic. I'm a friend of Jenna's."

"She's not here." The door starts to close.

"Wait!" I say. "Please. It's you I want to see. Here." I thrust out the bouquet. "These are for you."

Mrs. Connor eyes the flowers, and I can see a debate churning in her mind. A gift was clearly the right idea; I just wish I'd sprung for the more expensive ones. I hold my breath, praying she deems them nice enough to buy her time. Finally, she opens the door.

Though we're still separated by the screen, I can see her properly now. She's wearing a white nightgown with a pink robe over it, un-tied and pilling. A cigarette is perched between two fingers, a plume of smoke curling to the ceiling. In her other hand, she holds a plastic mask connected by a thin tube to an oxygen tank by her feet.

"Well," she says, "*Maury* comes on in twenty, but I suppose you can come in till then." Without opening the screen door, she turns back into the house, dragging the oxygen tank behind her.

The floorboards creak beneath my feet as I step inside, the air hot and unmoving. The ceilings are low, and none of the lights in the house are on, so it feels a little like walking into a cave. The living room is off the right. Mrs. Connor has resettled on the couch, an overflowing ashtray on the upholstered arm beside her. The TV flickers with a commercial—she's the last living person paying for cable. To my left is a kitchen with linoleum floors and a metal table. Dishes litter the counter by the sink.

"There're vases beside the microwave," Mrs. Connor says. "You can put the flowers in one of those."

I open the cabinet to find a clutter of glasses and vases and sift through them, settling on a squat round one. But as I set it onto the counter, Mrs. Connor's voice barks out at me.

"Not that one! It won't balance out the stems. Get that nice, tall, curvy one."

"Oh. Right." I replace the round one and search for something that fits her description. "This one?" I say, holding one up.

From the couch, Mrs. Connor nods solemnly.

I arrange the flowers in the vase, then fill it with water. I'm about to leave them in the kitchen but think better of it and carry them to the living room with me, taking care to place them in the exact center of the coffee table.

"Thank you for talking with me," I say, sitting in the armchair adjacent to the couch.

Mrs. Connor gazes at the arrangement, bringing the plastic mask connected to the oxygen tank to her face, sucking in deeply. When she lowers it, she takes a drag of her cigarette. "No one brings me flowers anymore."

"Well, I . . ." My voice fades as I realize in horror that the rest of my sentence was going to be: *know you're dying.* "Jenna's mentioned you like flowers."

She snorts sarcastically, as if the idea is preposterous.

"So, like I said, I'm a friend of Jenna's, and I was wondering if I could ask you a few questions about her."

Mrs. Connor's eyes snap to mine. "What's she done now?"

"Oh, no. It's nothing like that."

I have no idea how to ask what I want to know. From the little Jenna has told me about her mom, and from what I've witnessed so far, it seems Mrs. Connor lives in a state of emotional volatility. I don't want to upset her by bringing up Jules before I have to.

"I noticed that Jenna's been acting off recently," I begin. "And I know she's been spending a lot of time over here, so I was wondering if she's confided anything in you? Anything that might be the reason behind it?"

"Even if she had," Mrs. Connor says, "I wouldn't believe her. She's a little liar."

I shake my head. "What do you mean? What does she lie about?"

"Every day, she walks in here, and she tells me she loves me, but I know she doesn't mean it. Lying through her teeth."

"Right." So, Jenna wasn't exaggerating when she described her mom.

"Jules was the one you should've been friends with," Mrs. Connor says. "Sweet as lemon meringue, my Julie. She died though. Few years back. Did you know that?"

"I did, yeah. I'm sorry."

"Killed by some son of a bitch."

"Do you . . ." I hesitate. "Do you have any idea who it could've been?"

"If I did, he'd be long dead. I would've hunted him down and killed him right back. If I weren't hooked up to this goddamn machine, that is."

"You know," I say—this seems as good an opening as I'm going to get—"Jenna and I—that's what we've been doing together. Looking into Jules's case. Seeing if we can figure out who took her."

Mrs. Connor studies me. "You're a good one." She points to my chest with her cigarette. Half an inch of ash falls onto the floor, but she doesn't seem to notice. "Julie would've liked you."

"It was Jenna's idea, actually." I try to hold her gaze, but she turns indifferently to the TV. "Has she mentioned anything to you about it?"

She turns back to me and there's an amnesiac look in her eye, as if she's forgotten both who I am and what we're talking about. I wonder if that's the cancer. "What?" she snaps.

"I was asking about Jenna. Has she told you anything about looking into Jules's case?"

Mrs. Connor barks out a laugh that turns into a hacking cough. "Jenna doesn't tell me shit. She comes over to police me. That's it."

"Police you?"

"Babysit me. You know. 'Stop smoking, Mom,'" she parrots in a whining voice. "'Did you take your pills? You know you can't drink when you're on medication.' If it were up to her, I'd sit here all day doing nothing but drink celery juice."

I thought my dad's silent treatment was bad, but this open hostility is so pointed, so cruel. "When she's over here," I say, forcing my voice to stay pleasant, "has she ever mentioned anything about someone scaring her?"

"Scaring Jenna? Please."

"Well, has she ever mentioned anything about me?"

"First I learned about you was when you knocked on my door.

Don't take it personally though. My Julie was sweet as pie, but not Jenna. It's why I always said I wish that man would've taken her instead."

I lurch out of my chair, a snapped mousetrap. Jenna hasn't confided in her, and it's no wonder why. Coming here was a mistake. "I need to go."

"You sure?" she says. "It's nice to have some decent company for a change."

But I'm already at the front door. I fling it open and am about to step through when I whirl back around. "You know what? Jenna is one of the best people I've ever met. You're lucky to have her for a daughter, and if you can't see that, then you're a fucking asshole. Thanks for nothing. Sorry about the cancer."

To my surprise, Mrs. Connor starts to laugh. "I told you Jenna's a liar."

My hand, which had been reaching toward the door, stills midair. She's baiting me, I know. And yet. "What're you talking about?"

"Like I said, if Jenna really loved me, she'd tell her friends about my cancer."

"She did tell me about it. That's why I brought it up."

"Not the diagnosis. The remission. If my daughter truly loved me, she would've told you my cancer was in remission, now, wouldn't she?"

"You mean . . ."

"That's right," she says. "Got the news three weeks ago. I'm clean as a whistle."

CHAPTER THIRTY-FOUR

I stare at Mrs. Connor, the word *remission* bouncing around my skull like a pinball.

She takes a drag from her oxygen mask, peering at me with a look of amusement in her beady, watery eyes. "What do you think now?" she says. "You still think Jenna's one of *the best people you've ever met*?"

I think of the tears on Jenna's face when she told me only last Monday that her mom was dying. *I'm not going to spend the last few weeks of her life chasing answers we're never going to get.*

Mrs. Connor laughs. "Like I said, liar, liar, liar."

I fantasize about striding to the kitchen and throwing open the drawers, banging around their contents until I find a pair of big, rusting scissors. In my mind, I grab them, go to the living room, yank the plastic tube of Mrs. Connor's oxygen mask, and snip. I see the tube flailing around the old rug like a snake with its head cut off. I see Mrs. Connor smacking her lips open wide, sucking in air that isn't enough. A fish in the bottom of a boat.

I open the front door and walk through without another word.

At the curb, I throw myself onto my bike and pedal fast out of the neighborhood. Within minutes, my muscles are on fire and my lungs are tight. It's not smart to bike this recklessly on the busy roads between Mrs. Connor's home and mine, but I need to feel the distance between me and her growing, need to focus on my burning thighs instead of that word: *liar.* I'm so preoccupied, I swerve into a lane of traffic and a car slams on its brakes, its honk loud and long. I swerve out again, waving an apologetic hand as it passes. The driver flips me off.

A sweaty half hour later, I'm back in my apartment, my helmet and bag dumped by the door. I pluck my shirt from my damp skin and billow it back and forth.

Before today, I assumed Jenna was lying in order to get me off our sisters' cases because she thought it was dangerous. But that conviction is waning with every passing second. If that were the case, why would she be pursuing the investigation on her own? Because she clearly used her mom's cancer as an excuse to buy herself time. It's possible, I suppose, that she could be keeping me safe and not herself. But another possibility, the one that's seeping into my mind like poison, is that she has a more self-interested reason for lying.

The deception is like a switchblade between my ribs. Jenna has confided in me about Jules and opened me up about Kasey. She's given me rides, laughed when I tried to be funny, she's talked straight to me instead of dancing around all my shit like everyone else. More than that though, she's inspired me to be better, to stop running away from my problems and commit to our sisters' cases. How could the person who did all that possibly be the same one who lied about her mom's impending death?

But then I think back to the first day I met Jenna and the way she dangled a made-up development about Kasey's disappearance just to get me to talk. So I guess it's my fault for giving her a second chance, for letting her in. But even so, I keep coming back to *why.* The first time Jenna lied, she was trying to get information about Jules. Why is she doing it now?

My instinct is to call her this very moment, to demand answers, but if there's one thing I've learned from Jenna, it's not to be rash. *Come up with a strategy first,* I imagine her telling me. *Get the facts before you go confronting someone.*

I think through all the possible ways I could learn the truth, but none of them seem even remotely likely to work. Jenna's not going to get tricked into letting something slip, nor do I think she'll break no matter how many times I ask her. I could straight-up tell her I know she's lying, but she's fast enough to come up with some plausible excuse to explain it away. She probably already has another lie ready in the event I do just that. And there's no point in me threatening to walk away from the investigation, because it's clear that's exactly what she wants me to do.

I see a flash of that wall in her living room, the one with all the research, and one final possibility pops into my head. It's shitty and sneaky and I don't want to do it, because even after everything, I still care about Jenna. I want to trust her. But whatever she's lying to me about has to do with our sisters' cases, and everything we know about them is on that wall.

I glance at the clock on my stovetop. 4:40 P.M. Jenna gets off work at five, and if she goes straight home after like she usually does, she'll probably get there around 5:15. Which means I'll have to wait until tomorrow. I don't want to be rushed when I break into her house.

I leave my apartment at eleven the next morning to catch the bus to Osceola. I'm skipping work again today, but Brad's in a pretty bad position to make any noise about it, and he doesn't. Take as long as you need, he texted yesterday afternoon when I asked for some time off. I didn't respond. I still need a job, but I don't know if I'll ever be able to return to Funland. My relationship with Brad and Sandy will never recover.

We get to my stop and I step off the bus, my backpack heavy with the hammer I found gathering dust in my hallway closet. I won't use it—I brought it only as a last resort—but still, it serves as a reminder of the seriousness of what I'm planning to do. My handlebars slip through my sweaty palms as I heave my bike from the bus's front rack.

You have plenty of time, I remind myself as I hop on and pedal toward Jenna's house. And the truth is I won't need much of it. Once

I've broken in, I'll go straight to the living room where Jenna has as-sembled her wall of research. Since I've seen it before, anything new should stand out. I'll find whatever she's hiding from me, take a pic-ture of it, and leave. I'll be in and out in under five minutes.

When I round the corner onto her street, I slow, passing her neighbors at a crawl and craning my neck to catch a glimpse of her driveway. I can't think why her truck would be there, why she wouldn't be at work in the middle of a Tuesday, but I'm about to break the law. I'd be an idiot not to be cautious. When I get close enough to see her house, my shoulders slump with relief. The drive-way is empty. I turn around and pedal a block and a half to the copse of trees Jenna once told me she liked. I can't imagine any of her neighbors would think twice about an unfamiliar bike left on the curb, but, again, I'm not taking any chances. Hopping off, I walk it over, then weave my handlebars through the tree line and lean my bike against a cluster of trees at an angle perpendicular to the curb. Not foolproof, but it's something.

I make my way quickly to Jenna's house and up to her front door. The driveway is still empty, but I knock anyway, just to be safe. A small part of me hopes she'll answer. I imagine her swinging open the door with an expectant smile that turns contrite at the sight of me. I envision her ushering me inside, pouring me a cup of coffee, telling me how all of this is just some big misunderstanding. I would believe her. I would.

The door remains closed, the house dark. I knock again for good measure, call out her name, but I'm met with silence. I try the knob. It's locked. I look around for a place where she might hide a spare key, and my gaze catches on the welcome mat beneath my feet. It's one of the cheap kinds made from synthetic fiber, old and fading. I flip it over, but there's nothing there. I stand on my tiptoes to check above the doorframe. Nothing. There's no flowerpot or fake rock or any sort of chip in the exterior wall where she could slip a key. Not that I was expecting one. When you lose your sister to the worst kind of evil, you understand how precarious your own safety really is.

I walk around the side of the house to find a gate in the wooden fence and quickly slip through. In the backyard, I spot four possible ways into Jenna's house—three windows and the back door. I try them all. Unsurprisingly, they're locked. I knew I was going to have to break in, but this is officially where my plausible deniability ends. No longer can I tell a passing neighbor that I'm just a friend of Jenna's, picking something up from her house with a spare key. No longer can I say she left the back door open for me—not if, when I'm caught, I'm jimmying its lock.

When Kasey and I were young—she was probably nine or ten, I was seven or eight—she discovered Nancy Drew at our local library and decided she wanted to be a detective. Then she passed the books on to me so I could be one too. The idea that our little world was riddled with mysteries to be solved was irresistible to us, and soon we were writing notes to each other using a made-up code, searching the neighborhood for where someone might hide their secrets, shining flashlights into every hole of every tree, so sure we'd find a map to treasure. Most practically, we learned how to use a card to open a locked door, and even after all these years, I've never forgotten the way you have to bend the corner just so in order to slide it smoothly into place.

The back door to Jenna's house is old and wooden, clearly the original, its knob rusted brass. I peer into the sliver of space between the door and the frame and am relieved when I don't see a deadbolt.

I pull my wallet from my backpack and find the card I tested out on my own door last night—an old expired debit card I forgot to throw away. As I re-bend one of its corners, I hear a car on the street out front, and I freeze. What if it's Jenna coming home for lunch or to pick something up? I listen, the sound of the engine getting louder and louder until it is right in front of the house. Then it fades.

"Chill," I say aloud as I shake out my hands, trying to purge the sudden adrenaline.

I slide the corner of the card into the doorframe above the lock. With my free hand, I grab the doorknob and start to jimmy it around, but the card's not catching. The brass knob is old and rusted and it twists jerkily in the plate surrounding it. I rattle it harder, but still, the lock doesn't budge. I pause, thinking of the hammer in my back-pack. But if Jenna has an alarm, smashing a window will have the cops here within minutes. I loosen my grip on the doorknob and shake it more gently this time, working the card slowly downward.

And then, finally, I feel it—the thin plastic sliding behind the lock. The knob twists in my hand and the door creaks open.

CHAPTER THIRTY-FIVE

With one last glance around the yard, I slip my backpack on, step into the kitchen, and click the door shut behind me. Jenna's house is quiet. The lights are off, but the midday sun is bright through the windows, and I can see that everything looks neat and tidy. The edges of the cereal boxes are aligned, the counters are clean, and the kitchen chairs are tucked beneath the table where, not long ago, I sat and told Jenna if she ever lied to me again, I'd make her regret it.

I move quickly through the kitchen. Now that I'm in, I can feel the clock ticking, and I don't want to risk spending a single minute more than I have to here. But when I round the corner into the living room, I stop short.

The wall that used to be cluttered with articles and sticky notes and highlighted maps is empty. I turn dumbly in a circle, as if the collage of evidence will suddenly pop up somewhere else, but there's no trace of it anywhere. I look in the console beneath the TV and riffle through the things on the coffee table. I even look beneath the couch and behind the chairs. Nothing.

The only reason I can think that Jenna would have taken down that research is if she believed she didn't need it anymore. Is it possible she thinks she figured it all out? Is that what she's hiding from me, the name of the man who took our sisters? But why? I stare at the blank wall where all that evidence used to be. I have to find it.

The living room bleeds into the entryway, and on the other side of that are two doorways, which are currently closed—Jenna's bedroom and Jules's old one. I don't know which is which, so I head to the closest.

When I open it, it's immediately apparent that I'm standing at the threshold of the room where Jules used to live. The floor and bed are littered with things—old makeup, clothes, cardboard boxes—as if Jenna started packing up her sister's life, then quit halfway. It's an instinct I understand well. When all you have left of someone are the objects that made up their life, those things become precious.

Other than the brief interactions I had with Jules when I used to go to Harry's Place, I never knew Jenna's sister, but she comes alive now. The far wall is lined with dozens of drawings, their corners curling, overlapping, and I remember the time in Jenna's truck when she told me her sister had started to pursue art. The drawings don't seem technically accomplished, but there's something about them that grabs me. There are a few cityscapes and landscapes, but mostly they're of people. One is of a woman with a shaved head, her chin tilted up, hooded eyes locked on mine. Another shows a man lighting a cigarette in profile. Another is of a child, their knees to their chest, their face buried between them. Darkness crowds at the edges of the paper like a swarm of bats.

I scan the rest of the room for anything that might catch my eye, but I feel instinctively that Jenna doesn't come in here often. If she found a piece of evidence that unlocked the answer of what happened to our sisters, I think she'd keep it somewhere closer. Quietly, I click the door shut.

The other room is Jenna's. And just as her sister's was so idiosyncratically Jules, this bedroom is the epitome of the woman I've come to know over the past month. The queen bed is made, its blue quilt smooth. A desk is pushed against one wall, an organized clutter of pens and sticky notes surrounding her laptop. A gallery wall of framed art hangs on the space above the bed, and the biggest piece is clearly a Jules original—a drawing of the two sisters, arms around each other's necks, their faces animated with laughter.

I start with the desk, scanning the sticky notes, but they're just scribbled reminders—to-dos, grocery lists, and what I'd guess to be a handful of unlabeled passwords. There's a book beside her laptop with a title I don't recognize. I flip through its pages, but the only thing that falls out is a bookmark. Just as I'm stepping forward to open her laptop, the toe of my shoe knocks into something tucked beneath the desk. I bend down to look and find a clear plastic box the size of a printer. Through the side, I can see it's stuffed with papers, everything from newspaper clippings to computer printouts. This is it.

The box feels so final, the way it's pushed under the desk, its yellow top closed tight, and I think back to the last time I was here, when Jenna told me she was taking a break to care for her mom. I remember this evidence was still up on her living room wall that night. I clocked it the moment I stepped into her house. So, what changed between then and now? What did she find that has her so convinced she's done investigating? And, as all my questions have since yesterday, this one dovetails into my biggest point of confusion: Why is she hiding it from me?

I slip my arms out of my backpack and drop it to the floor. Then I pull out Jenna's desk chair to sit and tug the box onto my lap, prying off the lid. The newspaper article on top is one I recognize. Its headline reads: "Missing Mishawaka Girls." Beneath it is the picture of Kasey in her jean jacket. I place it on the laptop and move to the next, a printed Google map of the road where Jules went missing, the exact location marked with an X. I've seen this too.

Carefully, I go through it all, but with each subsequent piece of paper, my hope sinks a bit further in my chest. I already know everything in here. I check my phone and see that it's almost noon. Jenna won't be home for hours, yet with every passing minute I'm here, my anxiety kicks up a notch. I flip through the remaining documents quickly, but they're all dead ends.

I was so sure.

I pack everything back up and put the box where it was, then turn to the laptop, closed on the desk. I open it and tap the power button, chanting a silent prayer that it isn't locked. But it is, the empty password box staring back at me like a challenge. I hesitate for a moment before remembering the sticky notes. I sort through them again, finding all the slips of paper with the random lines of writing—letters, numbers, and punctuation combined. Total, there are what appear to be five passwords, but maddeningly, not a single one is labeled. I flip over the pieces of paper. All blank. I wonder how many failed attempts I have before the computer locks me out.

I type in the first one, a long line of meaningless characters. I double-check it before hitting the sign-in button, but when I do, the password box shakes back and forth. A technological chastisement. I grab the next sticky note, type the digits into the little box, but again, it shakes its disapproval. The next one is the same. There's the obvious possibility that none of these are right, but there's nothing I can think to do but keep trying.

Finally, on my fourth attempt, the screen suddenly brightens. I let out a sigh of relief.

Jenna's desktop photo, one of those default images of a waterfall, is the backdrop to an internet window with a handful of open tabs. One is for her email, and I skim through the recent messages, though nothing catches my eye. Another is the website of some car repair shop, another is her Facebook page. I scan her profile, but don't see any unusual-looking posts, and when I click on her message inbox and glance over the last few exchanges, there's nothing out of the ordinary.

I run a frustrated, jittery hand through my hair. It has to be here.

I look around the screen for any other open tabs and find a little minimized one in the bottom right corner. I click on it, and when it expands, the first thing I see, to my utter surprise, is my name.

Slowly, the rest of the box's content registers: On the left is a list of phone contacts. On the right is a message thread—Jenna's texts.

My name is the second on the list, sandwiched between two I don't recognize, Shawna Jackson and Amy Miller, then Mom. Beneath each of these is a preview of the text thread in smaller, lighter font. What's going on? the line under my name reads. Are you okay?? It's from the night she didn't show up at my dad's, a little over a week, and a lifetime, ago.

I'm about to read her most recent conversation with Shawna when I spot two words beneath Amy Miller's name, and my heart jumps into my throat. I click on their thread and it appears on the right. I skim the last message to Jenna from Amy, but out of context it makes no sense, so I scroll to the top of the conversation. The whole thread is relatively short, and I'm at the start within seconds.

WED, AUG 14 AT 10:09 A.M.

JENNA: Hey Amy, this is Jenna Connor. Just wanted to reach out via text like you asked. Do you have any time to meet up this week to talk about Jules? I'd really appreciate it.

AMY: Lemme get back to you

THU, AUG 15 AT 1:14 P.M.

JENNA: Hi, checking back in. Do you have any time to meet up this week? Can talk over the phone if it's easier.

AMY: Sorry. Been super busy. Yes, phone's better.

JENNA: No problem. Can you talk now?

AMY: Nows not great

JENNA: Name a day and time and I'll make it work.

JENNA: Hey, Amy, I'm sorry to keep bugging you, but this is my sister and I know you guys were close for a while when you were working together at Harry's. I just have a few questions. It would mean so much to me if we could talk.

AMY: Sorry sorry! Lifes been crazy. Maybe you could text me your questions? At work and can't talk on phone

I imagine Jenna flaring with frustration as she read this. But she wouldn't let on. She'd take what she could get.

JENNA: Sure, np

JENNA: Before she started at Harry's, Jules went through a weird spell. She got quiet, stopped going out, quit her job and moved across town. Did she ever mention any of that to you?

AMY: Yes. Not at first, but when we got close she did

JENNA: Did she tell you why?

JENNA: Amy? You there?

AMY: Sorry. I assumed you knew

JENNA: Knew what?

JENNA: ???

JENNA: Amy, please. If you know what happened, just tell me.

AMY: Jules told me she was raped

Everything in me contracts, sorrow and grief crushing against my body from all angles. And yet, at the same time, it somehow doesn't feel like a surprise. It feels as if the truth has been obscured behind a veil, just out of sight. Jenna and I could feel its presence, sense it, but we never wanted to look at it head-on.

Even though I already know what they're going to say, I read the last few texts, and all my sadness calcifies into rage.

AMY: I'm sorry

AMY: I thought you knew

JENNA: Did she tell you who did it? Did she give you a name?

AMY: She said it was someone she used to work with. I'm not sure if she ever told me his full name. We just used to call him Skeevy Steve

CHAPTER THIRTY-SIX

I stare at Jenna's computer screen, rage pooling in my gut, hot and choking like blood. I can't imagine the pain Jenna must have felt when she read those words, when she learned Jules's already too-short life was filled with such violence. I think of Steve fucking McLean at the bar that night we tracked him down—the way his gaze traveled leisurely up my body, the way he sat across from me licking his lips. I close my eyes and see the exact moment his laughter died and that unnerving coldness took its place.

This is what Jenna has been hiding from me.

I'm not sure how all her lies fit around it yet, but I know now she didn't deceive me to preserve some dark secret of her own. She did it, just as I first thought, to protect me. She didn't want me to know about the horror that had been done to her sister, in case I assumed the same thing happened to mine.

I'm jumping to conclusions, I know, but now it's all I can see: McLean slinking up to Kasey one night in the alley as she took out the trash. How would he have done it? Would he have offered her a cigarette first, or would he have just reached out and touched her face, a dirty fingernail pressed into her cheek?

An assault would explain everything—Kasey's sudden shift in

mood, her slip into isolation, the fear in her eyes when I went out at night. *Don't go anywhere alone.* Because a girl alone, everyone knows, is never safe. It could even explain why she asked Sandy for all that money. Because she was trying to run away, to escape McLean. She just never made it that far.

While I would like to think none of this could have happened, because surely, if it had, Kasey would've confided in me, I know better now. My sister wanted me to navigate the world ensconced in bubble wrap. She wouldn't tell me she was raped because it would've hurt me too much to hear. Even in their lowest moments, both Kasey and Jenna chose to protect me. Me, me, me, me, me. I want to be angry at them for their lies, but instead I just feel sick. If I'd been better, stronger, more capable, they wouldn't have felt the need to keep me in the dark.

I feel a tear fall onto my thigh and realize I'm crying. Hastily, I wipe my face with the back of my hand, then move the cursor to the column of contacts next to the text thread. The walls of Jenna's room suddenly feel as if they're closing in, and I want nothing more than to retrace my steps out of her house and put this behind me. But I need to keep digging.

Amy's texts had to have made Jenna focus on McLean, and I want to know what else, if anything, she uncovered. Because while this obviously makes him look even more suspicious than before, it's not proof of anything. And the finality of all the evidence tucked away in that plastic box makes me think that Jenna found something concrete, that she knows without a doubt who killed our sisters.

I click on the first name in the list of contacts—Shawna Jackson—and a new conversation replaces the old one. Despite my blurred vision, it's immediately apparent from their exchange that Shawna works at the dentist's office with Jenna. Dr. Spencer was being such a dick today! Shawna texted, to which Jenna responded, Right??? I am about to click back out when I see Jenna's latest text, sent yesterday morning:

Taking a half-day tomorrow. Planning to leave office at noon. Sorry to leave you in the lurch last-minute. Something of an emergency.

I only vaguely register Shawna's response—Np. Hope everything's ok—because my heart is suddenly racing. Jenna was talking about today. And the clock on her computer reads 12:11. If she comes straight home, she'll be here in less than five minutes.

I minimize the text thread, lurch to my feet, and hurriedly tuck the chair beneath the desk. My hands are jittery as I try to put everything exactly as it was, closing the laptop and straightening the pens. I should've taken a picture so I wouldn't have to rely on my memory, but this will have to do. I grab my backpack and am slipping my arms through the straps when I notice that the drawer of Jenna's bedside table is ajar.

I'm not sure what about this makes me pause, but it does, and I find myself walking that way instead of toward the door. I step beside the little table, lean over to peer into the open drawer, and see, tucked inside, a blue plastic box with a small white sticker. On it is a series of digits in large type, and beneath it, the words Smith & Wesson. I hear Jenna's voice in my mind. *I'd buy a gun,* she said. *I'd drive to his house and shoot him in the head.*

Finally, understanding dawns, and the weight of it almost buckles my knees. Jenna told me she needed time alone to take care of her mom, when really, she needed it to gather evidence on McLean and hunt him down. Not only was she protecting me from the knowledge that McLean is a rapist, she was preventing me from being complicit in her crime, safeguarding me from the violence of getting even. Just like Kasey always did, Jenna has been trying to keep me safe. Guilt swells inside me at the thought that I ever suspected anything else.

I stare at the gun box, fear screwing my feet into the floor. For a moment, I can't move, panic turning my mind blank.

But then I hear it: the sound of a vehicle approaching and turning into the driveway.

Jenna is home.

CHAPTER THIRTY-SEVEN

I stride to the open doorway of Jenna's bedroom and shoot a frantic glance around for the nearest way to get out. I don't know what to do about the gun or what I assume to be Jenna's plan or any of what I have just discovered. All I know is that she can't find me here, having broken into her house, snooping in her room. I can't leave through the front door—she'll be walking in in a matter of seconds. There's the back door in the kitchen, but it's across the house, which risks her spotting me. The only other plausible exit is the window in her bedroom.

Outside, I hear her truck door open, and I make a split-second decision.

I close the bedroom door, spin around, and dart across the room, the carpeted floor creaking loudly beneath my feet. When I make it to the window, I realize that there's a screen on the other side. My mind screams at me in frustration. How could I have forgotten about fucking screens?

I grab the bottom of the window and yank, but it's locked, so I have to fumble with the latch on top. As I do, I hear the deadbolt of the front door turn. I finally manage to tug open the window, then push my palms against the screen. It pops out of the frame with a clatter and falls to the ground below. In the house behind me, I hear the front door open. As quietly as I can, I clamber through the window and land in a heap on the ground, the hammer in my backpack knocking hard against my spine. Scrambling to my feet, I yank the window down, then go to replace the screen. But my hands are too jittery, and I drop it just as Jenna's bedroom door swings open.

I whirl away from the window, pressing my back against the wall, chest heaving. *Please don't have heard me,* I think furiously. *Please don't notice the screen.* I wait for the moment when Jenna spots it, then flings open her window and sees me.

But it doesn't come.

I hear her bustling around her room, her movements casual and routine.

I don't wait to catch my breath. She may not have seen me yet, but with every passing second, the likelihood that she will goes up.

I'm on the opposite side of her property now, far from the gate where I came in, and it feels too risky to retrace my steps. Instead, I stride to the right side of the house. When I turn the corner, I see another window. It has to be the one in Jules's old room, but to be safe, I crouch to my hands and knees and crawl beneath it.

When I stand up, my mind shouts again in panicked aggravation— there's no gate in this part of the fence, just an HVAC unit tucked between it and the house. My only option to scale the fence is to climb on top and launch myself over. As quietly as possible, I heave myself onto the hunk of metal, then grab the top of the fence. The edge is ridged and digs painfully into my palms as I bring one foot up. Using the side of the house for balance, I lift my other foot and realize suddenly how high up I am. It will hurt when I hit the ground.

I take a deep breath, then jump, landing hard on my hands and feet. When I lift my palms, I see blood beading through the dirt that now covers them. Quickly, I stand and dart in the direction of my bike, but I only make it to the edge of the driveway before I hear the front door open.

Why is Jenna coming back out? Did she hear me?

There's no time to run, so I crouch behind the bed of the truck, listening as her footsteps get closer. After a moment, the truck door opens, and I hear a muffled sound as Jenna tosses something onto the seat. This is it. The second she reverses out of the driveway, she'll see me. I look around for somewhere to hide—there's nowhere.

But the engine doesn't turn on.

Instead, I hear her footsteps retreat.

My body slackens with relief, and I straighten, which is when I notice the mound of tarp in the back of Jenna's truck. I've never seen it there before, and it sends a bad feeling through me. I turn to peer through the truck window and spot an overnight bag on the seat. It's zipped halfway, as if Jenna packed it in a hurry. Inside is a tangle of clothes, a pair of tennis shoes, and the corner of the blue plastic box.

So that's why Jenna's taking a half day—she's planning on doing it right now. She's going to McLean's and she's going to kill him.

I stand frozen with what feels like indecision, but deep down, I already know what I'm going to do. At minimum, McLean has fifty pounds on Jenna. A gun won't be able to guarantee her safety. I can't let her go to his place alone. I wouldn't be able to live with myself if she got hurt all because I was too scared to intervene. And after everything she did to shelter me from her plan, she's not just going to let me come along—especially not after I broke into her house.

I don't let myself give it another thought. I step up onto the back wheel and hurdle over the side into the hard flat bed. Crouching down, I grab the edge of the tarp and throw it over my head, and suddenly I'm awash in hot, plastic-smelling air. The front door of Jenna's house opens again, and I listen to her footsteps approach. She slides into the truck and slams the door behind her.

And then the engine is kicking on, and it's too late to wonder where McLean lives or how long it will take to get there. Too late to wonder what the fuck I've gotten myself into.

CHAPTER THIRTY-EIGHT

We lumber out of the driveway and the side of my head clatters against the truck bed. Wincing, I slip my arms out of my backpack and bunch it beneath my head for a pillow, but it's flimsy padding, and the metal surface where I lie digs into my hip and shoulder. We turn right out of the driveway, then left. I try to keep track of the navigation, but within minutes, I'm already disoriented. Suddenly, we're accelerating, the tarp whipping violently against my skin, and I know we're on the highway.

I reach my hand into my backpack to pull out my phone. I open my maps app, and after a confused moment of zooming in and out, I see we're heading south. Odd. McLean works north of Jenna's place, so it would stand to reason he'd live north too. Then I remember the property his family owns in Kentucky. Is that where we're going?

The minutes turn to hours.

My body is past the point of aching, my joints stiff and screaming. Every once in a while, I shift on the metal truck bed, and I can feel bruises blooming beneath my skin. My mouth grows dry and my head throbs from the constant bumps in the road. At some point we stop for gas, and I use the time Jenna's inside the station to check my phone, but the GPS must have drained it, because it's died.

It's another few hours before we stop again, and this time, Jenna doesn't get out of the truck. Slowly, I bring my hand to the edge of the tarp and pull it back. From my vantage point, all I can see is the evening sky and the tops of buildings. We're in a commercial area, I think, somewhere with shops and restaurants, but I have no idea which state we're in, let alone which city.

The minutes tick by.

What are we doing here? Why is Jenna not getting out of the truck? It feels as if ants are crawling beneath my skin I'm so desperate to move. Finally, mercifully, the engine turns on and we're driving again. Twenty minutes later, Jenna is putting the truck in park and unbuckling her seatbelt. I hear the sound of a zipper, then a rustling. The truck door opens, her feet touch pavement, the door closes. Not a slam but a quiet snick.

I hold my breath as I imagine Jenna reaching toward the tarp and pulling it back to discover me beneath it. *What are you doing here?* she'd ask, eyes wide with shock. But that's where the scene grinds to a halt. Because even after what feels like an entire day to sit with my thoughts, I don't know how to answer that question. She is here to kill McLean—of that I have no doubt.

But am I here to stop her, or am I here to help?

To my surprise, Jenna doesn't come around to the truck bed. Instead, her footsteps fade and then disappear. The quiet snaps me out of my rumination. I sit up and yank off the tarp.

It's night now, the sky above me a velvety black. With the dim light of the moon, I can see that we're pulled over on a country road. On one side is a sprawling field; on the other is a gravel drive leading to what appears to be a garage apartment. I look around, but I don't see any more buildings. The closest neighbor is nowhere in sight. Is this where McLean brought our sisters, this isolated piece of land where no one could hear their screams?

Peering through the darkness, I can just make out Jenna's figure walking across the yard, about forty feet from the road. My plan was to confront her once we got wherever we were going, but I can't call out to her now without revealing both of us to McLean. I'll have to follow her.

My body seizes with panic at the thought. What the hell am I doing here, in the middle of nowhere without a plan? Maybe I should just find the nearest gas station and ask them to call me a cab. I could do it. No one knows I'm here. But then I think of Jenna. I think of the money she took out for my bail and the rides she's given me so I don't bike home alone in the dark. I think of all the lies she told just to keep me safe, and I know I won't abandon her—not now when she needs me most.

My mind flashes to the hammer tucked inside my backpack. The thought of using it as a weapon floods me with fear, but I'm not going to confront McLean unarmed. I unzip my bag, pull it out, then quietly crawl over the side of the truck.

As I step onto the gravel road, the yard near the garage apartment is suddenly bathed with light. I flinch, then quickly duck behind the truck bed. Peering over it, I see the source—an illuminated bulb on the side of the building. It's clearly motion activated, because Jenna stands frozen in its beam. She's wearing loose-fitting jeans and a gray T-shirt, her hair pulled into a ponytail. Beside her is a wooden staircase leading to a door on the second level.

Jenna slips out of the beam of light. After a moment it goes off, and the yard is black again. I inch gingerly around the truck, the hammer heavy in my hand. As my eyes readjust to the dark, I can just make out Jenna stepping onto the staircase. I don't want to startle her, but I can't let her walk up to McLean's door alone, so I plant my next footfall in synchronization with hers, the sound of her step masking my own. Slowly, I pick my way through the overgrown lawn, moving whenever she does.

Jenna is almost at the top landing by the time I make it to the garage door, carefully avoiding the spot where she activated the light. As I reach the bottom of the stairs, a loud knock reverberates through the night.

This is it.

McLean is about to answer the door, and I still don't know what I'm planning to do. The idea of Jenna pulling the trigger, of McLean's brains blowing out the back of his head like bloody confetti is so violent, I can't wish that upon her even if I can wish it upon him. I can't intervene now though; startling Jenna when she has a gun would be akin to suicide.

Before I can do anything, she knocks a second time. It's louder now, urgent and angry. Yet again, there's only silence. Maybe he's not home. Maybe Jenna will turn around and I can confront her without the threat of McLean. We can go to the truck together and talk through what we want to do next.

But then a light turns on, washing Jenna in a white glow, and I hear it: the *thunk* of a deadbolt flipping, the door opening.

I squeeze my eyes shut, anticipating the gunshot, but it doesn't come. Instead, I hear someone say, "Can I help you?" and my body goes cold.

The voice is so familiar to me, I could pick it out of a lineup of a thousand. I just never thought I'd hear my sister speak ever again.

CHAPTER THIRTY-NINE

An enormous wave crashes inside me. It should be relief, but it is far too visceral, too violent for that, and in some dark, far-off part of my brain, I realize that it is love, deep and bottomless, for the owner of that voice. For Kasey, who plastered her walls with posters of musicians, Kasey, who saved me from the world's worst self-inflicted haircut, Kasey, who gave me medicine the first time I was hungover, who stayed in bed with me and watched nineties rom-coms till finally I felt better, Kasey, who wanted to be a nurse, to help people when they were sick, Kasey, who felt too old for her age and too big for our town. Kasey, my sister, the greatest love of my life.

She was dead. For seven years, she was buried in the ground.

For a moment, I think I must be hallucinating, but then I hear her voice again—cautious this time—and I know I'm not.

"Who are you?" Kasey says.

But Jenna seems to be frozen and doesn't respond.

I never allowed myself to imagine a reunion with my sister. The comedown from a fantasy that bright would have simply been too painful to bear. If I had, though, I would have envisioned something soft and shimmering: Kasey sitting on the back of an EMT truck, a foil blanket wrapped around her shoulders, a tin mug of coffee in her hands. She'd lift her head to see me running toward her and give me a weak smile. I'd launch myself into her arms and only let go when somebody pried me off.

But some deep instinct tells me to stay hidden now, because something is wrong about all of this. Something isn't adding up. This clearly isn't McLean's house, not with my sister opening the door. And Jenna doesn't seem confused or even surprised to find her here. If I could just see Kasey, maybe I could understand. But from my vantage point at the bottom of the staircase, I can only see Jenna. Her body is so tense, it's vibrating.

"Who are you?" Kasey says again.

Jenna finally finds her voice. "I'm Jenna Connor. Jules was my sister."

"I'm sorry, I don't know who that is."

Kasey must start to close the door, because Jenna throws out a hand, her palm slamming hard against it. "Don't," she snaps. "Don't do that." Her snarled tone prickles up my spine like the edge of a knife. What the fuck is going on?

"I don't know who you're looking for," Kasey says, "but you have the wrong—"

"Stop it!" Jenna shouts. "Stop doing that. I don't have the wrong person. You may have cut your hair, you may be going by your middle name now, but you're Kasey Monroe."

Kasey says something unintelligible, but Jenna barrels through it.

"You were born in Mishawaka, Indiana, you were in nursing school at Arizona State, you were one of the two Missing Mishawaka Girls—you and Jules. This whole time, everyone thought you were dead, but really, you were just working at a record store in Nashville, Tennessee."

I am in a fun house. A carnival ride that scoops out your stomach every time it dips.

"How . . ." My sister's voice cuts out. "How did you find me?"

Jenna shakes her head. "I'm not here to answer your questions."

But in light of everything she just said, I'm starting to suspect I already know. My mind flashes to that day in Jenna's truck, after she picked me up from jail and all but forced me to close my eyes and picture Kasey somewhere she'd always wanted to go. I envisioned her in Nashville. And then there was that first conversation Jenna and I had with Lauren outside her church, when she told us Kasey loved working at the record shop so much, she started joking about doing it full-time. I don't understand how Jenna knew Kasey was going by her middle name, Marie, but the name itself is all over the internet. She could've just seen it enough and guessed. With those few pieces of information, it would've been hard, but not impossible, to track down someone who fit the parameters.

And yet none of that explains how Jenna knew to look for Kasey in the first place, or what she's doing here now, or—most disturbingly—why she has a gun tucked into the back waistband of her jeans.

"What—" Kasey begins, but Jenna cuts her off.

"I just fucking said I'm not gonna answer your questions. You're the one who killed Jules. You're the reason my sister is dead."

CHAPTER FORTY

The words ring through the night like a gunshot, and everything feels suddenly surreal. The accusation is absurd, like the punchline of some horrible, sick joke. I envision Jenna taking out her gun and pulling the trigger, only to see a stream of water come out, or a little flag that says *Bang*. But her face is contorted into an unfamiliar mask of rage. Something dangerous is building inside of her, a snake coiling tighter.

"You killed Jules," she says again.

"W-wait," Kasey says, her voice trembling. "Please. It's more complicated than that."

"Is it?" Jenna snaps. "Because now that I've got it all figured out, it seems pretty fucking simple. You hit my sister with your car that night, and when you realized you'd killed her, you got rid of her body."

"I didn't—"

"I *saw* you," Jenna shouts. "When Jules didn't come home that night, I went looking for her and just before I found her car pulled over on the side of the road, I saw another one driving off. It was spectacularly bad timing on your part. If you'd left even sixty seconds earlier, I probably never would've seen your car, but I did. I remember it because of its bumper sticker. In the beam of my headlights, that's all I saw—a big white sticker against dark metal. *We are not two, we are one.* That's what it said. I looked it up later and found out it was a line from a song."

Standing in the shadow of the stairway, I feel as though the earth is tipping beneath me. I never told Jenna about that bumper sticker.

"I told the police about the car," she continues. The words are pouring out of her in angry spurts as if she's not entirely in control of what she's saying. "But I couldn't remember anything else, not the make, the model, nothing. And so nothing ever came of it. I all but forgot about it until two weeks ago when your sister went through your old car, and I found a CD you'd burned. You'd decorated it with that line."

I think back to that night in my living room, to the way Jenna's smile had dropped when she saw that CD. *It reminds me of Jules,* she'd said, and I thought I knew exactly what had happened. Nostalgia turned to grief. *Kasey loved it too,* I told her, trying to be comforting. *She wrote out the lyrics to it all the time.*

"Wait," Kasey says. "You said my sister? What does Nic have to do—"

Jenna's body jolts at the sound of my name, and she cuts Kasey off. "You don't get to worry about your sister, okay? Not in front of me. Your sister is alive, and mine is dead—because of you."

"I didn't—"

"Stop denying it! I have proof."

"That you saw my car that night?" Kasey says. "That doesn't prove anything."

"You're right. It doesn't." There's a sudden coolness in Jenna's voice that scares me more than if she'd shouted. "That same night, when your sister and I were going through the rest of the stuff from your car, I found a business card for an auto shop out of town. It didn't mean anything to her, but after seeing that lyric, I was starting to get suspicious. I went to the shop the next day and offered the guy working there two hundred dollars to show me their records between August 4th and August 17th, 2012—the day my sister went missing and the day you did. I found it within ten minutes. A black

Honda Civic with a banged-up front bumper. The repair shop had taken dozens of photos of the car. Most were of the damage, but there was one picture of the back, and there it was—that fucking bumper sticker."

Finally, everything that's happened over the past week clicks into place. Jenna *was* trying to get me off the case when she told me she was taking a break to care for her mom, but she wasn't doing it to protect me—from McLean or anything else. She was doing it to get me out of the picture while she investigated Kasey.

"I'm right," Jenna says. "Aren't I? You hit her. You hit her that night and then you hid her body to cover up what you'd done." Anger is consuming her body like fire eating through wood. "I need to hear you say it." Then she reaches behind her and pulls out the gun. "Say you killed my sister."

CHAPTER FORTY-ONE

ight from the outside bulb glints off the shiny black metal in Jenna's hand, and the air around me electrifies.

"Wait," I hear Kasey say from the doorway. "Please, just—wait." I've never before heard her sound so scared, and it's this, almost more than the sight of the gun itself, that clarifies what, deep down, I already knew but wasn't willing to believe: Jenna isn't here to get a confession out of my sister. She's here to kill her.

For close to a decade, I've lived with a hole in my heart, the space carved out when Kasey disappeared. Now, after all that time, we've found our way back to each other and that emptiness in my chest has filled. I'm not willing to lose her—not again.

My world narrows to one objective: Get the gun out of Jenna's hands.

"Just say it," Jenna says. Tears are choking her speech now, slurring her words. The gun, which she's pointing somewhere between the floor and Kasey, looks heavy in her hand. "Say you killed my sister."

Holding my breath, I take one tentative step up the stairs. It's impossible to be completely soundless, but the edge of the staircase is more fortified than the center, and I'm praying that Jenna's too distraught to hear the almost imperceptible noise it makes. Plus, I'm still hidden in the house's shadow, which should obscure her peripheral vision.

"You took away the one thing in this world I loved most," she says, and I take another step, the sound of her voice masking the slight creak of wood beneath my weight.

"Please," Kasey says. "Let me explain."

Jenna lets out something between a scoff and a sob. "Explain what? What could you say that could possibly make a difference?" She's shouting now, tears streaming down her face and into her open mouth.

I use the opportunity to keep moving.

"It was an accident," Kasey says.

"Do you honestly think that changes anything?" Jenna waves the gun wildly through the air. "She was going to be an artist, did you know that? She was supposed to have a goddamn life."

"I . . ." Kasey's voice chokes out.

Finally, I am close enough to lunge at Jenna, but just as I'm about to try to knock the gun out of her hands, she walks over the threshold and disappears from my sight.

"Say it!" I hear her shout from within the house. "Just fucking say it!" She sounds unhinged. There's no time to rethink my plan. I take the final steps onto the landing and turn to face the doorway. Jenna's back is to me, her body shaking.

And there, over her shoulder, is Kasey.

Her hair is in a pixie cut, much shorter than I've ever seen it before. Her cheeks are slimmer too. I've thought of her face many times over the years, but it is so much more nuanced in real life than my own memory could ever conjure, more alive than any photo ever captured. My heart clenches at the sight—she looks terrified.

"Please." Kasey lifts her palms, and it's then that I see her register my presence, her gaze flickering with confusion.

Stall, I try to tell her with my eyes. *Buy me time.* Jenna's still pointing the gun down toward Kasey's legs. If I can get it out of her hands, I can save them both.

"Give—give me a minute . . ." Kasey stammers out. "Give me a second. To explain."

"You've had seven fucking years," Jenna says, lifting the gun and aiming it at Kasey's head. "Your time's up."

There's a metallic clicking sound as she cocks the gun, and I realize there is no saving them both. If I spare Jenna, she will kill my sister. To spare my sister, I'm going to have to kill Jenna.

It's as if I'm suspended in time. I see Jenna bringing me a bag of peanut M&M's, Jenna slipping her arms gratefully through my cardigan, Jenna throwing her head back and laughing at my joke, Jenna smiling softly as Banksy curls into my lap. For these past few weeks, the woman in front of me has become the closest thing I've had to a sister since my own went missing. I realize now that I've come to love her.

Tears stream down my cheeks as I lift up the hammer, impossibly heavy in my hand. And then, with all my might, I swing it down on the back of Jenna's skull.

CHAPTER FORTY-TWO

Jenna's body crumples. I have the inane urge to reach out, to guard her head from the fall, but I'm too late, and it cracks against the faux wooden floorboards like a ceramic bowl. The gun drops from her hand and skitters into the baseboard, black and glinting but no longer ominous—a defanged snake. Without Jenna between us, I'm suddenly face-to-face with Kasey for the first time in seven years.

Without preamble, she crouches down to press two fingers deep into Jenna's neck. "She's dead," Kasey says, the first words she's spoken to me in almost a decade.

My stomach lurches.

"No!" She throws out a hand. "Don't do it near her body. Vomit contains DNA."

The implications of this seem abstract and faraway, but even after all this time, it feels natural to take instructions from my big sister, so I whirl around to the open doorway behind me and stagger out, a hand clamped over my mouth. I make it to the wooden railing and lean over, retching into the yard below. Like an echo in my right arm, I can still feel the force of the hammer colliding with bone, as if my body is memorizing what it's like to inflict such violence. I throw up again.

"Close the door behind you," Kasey says when I step back inside. Blood is pooling around Jenna's head, crimson and slick. Her face looks blank—not peaceful or sleeping, like corpses in the movies, but hollow. The hammer, which I don't remember dropping, is on the floor beside her, the metal stained red. "Lock it."

Everything is moving too quickly, as if I'm in a film that's being fast-forwarded. I need to pause, rewind. "Wait, Kasey . . ." I don't know how to finish. I know she pressed her fingers into Jenna's neck, pronounced her dead, but my brain is sludge, and the words aren't making sense.

"We don't have time for all that right now," Kasey says, and that's when I notice the wad of towels in her hands. She must have gotten them when I was outside. Gingerly, she steps around Jenna's body and crouches down to lay a towel on the floor by her head. The blood seeps into it, turning the brown terry cloth black. With the other towel she grabs the hammer and begins to rub it down. "We need to do this first, then we can talk."

"Do what first?" I say.

Kasey looks up. On her face is a mixture of pity and impatience. "We need to get rid of her body."

"Wait. No. Shouldn't we call the police?"

"And tell them what?" she says. "That you hit her in the head with a hammer? And now she's dead?"

"B-but," I stammer, "she was going to kill you. That's self-defense, isn't it? I mean, not *self*-defense, but something."

Slowly, Kasey stands up. "Nic, what she said is true. The car crash may have been an accident, but Jules died that night, and I covered it up."

Everything inside me sinks. Even in the face of all Jenna's evidence, I'd been clinging to the hope that she'd gotten something wrong, that Kasey hadn't killed Jules that night after all. But with my sister's words, the last of that hope fades.

"So, if we call the police," Kasey continues, "I go to jail for a very long time. And"—she nods at Jenna's body—"so do you."

I stare at the blood-soaked towel by Jenna's head, and the word that has been crowding at the edge of my consciousness since I swung the hammer mere minutes ago finally crashes through: *mur-derer.* Jenna is dead, and I killed her. I gulp in a breath, then another. My hands start to tingle. Blackness swoops into my vision.

"Hey," Kasey says, and her voice is softer now. Through the haze of my confusion and distress, it reminds me of our childhood, when I'd crawl into bed with her after a nightmare and she'd murmur to me, the sleepy words comforting and warm like honey. "You saved my life tonight. That woman was going to kill me."

But she wasn't *that woman*, I think. She was Jenna. And I loved her.

I must've voiced this out loud, because Kasey says again, "She was going to kill me."

She's right, isn't she? Hadn't I waited until Jenna cocked the gun? And if faced with the same choice now, between Jenna and Kasey, wouldn't I choose the same thing? The answer feels so deeply ingrained in me, articulating it is like trying to describe what it feels like to breathe: Jenna may have become like a sister to me, but Kasey is blood, and I will always choose her. Again and again and again.

Still, I am a killer now. For the rest of my life, Jenna will be dead and I will be the one who murdered her. It is depraved what I have done, evil. It will twist around my DNA and change me from the inside out. The thought makes me start to hyperventilate again.

"Nic," Kasey says. "I need you to hold it together. You can react to all of this later, but right now I need you to trust me and do what I say."

I stare into my sister's eyes, feeling as if I'm standing on the edge of a great precipice. If I take one step forward, I'll go into free-fall, with God knows what waiting for me at the bottom. But this is my sister. And right now, she needs me.

"Okay," I say. "What do I do?"

CHAPTER FORTY-THREE

I get the tarp from the back of Jenna's truck while Kasey cleans up the rest of the blood, then together we move the body. Jenna is far heavier in death than I ever could have expected, and Kasey and I have to wedge our arms beneath her torso to flip her over onto the tarp, her hands falling onto it with fleshy thuds. I swing violently from sorrow to disgust and then back again.

Slowly, we heave her body down the stairs of the garage apartment, across the lawn, and into the truck bed. I climb into shotgun and Kasey slides into the driver's seat, using the key she found in the back pocket of Jenna's jeans to turn on the engine.

As we pull out of the yard, I study my sister's face. What I did to Jenna is looming at the edge of my mind like a storm on the horizon, but for now, I hold on to the distraction that is Kasey. For years, I tried to numb the pain of losing her with alcohol, but it never came close to the feeling of being in her presence. I drink everything in: her hands, her fingernails, the curve of her ear, the soft, peachy, all-but-invisible hair on her cheek. She's wearing jewelry I've never seen before, and something about this makes me ache. Her arms are slimmer than they were in college, more muscular too.

There are so many questions I need to ask her, but before I can verbalize any of them, she says, "How do you know Jenna Connor? She said you were going through the stuff in our car together? And how did she find me after all this time? How did *you* get here?"

All of that feels like so long ago now. I quickly tell her the basics, how Jenna and I teamed up to look into her and Jules's disappearances, how Jenna, I assume, pieced bits of information together to find her, how I jumped in the back of Jenna's truck when I saw the gun in her bag. "I didn't know it was you she was coming to kill," I say. "I didn't even know you were alive. I can't believe you're alive."

My voice is thick with incredulity and relief and gratitude, but beneath is a thread of anger. Kasey's been alive this whole time, and she never once reached out. She looks over at me, and I can tell she knows exactly what I'm feeling.

"I know," she says. "I'm sorry."

"But I don't understand." The conversation I overheard between her and Jenna earlier had major gaps, and I'm growing more and more impatient for her to fill them in. "What happened that night after . . . after you hit Jules with the car? What did you do?"

Kasey shoots me a sideways look I can't read. "What Jenna said was true," she says. "I hid Jules's body. I was going to call 9-1-1— I was—but it was clear she was dead. There was no chance of saving her. If I called the police . . . well, everything would've been ruined, and for what? A split-second freak accident."

Beyond my window, the black sky blurs with the dark wash of trees. None of this is what I imagined. This whole time, Jenna and I were looking for a depraved man, someone evil and sociopathic, and it turns out the person we should have been looking for—the person responsible—was my sister. "So, you hid her body and staged the car so it would look like she'd been taken."

Kasey nods.

"And then what?" I ask, but suddenly I realize I already know the answer. If Kasey faked Jules's abduction, it means she faked her own too. The truth has been staring me in the face since I learned about the accident earlier, but until this moment I'd been too addled by shock to see it.

"Even after hiding the body," Kasey says, "I thought it could still look like a hit-and-run, and I was scared it would come back to me. We lived in such a small place, I didn't think it would take much for the police to learn about the damage to our car and link it to Jules. But *two* missing girls—that looks like something else entirely. I thought if I could make the circumstances of our disappearances look similar enough, the police would start looking for some guy. Instead of a reckless driver, they'd be looking for a kidnapper, a killer."

Tears are spilling onto my cheeks. Kasey wasn't taken from me. She left. "What the fuck?" I choke out. "How could you just leave like that?"

"I didn't want to, Nic," she says. "I promise. It was the only thing I could think to do."

"But the police never even suspected Jules was hit by a car that night. They thought she was taken—because that's what you staged it to look like."

"I couldn't be sure what the police were thinking," she says. "For all I knew, they were getting close to the truth."

"Why didn't you at least tell me?" My voice is pleading, desperate. "I'm your sister. You could've trusted me."

"I know that," Kasey says. "I do. But . . . I needed the whole thing to be as real as possible. Let's face it, you've never been great at hiding your emotions, and I didn't want to put you in the position of lying to the police. It wouldn't have been fair to you."

"And you think it was fair to let me believe you died? Because that is what I thought. For years."

I'm expecting this to jolt her into an apology, but instead, she says, "I did what I thought was best."

I want to yell. I want to swing my fists against the dash of Jenna's truck, but something stops me: Beneath all my anger and frustration, something feels off about all of this. I just can't put my finger on what. It feels as if Jenna and I put together a puzzle with one final missing piece, which Kasey is handing over, only for me to find out it doesn't actually fit. "Why did you wait?" I say. "You went missing two weeks after Jules did."

Kasey hesitates.

"Were you waiting for the money from Sandy?"

She snaps her head sideways to look at me. From the horrified expression in her eye, it's clear she understands the implication of my question. I don't just know about the money. I know about the affair too.

"I regret that," she says eventually.

"What? The money or the affair?"

"Both. But the affair."

"How did it even happen in the first place?" I say. "Brad's practically our uncle."

"Believe me, Nic, I already feel shitty enough about it. It was . . ." She shakes her head. "I don't know. I was home from college for the first time, and I felt antsy, out of place, like I'd outgrown the person I was before I left. And I think I wanted something to match that, something I thought was mature." She lifts her fingers from the steering wheel. "I know, I know. Sleeping with Brad was the most immature thing I've ever done. Then Sandy caught us and the accident happened and suddenly the police were investigating Jules and that's when I got the idea to leave. I knew I could get some money from Sandy, which would help me start over. And I knew she'd never tell anyone about it, because if she did, she'd have to explain that her husband had slept with his best friend's daughter."

"What about Lauren Perkins?" I say. "She knew about the affair. You weren't worried about her talking?"

Again, Kasey shoots me a surprised look. "How did you . . ."

"I told you," I say. "Jenna and I were looking into your disappearance. Yours and Jules's." *Look at how hard I worked to find you,* I think. *And here you've been all along. Seven hours away.* "We found out a lot. About the affair, you fighting with Lauren, McLean—"

"Who's McLean?"

For a moment, I'm speechless. Here I'd been convinced McLean was the one who took Kasey, meanwhile she doesn't even recognize his name. "Steve McLean. He worked at the barbecue place next to the record store. You guys used to call him Skeevy Steve."

"Why were you looking into him?"

I let out a small, hysterical laugh. "Because I thought he killed you, Kasey! Because I thought you were dead! Because he raped Jules and I didn't know you hit her with your car and got rid of her body because you lied to me!"

"What was I supposed to do, Nic? Huh? I'd slept with a married man. I got rid of a body to cover up a crime. I didn't want to burden you with any of that because it would have ruined your life."

"You know what ruined my life?" I say. "Losing my only fucking sister. Did you really not consider the damage that would do?" The words are spilling from me now like blood from sliced skin. "Did you honestly think I'd just get over it? Here I've been mourning your death, and the whole time you've been selling records in Nashville fucking Tennessee?"

Kasey's knuckles are white around the steering wheel. Her mouth is clamped shut.

"I get that you were trying to protect yourself," I continue, "but you were pretty selfish."

"Don't," she says. Her voice is like venom.

"Don't what? Call you selfish for letting everyone in your life believe you were dead? Your disappearance tore apart our family, Kasey. Mom's gone, did you know that? She left a year after you went missing. Dad can't even say your name, and I—" My voice cuts out. I am a mess. I am a walking wound, a collection of pain. "So, yeah. I think *selfish* is pretty fucking spot on."

"Everything I did," she says through gritted teeth, "all of it, was for you."

"Right, I forgot. You were saving me from the secret of your affair. And from lying to the police. That would've really ruined my life, Kasey. I much preferred believing you were dead. Thank you so much."

"You honestly don't know what happened," she snaps. "Do you? You honestly have no idea."

I freeze.

This is it—I can feel it—the piece of the story she's been hiding, the reason her explanation hasn't quite fit.

"What do you mean?" I say slowly.

She is silent.

"Kasey?"

"Never mind. Forget it."

"No. Tell me."

"I'm just upset," she says. "I was lashing out."

But I know she's lying. The story she's told me is a like a crumbling house, and I'm standing inside it, watching as the shingles drop from the roof.

"Tell me," I say again.

"There's nothing to tell, Nic." Her voice sounds strained, as if I'm squeezing my hands around her neck. "I told you everything already."

My gaze darts around the inside of the truck, and an idea hits me. It's idiotic and dangerous, but at this point I don't care. Without letting myself second-guess it, I lunge sideways and grab the steering wheel with both hands.

Kasey screams.

I jerk the wheel to the left—she wasn't expecting this, and her grip gives little resistance—then I swing it back to the right so we don't crash off the side of the road.

"What the fuck, Nic!" she shouts. "Let go."

"Tell me the truth and I will."

"You're going to get us killed!"

I spin the wheel again. This time, though, she's gripping it hard, and it's a fight. The truck lurches off the edge of the road, then lumbers back on. I hear a tumbling sound from the back and realize with a sickening jolt that it's Jenna's body.

It reminds me of all the ways she kept me in the dark. But while Jenna might not have done it to protect me, as I originally suspected, I know with a bone-deep certainty that's what Kasey's doing now. I'm so sick of being lied to, sick of being condescended to and coddled. I have not been the same since the summer of 2012, and if anyone deserves to know the truth about what happened, it's me.

"I know you think you're doing what's best for me," I say. "But you're not."

She scoffs.

"I don't need you to take care of me, Kasey. I never have. So just tell me the truth!"

"I've already told you—"

I jerk the wheel again and she shrieks.

"Like fuck you have!" I shout. "You're still trying to shelter me. And you know what? I always thought the reason you did everything for me when I was younger was because I couldn't take care of myself. But it's the other way around, isn't it? I couldn't take care of myself because you did everything for me." I'm so angry now, so desperate for answers, I'm not even sure I believe the words pouring out of my mouth, but I don't stop them. This is Kasey's button, and I'm going to push it. "You're the reason I'm like this. You're the reason I'm such a fuckup, because you babied me and then you abandoned me."

"Stop it," Kasey says.

I wrestle the steering wheel and we veer sideways. "If you hadn't shielded me from everything all the time, I might've actually done something with my life."

"Shut up!"

"Without you—"

But Kasey cuts me off. "You killed Jules! Okay? Without me, you'd be in fucking prison."

And with that, the last of the crumbling house shatters to the ground.

CHAPTER FORTY-FOUR

KASEY, 2012

The sound of her cell vibrating on the bedside table lurched Kasey from sleep. She blinked blearily, her eyes adjusting to the dim light of her room. She'd forgotten to turn off the lamp, and the textbook she'd been studying when she drifted to sleep was open beside her. The night outside her window was still and black. It must have been late.

Yawning, she grabbed her phone and glanced at the screen. Her first reaction at seeing her sister's name was relief that it wasn't Brad. He hadn't called her since she'd broken things off last week, but she kept anticipating it. He'd actually cried when she told him it was over, and every bit of attraction she'd ever felt for him had turned in that moment to pity and disgust. Just because he was older, she'd realized, didn't mean he was wiser or more mature. He was just lost—like her, like everyone.

Her second reaction to seeing Nic's name was annoyance. Her phone's clock read almost 2 A.M., which meant her sister was probably at a party somewhere and wanted a ride home. Kasey had gotten the same call many times from Nic over the summer, and no matter how frustrated it made her, she always got out of bed. But the moment she heard her sister's voice over the phone, Kasey knew something was different.

"I need your help." Nic's words were slurred, frantic.

Kasey sat up and the textbook fell to the ground. As it did, she caught a glimpse of the circulatory system diagram she'd been studying earlier, the network of blood in the human body.

"What happened?" she said.

Nic let out something between a sob and a groan.

"*What happened?*" Kasey repeated. Her mind was already spinning with scenarios—greedy boys drunk on beer, dares gone too far. "Are you hurt?"

"I fucked up," Nic said, starting to cry.

"Take a deep breath." Kasey waited for her sister to do as she said. "And another . . . Okay. Now tell me what happened."

"I was at Harry's Place, y'know that bar we sometimes go to, the one that takes our IDs? Well, I was driving home and I . . ." Nic hesitated, and Kasey closed her eyes, the nightmare scenarios shifting. She hadn't even remembered that Nic had the car. "I hit something," Nic finally finished.

"Are you hurt?"

"No."

"What did you hit?"

"A tree." Nic sobbed again. "Mom and Dad are gonna be so pissed."

Kasey slumped with relief. Her sister was an idiot. A reckless, careless idiot who risked too much for nothing. But nobody had gotten hurt. "Where are you?" she said. "I'll come and drive you home."

The night was pitch black, but Kasey had a small light affixed to the front of her bike, and it didn't take long for her to find their old Honda Civic. It was pulled off the pavement near a dense wooded area. Trees towered beside the car, swallowing the light from the moon and stars.

"You came," Nic said after Kasey got off her bike and walked up to the driver's side window. Her sister's eyes were unfocused, their lids heavy. Her smokey makeup was smudged, making her sockets look black.

"Jesus Christ, Nic, what were you thinking?" By now, all Kasey's relief had curdled to anger.

"I know," Nic said. "I'm such a fuckup. You should disown me."

Kasey rolled her eyes. "Just get out so I can drive."

She opened the door and Nic slipped out, then Kasey helped her walk around the front of the car to the passenger seat. As if she were a toddler, Nic grabbed Kasey's hand in hers then pulled it up her face, rubbing the back of it against her cheek. Her skin was sticky with tears. "I'm sorry you're always taking care of me, Kase. I don't know what I'd do without you."

Kasey was too furious to speak. Plus, there was no use reprimanding her sister when she was like this. Nothing would sink in, and she probably wouldn't even remember it in the morning. Tomorrow, Kasey would have a real conversation with her. She'd tell her she had to stop drinking so much, tell her she couldn't use the car anymore, not when she was going out. Kasey opened the passenger side door, scanning the car for any evidence of the accident. It looked like the right side of the front bumper was dented, but that was it—surprisingly little damage considering how enormous the trees along the road were.

"Really," Nic continued as she slid into the seat, her body boneless. "I'd be such a fucking mess without you."

"You're a mess with me, Nic." Kasey buckled her sister's seatbelt, then closed the door.

As she walked back to her bike, she studied the gaping blackness of the road behind her, the slightest hint of unease crawling up her spine. Where was the tree Nic had hit? Kasey had assumed it'd be obvious to spot—the one that stuck out from the rest—but she could hardly make out anything at all. She pulled her phone from her pocket and shined the flashlight toward the woods. The tree line was still a dark blur, but with the light, she could tell that it was far from the road, at least ten feet. Even in Nic's state, it seemed unlikely that she would've swerved so violently.

Kasey aimed the flashlight toward the road behind her, illuminating the pavement and the dirt shoulder. Nothing. She took a few tentative steps forward, gravel crunching softly beneath her tennis shoes. Was it possible Nic had actually hit a deer and, in her disorientation, hadn't seen it? It could've limped off into the woods before Kasey got there.

But then her light caught on something just off to the left. At first, Kasey didn't understand what it was. It was small and white and so out of place here in the middle of the night, it took a moment for her brain to register that what she was looking at was a human hand.

She gasped, stumbling backwards, then fell to the ground, her phone clattering to a stop in front of her. Kasey stared horror-struck into the beam of light, which was now illuminating a woman's face, one cheek pressed into the dirt, a cluster of grass grazing her parted lips. Her eyes were open in a vacant gaze.

Kasey tried to scramble to her feet, but her legs were limp and she sunk back to the ground. When she was finally able to stand up, she inched toward the body, snatched up her phone, then clambered backwards again. She needed space between her and this horrible, unnatural thing.

At the distance of a couple feet, her phone's flashlight revealed the scene in full—a woman prone on the ground, her arms flung wide, legs akimbo. Kasey forced herself to look away, to focus instead on dialing 9-1-1. But just as she was about to hit the call button, she paused.

The woman was clearly dead.

Nic had killed her.

The police would come, take one look at Nic, pronounce her wasted, then slap handcuffs on her. They wouldn't be able to save the woman. And Kasey would be responsible for sending her sister to prison.

She bent over, hands on her knees, head spinning. Who was this woman? Where had she come from? The closest house was half a mile away, and it wasn't like she'd gone out for a late-night stroll. Not on a road with such bad visibility and this close to the woods. The woman was wearing black jeans, tennis shoes, a thin black T-shirt that clung to her skin. She would've been nearly impossible to see in the dark. There was also, Kasey noticed, a phone near the body. It was miraculously intact, without even a crack.

A small yellow light in the distance caught Kasey's eye. When she squinted at it, she could just make out the interior of a car. Carefully, she stepped around the woman's body, giving it a wide berth, then walked until the beam of her phone's light caught on a metal bumper. The car was pulled over on the side of the road, the driver's door open, the dome light flickering. When Kasey looked inside, she spotted a purse on the passenger seat and a key in the ignition, a small heart-shaped keychain dangling from it.

It was all starting to make sense. The woman's car must have broken down, and she'd gotten out to walk. The whole thing looked eerie, as if the driver had simply vanished.

And that was when the idea came to her.

Kasey could remember this time when Nic was three or four, she was five or six, and their mom had taken them to a pool party at some neighbor's house. Kasey was comfortable in the shallow end by then, but Nic, still a toddler, wore floaties whenever she went in the water. Kasey had been splashing around on the pool steps with some of the other kids when she noticed the little body floundering beneath the surface. It was Nic. For one heart-stopping second, Kasey was paralyzed, looking around as if her sister might actually be somewhere else, playing with the hose in the yard or eating a popsicle on the deck. But then she saw them—Nic's *Little Mermaid* arm floaties discarded on the edge of the pool. Kasey gulped in a breath, dove beneath the water, and looped her arms around Nic's waist. They breached the surface moments later, both gulping for air. As she dragged Nic to the edge, Kasey spotted their mom in a lawn chair, in the middle of a conversation, a drink in her hand. It took another few seconds of Nic spluttering for her to notice her youngest had almost drowned, and in that moment, Kasey understood that her sister was her responsibility. She was the one who was going to have to keep Nic safe.

The idea Kasey had was wrong and fucked up. She knew she shouldn't do it. She also knew, without a flicker of a doubt, that she would.

Quickly, she walked back to the woman's body. If anyone caught her now, it wouldn't just be Nic who went to prison. She had to move fast. Kasey grabbed the woman's phone from the ground—it was dead—and put it in the purse in the woman's car, using the edge of her T-shirt to wipe the phone and door handle afterward so she wouldn't leave any prints.

Then she hurried back to their Honda. Peering through the driver's side window, she found her sister slumped in shotgun, her eyes closed, her chest rising and falling with the slow, melodic rhythm of sleep. Good. Quietly, Kasey opened the car door and slid into the driver's seat. She wanted to shorten the distance between the woman and the car's trunk so she didn't have to waste time dragging the body over. She just prayed Nic stayed asleep through it all. Her sister thought she'd hit a tree, and for Kasey's plan to work, she needed to keep it that way. But when she turned the key in the ignition, Nic stirred.

"Kase?" she muttered. "What're you doing?"

"I'm gonna put my bike in the car," Kasey said. "But I have to take the front wheel off first, so it'll be a few minutes. Go back to sleep."

"D'you need any help?"

"No. Go back to sleep."

"You're a good sister," Nic said as her eyelids drooped, then slowly shut. "Just don't let it go to your head."

Kasey stared at her sister's peaceful face and felt as if a deep fault line were tearing through her—love on one side, loathing on the other. *You killed someone,* she thought. *A woman is dead because of you. I am about to become a criminal because of you.* But she didn't have time for any of that. Not now. She put the car in reverse and tapped the gas until the body appeared in the rearview mirror.

If it hadn't been for the immense amount of adrenaline coursing through her veins, Kasey wasn't sure she would have been able to heave the body into the trunk. It was far heavier and more cumbersome than it looked, and by the time she'd pushed the woman's limp feet inside, her chest was heaving, her body damp with sweat. She gazed down at the corpse, the fingers white and curling in on themselves, the hair spiderwebbed over the woman's face, obscuring everything but that pink, gaping mouth.

Kasey pulled out onto the road a few minutes later, after taking the wheel off her bike and stuffing both parts into the back seat. She decided to make a U-turn so she could drive by the scene one last time and make sure she'd covered her tracks. But just as she was about to pass the woman's car, Kasey saw something in her rearview that made her flush with hot fear. Headlights were approaching from behind.

Don't be a cop, she thought furiously as her panic-riddled brain envisioned sudden flashing lights. White, blue, red. A siren. But the car remained dark except for the two bright beams of its headlights.

Kasey breathed in relief—she'd gotten away with it.

And yet, as she drove, her brain kept sticking on a moment earlier as she closed the trunk. Had she simply hallucinated it, or had that tiny movement in her periphery been the woman's hand twitching with life?

In the days after, Kasey couldn't sleep. Every time she closed her eyes, she saw the woman's face, pale and soft in death. When she did eventually pass out from exhaustion, she'd wake up not long after gasping in panic, covered in sweat. She kept waiting for the police to knock on their front door asking for Nic, for her. But they didn't come. She kept tuning in to the local news stations, but no one seemed to be covering the case of the woman who'd disappeared from the side of the road. She began to compulsively google "missing woman + Mishawaka + abandoned car," but there was nothing. Then finally, on the third day, the woman's face appeared on the screen in front of her. *Jules Connor,* the text read, *age 24.*

Kasey was keeping a close eye on Nic too. The morning after that horrific night, she knocked on her sister's bedroom door, and from the way Nic moaned for her to come in, Kasey knew she was regretting how much she'd drunk.

"How're you feeling?" Kasey asked, fighting to keep her voice neutral.

Nic moaned into her pillow.

"You were pretty drunk last night. Do you remember what happened?"

"Oh god," Nic said. "No. What did I do? Was I awful?"

Kasey watched Nic's face for any glimmer of recollection, but it was clear the only thing her sister was preoccupied with was her hangover. "No," she said. "Well, I mean, yes. You called me from the bar to pick you up, and I had to bike all the way to South Bend. Other than that, you were fine."

Having kept the affair with Brad from her sister all summer made hiding this secret a tiny bit easier, but lying to Nic didn't come naturally. And the horror over what she and her sister had both done felt like a fever—a disease that wouldn't go away. Kasey stopped taking Nic up on offers to hang out, claiming school was too stressful. She stopped going out at night, stopped seeing her friends. The idea of continuing to live in the same house as the person who put her in this position felt unbearable, but neither could Kasey imagine going back to college. She didn't want to go to parties where people drank from Solo cups and yelled at each other over bad music. She didn't want to sit in class taking notes on how to save lives—not when Jules Connor's twitching hand haunted her every waking moment.

And then one morning, something happened that changed everything.

Nic was in the shower while Kasey got dressed for work. She was looking for her old Rolling Stones T-shirt when she remembered that Nic had borrowed it a few weeks before.

"Nic!" she called through the bathroom door and over the running water. "I want my Stones shirt back. I'm going in your room to find it."

Kasey didn't wait for an answer. She just opened the door to her sister's bedroom and went to her closet. When she didn't find the shirt hanging up, she bent down to sift through the clothes in the dirty hamper. As she did, she spotted something on the floor—a business card. She picked it up, flipped it over, and her breath caught in her throat.

MISHAWAKA POLICE DEPARTMENT, the card read. Then, beneath that, PHILLIP JOHNSON, DETECTIVE.

Kasey knew from her online searches that Detective Johnson was the one investigating Jules's case. How much did he know? What questions had he asked Nic? More terrifying still, how had she answered?

This whole time Kasey had thought Nic's greatest defense was that she believed herself to be innocent, that she wasn't even aware a crime had occurred. But if the police asked her about the night Jules disappeared, Nic would have no reason to hide that she'd been at Harry's Place. Would they put two and two together? Would they pull up a map and see that the most direct route from the bar to Nic and Kasey's home was the road where Jules's car was found? Had they done all of that already? With the business card in her hand, Kasey understood the unnerving reality: If the police had Nic's name in association with Jules's case, surely it was only a matter of time until they uncovered the truth.

Kasey fought back the weary tears that had begun to fill her eyes. After everything she'd done to insulate her sister from the accident, it wasn't enough. But what more could she do? The only thing she could think of was to somehow bolster the image that Jules had been taken, to do something that would steer the police away from the theory of a drunk driving accident and toward an abduction.

Another missing girl.

The idea was impossibly heavy. Disappearing would mean Kasey would never see her friends or parents again. She'd never finish college. She'd miss Nic's life, her future. But at least Nic would have one. Plus, if Kasey were being honest, a very small part of her felt relieved at the thought of the anonymity disappearing would afford her. No longer would she have to look her dad in the eye while thinking, *I fucked your best friend.* She'd never have to see Sandy and witness the pain she'd caused. She wouldn't have to study for school when all she could think about was Jules Connor's face as she lay curled inside the trunk. She'd no longer run into Nic in the hallway and feel her chest constrict with everything she'd lost.

Kasey didn't want to leave forever. She didn't want to vanish from her own life. But as she looked down at the word *detective* staring up at her, she realized she didn't have any other choice. This was the only way to protect her sister—and she'd do anything to keep Nic safe.

CHAPTER FORTY-FIVE

When Kasey stops talking, the only sound is the distant buzz of insects, the night unfurling quiet and expansive beyond the truck windows. But I feel suffocated—as if all the loose threads I've been working so hard to weave together are forming a straitjacket around me.

There's that time Kasey had said, with a look of fear in her eyes, *Be careful tonight. Don't drink too much. Don't go anywhere alone.* She hadn't been trying to keep me safe from McLean or some stranger. She'd been trying to protect me from myself.

There's the business card that apparently scared her into leaving, the one I got one random night when my friends and I went to Harry's Place. I dredge up the memory, so benign I hadn't thought twice about sharing it with Jenna the first day we met. A detective had approached us at the bar, told us one of the bartenders had gone missing, and asked if we knew anything about it—but we didn't even know who Jules Connor was. Then he gave all of us his card in case we thought of something relevant. He hadn't been onto me; it had just been routine.

There are the headlights Kasey told me she saw that night as she drove off from the scene. They hadn't belonged to a cop car, as she'd originally feared, but to Jenna's.

And then there's the accident. Kasey assumed I'd blacked out the night Jules died, but as she relived it, the memory started coming back to me: swerving drunk in the dark, my tires squealing as I clipped what I thought was a tree. It's the same memory that's been haunting me since my DWI months ago, ever since I started trying to get sober and my mind started to get just a little clearer. The two accidents were so similar, I'd conflated the memories of them in my mind.

I push the truck door open and stumble out, the night spinning around me. I gulp in a breath, then another, my face tingling with the sudden influx of oxygen. A scream rips through me, cutting through the night like the wail of a wounded animal. After everything Jenna and I did to find the monster who took our sisters, it turns out the monster is me. Darkness fills me up, turning my insides black and rotten. I am nothing but a mixture of badness and self-loathing. I'm unforgivable, unlovable. *Killer,* a voice sneers inside my head. *Murderer.*

I scream until it gags me, then I contract over myself. But I vomited everything up earlier, and nothing comes out except saliva and the acidy dregs from my stomach.

Finally, I drag a hand over my mouth, then turn back to the truck, to Kasey. Wordlessly, I slide onto the seat beside her. All I want is to turn back time, to undo everything I did that summer, to start again. But there's nothing I can do or say to change all the damage I've done. I am scraped out by pain, hollowed by guilt.

"I shouldn't have told you," Kasey says.

Yes, I think. "No. You were right to. You shouldn't be the only one who has to live with the truth."

I look over at her. Her eyes are full of despair and pity, but there's a glint of something else behind that—something like relief—and I know a part of her must feel lighter to be telling the truth after all these years. To finally be sharing the burden.

"Fuck, Kasey, I— I'm so sorry." I will never be able to say it enough. "I ruined your life."

"It was my choice," she says. "To protect you. And me. Our futures."

I try to see my old life through her eyes, all the potential I had at seventeen. I could have left Funland, gone to college, made new friends who didn't drink for the fun of it. I could have done more, been more. But what Kasey failed to consider in all her careful preparations was how her supposed death would tear my life apart. She'd simply exchanged one life of pain for another. But I can't tell her that. Not when she sacrificed so much.

"I would've done anything to keep you safe," she says. "You would've done the same for me. You did. Tonight."

We share a fleeting glance, her words conjuring Jenna's ghost so tangibly between us that I can't hold her eyes, and we lapse into silence. *Where do we go from here?* I think. *What do we do?*

"We should get going," Kasey says eventually. "We still have a long way to go."

As we pull back out onto the street, I say, "Where did you go that night?" Those un-accounted-for miles on our odometer represent the last missing piece to this nightmare. "The night you—I—hit Jules? Where did you put her body?"

Kasey looks unbearably tired, so much older than her twenty-six years. She has long been ravaged by the guilt I am just starting to feel. It has robbed her of her youth. "Remember the road trips Mom and Dad used to drag us on when we were kids?" she says. "The ones to visit Aunt Jean in Dayton?"

"Yeah . . ."

"Do you remember what we used to say when we passed that one swamp?"

A shiver laces up my spine as I think back to those drives and the way the two of us would hold our breath, cheeks puffed out dramatically, as we passed the swamp—our twist on the cemetery classic. "Somewhere like that," I say, parroting our younger selves, "has to be full of dead bodies."

"It was the first place I could think of," Kasey says. "That's where we're headed now."

CHAPTER FORTY-SIX

We drive the rest of the way in silence. I still have one last question—or rather one last favor—to ask of Kasey, and I chew it over in my mind.

We reach the outer edges of the swamp hours later, when the moon is hanging directly above us in the sky. Other than it and the stars, the night is dark, the swamp an infinite blackness. I point the beam of a flashlight Kasey grabbed from her home earlier into the tree line, but the darkness swallows it. A cacophony of wildlife hums in the air, frogs trilling, mosquitos buzzing.

"You ready?" Kasey says. I try not to think about what we're doing, but it creeps into my brain regardless. We're hiding a dead body—Jenna's body. "We can't take the tarp. It'll stand out too much. We're going to have to move her as she is."

Kasey opens the back of the truck, and we stare at the roll of blue plastic. All I want to do is run back to the passenger seat and put my head between my knees until it's all over, but I can't let Kasey carry this burden for me. Not this time. Taking a fortifying breath, I climb into the bed of the truck.

"Let's get her out up here," I say. "Then we can push her to the edge together."

I reach a hand to help Kasey up, and her eyes widen ever so slightly in surprise. This is the first time she's ever seen me take the lead, the first time she hasn't had to guide me through my own mess. After a moment's hesitation, she puts her hand in mine.

Awkwardly, we unroll Jenna's body, then heave it out of the truck bed. I grab her ankles and Kasey grabs her wrists, and together we start to carry her to the tree line. Our only source of light is from the flashlight I hold with my mouth, and it shines an eerie spotlight on Jenna's corpse swinging in our grip. Her head lolls heavy on her bent neck, exposing the soft underbelly of her chin. Her hair drags through the grass on the ground. I'm grateful I can't see her eyes.

"Let's put her down," Kasey says through panting breaths once we reach the trees. "It's hard navigating in there. Most of it's just mud and water, and it's really dense."

Dense is an understatement. Within seconds of stepping through the tree line, I'm covered in stinging scrapes, the underbrush more like a wall than individual plants. We make it less than ten feet before we need to put the body down again.

"Shit," Kasey says, glancing over her shoulder. "We're already almost at the water." Sure enough, I look behind her and see moonlight bouncing off its black surface. I grab the flashlight from my mouth, and the bright beam turns the water a murky greenish brown.

We catch our breath, then continue deeper into the swamp. Soon the hard ground turns soft, our shoes squelching in mud. And then we're in the water. In all the dark places around us my mind conjures threats: snakes coiled in the earth, spiders hanging over our heads, fish slipping against our legs in the watery depths. This is how we make our slow progress—moving through the water to solid ground and then back to water again, catching our breath every few feet, Jenna's lifeless body suspended between us.

"What about here?" I say when we've made it to a patch of harder terrain. It feels as if an hour has passed. My clothes are soaked, my arms and legs sting with scrapes, and my muscles are starting to fatigue. Soon, I won't be able to lift Jenna anymore. "This feels far enough, don't you think?"

Kasey looks around. "Yeah, okay." She hesitates. "We need to weigh her down, make sure she doesn't float. I don't think anyone will find her back here, but we can't take the chance."

"Jesus," I say. I hadn't thought of that.

"We can do it with rocks. You know, fill her pockets."

I shine the flashlight in slow arcs on the ground so we can search for anything heavy. When we find a rock, one of us picks it up then tosses it into a pile.

"Hey, Kase?" I say after a few minutes. "If you never want to see me again after this, I'd understand." I have a new and painful thrum in my veins, as if my heart is pumping poison. *My fault, my fault, my fault.* If I were her, I don't think I'd ever be able to even look me in the eye.

Kasey is quiet for a long time, staring down into the mud. Finally, she says, "When I was here last time—with Jules, I mean—I was terrified. I was alone, and I didn't have a flashlight because I'd been in such a hurry I'd forgotten to bring one, and I kept thinking I was going to get caught. It was irrational—there was probably no one else around for miles—but I couldn't get it out of my head that someone was going to see my car and walk into the swamp and find me. And if that happened, I knew I'd go to prison for the rest of my life."

"I'm sorry," I say.

She shakes her head. "That's not why I'm telling you this. That night, I had this moment where I just . . . panicked. I thought that someone was right behind me and that I was going to get caught and my life would be over. And I realized then that if I went to prison, it was you I was going to miss most. Just the little moments, you know, the two of us hanging out, talking. Mom and Dad were in their own worlds, but you were always there next to me. You may have been the reason I was there in the first place, but it was still you I was going to miss." Her voice fades. "What I'm saying is, there's nothing you could ever do that would make me stop loving you. You're my sister."

Tears stream down my cheeks and into my mouth. It is unfathomable to me that I could be lovable after everything I've done, but perhaps that's what she's trying to say, that sisterhood is knowing someone fully and loving them anyway. "Thank you." It isn't enough. Nothing will ever be enough.

I look up to the sky, to the stars peeking out beyond the canopy of trees. It's time to ask my last question.

"Can I stay with you after this? I mean, like, live with you? I know I'll have to start over, to disappear like you did, and maybe you'll want to start over too, move to another city, get a new name. But I was thinking we could do it together this time. I . . . I don't know. What do you think?"

Kasey hesitates. "What about your life back home?"

I think of everything I have back in Mishawaka: a dad who's lost in denial, a dead-end job with a boss I used to love and now hate, a crappy apartment, no friends, no pets. I have nothing to go back to but a criminal record and legal red tape. I will tell Kasey all of it someday soon. But for now, I just say, "I'd rather start over with you."

She studies my face. "We can't do it right away. I need you to go back home after this and act like everything's normal. Just for a while. Just till we know no one is missing Jenna."

The idea makes me unbearably sad. I'll be missing her, at least.

"But eventually," Kasey continues, "if you want to come join me—"

"I do."

"Then . . . yeah. If that's what you want." She smiles and it looks sad, but there's something else there too, something brighter.

We tuck all the stones we've found into Jenna's pockets, her shoes, her bra. Then, together, Kasey and I roll her corpse into the water. For one sickening moment, I think she's not going to sink, but then the swamp gurgles around her and sucks her down. Soon, all I can see are the strands of her hair disappearing into the black. If I didn't know what it was, I might think it was nothing more than underwater grass.

I know we are not in the same exact spot Kasey put Jules's body all those years ago, but I can't stop the image that swims into my mind: Jenna's body settling beside her sister's at the bottom of the swamp, their ghostly hands floating side by side. It makes me think of that poem some stranger wrote in a card all those years ago:

> *Two branches of the same tree,*
> *two pieces of a soul.*
> *Where one sister goes, the other will be,*
> *for she is but half of the whole.*

I look to Kasey, and the two of us begin to retrace our steps back to the truck. Both sets of sisters reunited at last.

I'm just not sure the right ones survived.

ACKNOWLEDGMENTS

For someone who writes, speaks, and generally uses words to tell long and detailed stories, I'm pretty bad at expressing my feelings. So my acknowledgments are likely to be short and sweet, but to these people I owe my literary success and my sanity. They each hold a special place for me, and I reserve a special place in my life for only the most wonderful people.

To my husband, Erik, my daughter, Jo, and our dog, Chuck, thank you for giving me purpose and meaning and for believing in every dream I've ever had. Everything I do, I do for the life we are building together.

To my amazing team at Audiochuck, without your fierce commitment, passion, and drive, I wouldn't have the space to explore projects like this one. Sometimes I have to pinch myself when I think too long and hard about how much I enjoy being around you and living in the mission, vision, and values we have created together as a company. Changing the world is hard, but with you all by my side, it doesn't feel like work.

To my mother, Lisa, and my mother-in-law, Marsha, thank you for surrounding me and building me up as a mother. You not only give me the support to have a spectacular career, you encourage me to try and have it all. But that doesn't happen without both of you.

To my co-writer and dear friend, Alex Kiester, I, of course, am honored to get to have the continued opportunity to create magic with you. You are so talented and hardworking that you make some of the most difficult parts look easy. But I am most grateful for our friendship that has blossomed over the course of creating this second book. In writing about the bond between sisters, my soul found a sister in you.

To our editor, Jenny Chen, thank you for believing in my ability to tell stories since the beginning. Your ability to push when you needed to push and give room to things I fought for has created a great balance and a better book for readers. Thanks also to Alejandro Martinez and Jason English for lending your expertise for all the legal logistics within the book. Your insight was invaluable.

To my literary agent, Meredith Miller, at UTA, thank you for always respecting my content-first approach and helping me balance that with a business I'm still new to. You are smart and savvy and I really won big when Oren added you to my team.

And speaking of, I want to thank my podcasting agent, Oren Rosenbaum. Oren, you were the first person to bet on me and you've had my back every day ever since. Your unwavering belief in me and what I'm capable of, honestly, feels insane sometimes. But I'm grateful for it. To say I wouldn't be here without you feels cliché and frankly just . . . not enough. Our industry wouldn't be where it is without you, and I feel lucky to be in your orbit.

ABOUT THE AUTHOR

ASHLEY FLOWERS is the #1 *New York Times* best-selling author of *All Good People Here* and the #1 female podcaster in the United States, best known as the host of *Crime Junkie*. She founded Audiochuck, an award-winning media company with over 2.5 billion downloads, and Season of Justice, a nonprofit dedicated to funding DNA testing for cold cases. Flowers lives in Indiana with her family.

ashleyflowers.com
Instagram: @ashleyflowers
X: @Ash_Flowers

ABOUT THE TYPE

This book was set in Caledonia, a typeface designed in 1939 by W. A. Dwiggins (1880–1956) for the Merganthaler Linotype Company. Its name is the ancient Roman term for Scotland, because the face was intended to have a Scottish-Roman flavor. Caledonia is considered to be a well-proportioned, businesslike face with little contrast between its thick and thin lines.